# COVER OF DARKNESS

## J. Carroll

**Huntington House Publishers**

Huntington House Publishers
P.O. Box 53788
Lafayette, Louisiana 70505
1-800-749-4009


ISBN 0-910311-31-5
Library of Congress Card Number 90-85177


Printed in Colombia

# DEDICATION

To my wife, Dawn, for her patience and support. And to
Jay Gaines whose knowledge and wisdom made it all
possible.

# 1.

# Chapter One

**J**ack Clayburn knew Dr. Floyd Thacker was avoiding him. He had left message after message with the man's secretary and when Thacker did not return his calls, Jack tried to get an appointment for an interview. That too had been unsuccessful.

Thacker was the president of Waylanth College, located just outside Richmond, and he was also one of the top computer experts in the country. As such, he served on several government panels as a consultant, and it was in this capacity that Jack needed to make contact. His assignment was to research and produce a story concerning rumors about an infestation of a deadly computer virus that was affecting government computers.

From what Jack had learned, the "X-Y" virus existed; it was not a rumor, despite denials from Washington. He learned that the virus attached itself to the command prompt of any computer that used the Disk Operating System or DOS master control program. Then, when a user began work, the virus immediately attached itself to any file with the three-letter extension "COM" or "EXE" that was opened for use. That added roughly 4,000 characters of length to any such file as the virus replicated itself. If unnoticed, the addition of that much length to multiple files or programs placed a significant undisclosed burden on the computer system.

The repeated replication of 4,000 characters to files overloaded the mass storage capacity of any system. But because the attachment remained hidden from detection, the map that described where files were stored on a hard disk drive then became disrupted, halting operation and even ruining all files and programs stored in the computer.

The most intriguing aspect of the story, besides the possibility that all government files could ultimately be destroyed, was the hint or suggestion that the virus was not accidental. He had learned that the virus was smart enough to hide its tracks so that it was almost impossible to detect visibly. It was becoming increasingly obvious that someone had gone to much work developing this diabolical virus.

Jack was convinced Dr. Floyd Thacker could provide some insight into the virus situation. First, however, he had to meet the elusive college president.

Consequently, when he learned that Dr. Floyd Thacker would be attending the National College President's Conference in New York, Jack had arranged to obtain a press pass to attend also. He even arranged to stay in the same hotel as the visiting presidents. He needed to talk to Thacker and the fact that the man didn't want to talk to him only made him more persistent—and curious. Did Thacker have something to hide?

Now, as he carried his more than twenty years of journalistic experience slowly across the meeting room floor, maneuvering his way through the narrow aisles separating the white sea of banquet tables, Jack wondered if he could find Thacker among the crowd of college presidents. He had only a photograph from the network news files to go on, and it was a picture from several years previous. He had checked at the registration desk to see if assigned seating prevailed for the banquet and when told there was not, he proceeded on a search mission through the large banquet room.

As he threaded his way through the crowded hall, he paused occasionally to glance around, searching for his quarry. Those who saw him automatically assumed that Jack was one of the visiting university professors or presidents. He did possess a scholarly image—greying temples, horn-rimmed glasses, and a neatly tailored conservative suit. Some even recognized his Lincolnesque face from his infrequent appearances on the evening news; and although they might have wondered why he was present, his presence evoked no special interest. He was just another scholarly face in a scholarly crowd.

As Jack patiently continued making his way through the packed aisles, he entertained second thoughts on the wisdom of trying to find and (with a little luck) interview the man evading him. He was painfully aware that instead of fighting his way through a crowd of people he could have simply waited outside Thacker's hotel room until the meeting dismissed. But, he was not one to give up so easily. He strained his neck and even stood on tiptoe, trying to locate Thacker. The center was a sea of people and he was beginning to doubt if he would find the man he was seeking before the Friday evening program began.

Then Jack spotted him. Thacker sat alone at a table near the front center of the convention room. Quickly, Jack made his way in that direction, apologizing to those he brushed or shouldered out of the way. Finally, he reached the table and addressed the man sitting there, making notes on a small pad.

"Dr. Floyd Thacker?"

A pleasant, moon-faced man with a receding hairline looked up at Jack and without recognizing him answered politely, "Yes?"

"Dr. Thacker, I apologize for bothering you but I need a few moments of your time. Can you spare a minute or two?" He added quietly, "I'm Jack Clayburn."

Thacker frowned as he instantly recognized the name, but his expression quickly changed and he said, smiling, "Ah, the gentleman who has so persistently been pursuing me."

Jack laughed. "That's my job, Doctor, talking to people." Still smiling, but with a guarded glint in his eye, Thacker asked, "And why does a network news reporter want to talk to me? Surely, it's not about this College President's Conference?"

Pulling a chair back from the table, Jack eased his tall, lean frame into it and answered, "No, it has nothing to do with this conference. I wanted to talk to you about the computer industry. I thought you could help me with a story I'm working on."

A cautious look spread over Thacker's face. "What story is that?"

"I'm doing a piece on computer viruses," Jack answered.

Dr. Thacker reached over for a glass of water. Lifting the glass to his lips, he took a deep drink, placed the glass back on the table and asked, "Help you how, Mr. Clayburn?"

Jack didn't answer immediately. He had learned long ago that the moment he approached someone for an interview, they usually tensed up, fearing the worst. His reputation as a hardnosed newsman, capable of asking some extremely sensitive and embarrassing questions, did not defuse the situation either. Therefore, he always tried to put people at ease by telling a joke or asking the most absurd and ridiculous question he could conjure up. Certain that Dr. Thacker could help provide him with background information and anecdotes on the subject of computer viruses, and seeking to ease the tension, Jack blurted out something he thought would be absurdly funny. "I want you to tell me all about the conspiracy," he said with a big smile.

The immediate effect was anything but what he expected. The blood drained from Dr. Thacker's face and his eyes opened wide. His hand jerked up, knocking over the water glass and spilling water on the table and into his lap. He looked nervously around the room and then averted his eyes from Jack's as he answered weakly, "I don't have any idea of what you're talking about."

Jack was stunned. "My God," he thought. "What have I asked?" He watched the portly little man squirm around, a frightened look spreading over his little moon face. Jack didn't know what he had stumbled onto but he wasted no time following up on what he had thought to be an absurd question. He said again, "I want you to tell me all you know about the conspiracy."

Thacker's body remained rigid. If Jack Clayburn knew, it was only a matter of time before the entire country knew. He glanced around quickly, nervously. He suddenly realized he didn't want to be seen talking to Jack Clayburn. That could be dangerous. Deciding his best course of action was to leave immediately, Thacker attempted to make some sort of show that would indicate he wanted nothing to do with the network newsman; he rose from his chair. In his haste, however, his knee hit the edge of the table, tilting the table, causing the dishes, glasses, water pitcher, and silverware to crash to the floor, creating a loud clamor. People sitting at the adjoining tables stopped talking and turned to stare. Two security guards walked over to investigate and Thacker, realizing his action had only drawn attention to himself and Clayburn, reacted in a panic.

He said loudly, "I don't know what you're talking about. Just leave me alone. I have to get back to my room."

Jack rose from his chair and asked quietly, "Doctor, if you don't know what I'm talking about, why are you so scared?"

"I'm not scared and I don't know anything. Just leave me alone." With that, Dr. Thacker turned to leave, then remembered his note pad. He reached down, grabbed it, and began rudely pushing his way through the crowd, rushing to get away from Jack and the auditorium.

Clayburn watched him leave, but from the corner of his eye he saw two men talking excitedly to each other while both were looking directly at Jack. A sense of bewilderment spread through his mind. What in the world had he walked into? All he had asked was some silly question about a conspiracy and the good doctor had literally gone into a hysterical panic. Jack knew he had stumbled onto something, but what? Was the virus part of some conspiracy? If so, what kind of conspiracy? And where? Who is involved? The university where Thacker worked? A business firm? Was the government connected? Jack had a thousand questions and absolutely no answers.

Dr. Floyd Thacker exited the auditorium and was nervously waiting in the lobby for an elevator to carry him up to his room. He kept looking around, studying the faces of those near, trying to determine if anyone was watching him or displaying any unusual interest. He was scared. He remained scared from the first day of his involvement. He had always opposed the plan and he was well aware that many of the wrong people knew of his opposition. Originally, he had been scared of becoming involved. Now, he was scared for his life.

Thacker struggled to calm down. Maybe Jack Clayburn was sent to test him. Maybe that was it—and he passed the test with flying colors. Anyone watching, and there was always someone watching, could not accuse him of leaking any information. That had to be it. Jack Clayburn had been a test. There was no way Clayburn could have known of the plan. The secret was too well guarded. Reassured, he breathed easier; his heart stopped pounding in his chest and by the time the elevator arrived his metabolism had returned to a normal state. He was still scared but at least he felt safe. He had not said anything and his actions surely indicated he had not cooperated in any manner with Jack Clayburn. Still, as he stepped into the elevator, he looked carefully to make certain that no one was watching. The doors closed and he sighed. Once in his room, he could pack, leave, return to the safety of the university, and from there he could assure his former associates that he had not volunteered any incriminating information to the television reporter.

In the auditorium, Jack Clayburn still sat at the table. He had momentarily forgotten that he was working on the virus story and was, instead, trying to determine the significance of Thacker's obviously unintentional slip. He was not so engrossed in his thoughts, however, that he failed to observe that two men whom he had noticed earlier, standing near the stage, were studying him carefully. Nor did he fail to notice that when he did get up from his table and began moving toward an exit, both men discreetly fell behind him, following him from the auditorium.

Jack Clayburn had a naturally suspicious nature and to assure that his imagination was not playing tricks, he walked through the front door of the hotel as if he planned to leave. Once outside, he walked a few steps and then, as if he had suddenly remembered something, he turned and retraced his footsteps. Sure enough, the two men following him outside now turned to follow him into the hotel.

So, they were following him. Why? Had they seen him talking to Thacker? Obviously. But why the interest in him?

On a sudden impulse, he stepped into the small gift shop and walked immediately to the card rack. His eyes scanned the cards quickly and, seeing what he wanted, he grabbed it, walked to the cashier's counter and paid for the card. While she was ringing up the sale and getting his change, he wrote "Dr. Floyd Thacker" on the envelope. Smiling his thanks to the young cashier, he turned and walked back into the lobby. There was no sight of the two men who had followed him so, walking briskly, he proceeded to the registration desk.

Casually, he handed the envelope to the desk clerk and said, "I missed Dr. Thacker in the banquet room. Would you see that he gets this please."

The clerk assured him it would be taken care of and Jack walked away. He walked to the coffee shop, sat at the counter, ordered a cup of coffee, and patiently allowed five or six minutes to pass. When he figured that the clerk had had time enough to deposit the envelope, he arose, threw some change on the counter, returned to the registration desk, and, waving a folded sheet of paper, said, "I left an envelope a moment ago for Dr. Thacker and I forgot to include something. Would you get the envelope and let me add this?"

The clerk nodded and stepped around the privacy wall to retrieve the original envelope. He handed it to Jack, who slipped the blank sheet of folded paper into the envelope, casually noting the room number written on the front of the envelope. He knew no one would release Dr. Thacker's room number willingly, but his little charade always enabled him to find out the room number anyway.

Simple as that—Dr. Thacker was in Room 714.

Smiling to himself, he walked toward the elevator, carefully sweeping the lobby with his eyes, and, satisfied that the two men were no longer around, he bypassed the elevator and walked instead to the stair exit. Jack Clayburn did not stick to any regimen of exercise but he did walk as much as possible and this included always using the stairs rather than an elevator. He figured that during any week, walking up and down several flights of stairs provided him with as much exercise as any jogger. Occasionally, he even ran up the stairs but on this evening he maintained a normal pace, climbing steadily upwards, heading for the seventh floor, mulling over his meeting with Floyd Thacker. As he reached the third floor, his thoughts were interrupted by a sound from below. A door closed. He glanced downward just as one of the two men he suspected of following him out of the hotel—the one with the buck teeth and garish sports jacket—entered the stairwell. Jack moved back against the wall, out of sight, and quickened his pace up the stairs. He had the sudden, frightening thought that what was happening might be serious. He was not necessarily a coward but he was well aware of his limitations and he did not relish the thought of a confrontation with two thugs who both appeared to outweigh him by a considerably healthier number of pounds. He decided he needed to get to his room as quickly as possible—and stay there.

He dashed up another flight, eased the door open quietly and stepped into the hotel corridor. Within seconds he was in his fifth floor room, inside, standing at the closed door with his ear pressed against the door, listening intently for any sound that might suggest the man with the buck teeth had followed him.

Only after several minutes had passed without any sound did he allow himself to relax. Mr. Buck Teeth had obviously decided not to follow him to his room or had lost him completely. Relieved, he walked over and sat on the bed. He was still trying to figure out Thacker's reaction. He mulled over the problem for several minutes and then, picking up the phone, dialed room service and ordered a club sandwich, glass of milk, and a newspaper. Next, he called the network's research office, which was available to newsmen twenty-four hours a day, and within a few seconds a feminine voice at the other end identified herself. "Hello, this is Cindy."

Jack heaved a satisfied sigh. He knew Cindy and knew he could count on her to be thorough. "Cindy, this is Jack Clayburn."

"Mr. Clayburn. How the heck are you? Haven't heard from you in a while. I was beginning to think you were caught up in the purge. What can I do for you?"

Jack smiled at the mention of the "purge." There had been quite a reshuffling and reassigning of personnel lately. However, from his position he had viewed the many personnel changes without too much concern. He had learned that in the television business, people come and go. He had managed to achieve his status by minding his business, staying out of trouble, and maintaining a high level of performance in his work. If the network wanted to get rid of him, it would cost them plenty to buy out his contract and he doubted if they wanted to do that.

"Cindy, I need you to get together whatever you can on a Dr. Floyd Thacker. He's the president of Waylanth College and I need whatever background information you can come up with." He added, "And I need it on my desk in the morning."

"You'll have it, Mr. Clayburn. I'll get right on it."

He thanked her and hung up the phone. He walked over, turned on the television set, and began flipping through the channels, searching for anything that might prove interesting. As he flipped from network to network, he was reminded of Cindy's reference to the "purge." There were, indeed, a batch of new faces, not only on his network but the three others as well. He recognized very few of the newcomers and although he knew retirement and a few ill-timed deaths had depleted the networks' staffs, he had not been aware that the turnover within the industry had been so complete. Curious, he thought.

Suddenly, there was a knock on his door. With a start, he jumped up and warily asked, "Who is it?"

"Room service," a voice answered from the other side.

Jack unlocked and opened the door. The bellhop rolled the cart with his food order into the room, placed it near a chair, and asked, "Anything else, Mr. Clayburn?"

"No, that's it," replied Jack, reaching for the check. He added a gratuity to the amount, signed his name and room number, and handed it back to the young man. Thanking him, he escorted him out the door, locking it again, and turned his attention to the food on the cart.

While he ate, he thumbed through the newspaper. But his mind refused to concentrate. His thoughts kept returning to Dr. Thacker. Finally, in exasperation, he rose from the bed, threw the paper aside, grabbed his sports jacket, and prepared to leave the room. Thacker's room was only two floors above and he felt compelled to make at least another attempt to see the man. With a little luck, and with no audience, maybe Thacker would sit and talk to him. It was worth a try.

Easing the door open, he stuck his head out, glancing left and right, and seeing no one in the corridor, stepped out and quietly closed the door. He then walked immediately to the elevator, punched the button, and waited. He couldn't quite bring himself to use the stairs on this excursion, though he doubted anyone was sitting, waiting for him. Still, no sense being utterly careless—or reckless.

The elevator arrived, the doors opened, and he stepped in, joining a couple obviously returning to their room. He ignored them, as they did him, and within a few seconds, the carrier had stopped on the seventh floor. Stepping out, he studied the arrows and room directions for a moment, then turned right and walked toward Room 714. When he reached the door, he paused, looked around to make certain no one was watching—especially Mr. Buck Teeth—and then started to knock.

But the door was open. Just a crack, but open. Unusual, he thought. He knocked gently. There was no answer. Knocking a little harder the second time, he called out in a low voice, "Dr. Thacker?" There was no answer. Then he noticed that the door had been forced open. A knot grabbed his stomach and an inner voice urged him to get away quickly, but the reporter's curiosity in him was too strong. He pushed the door open and stood for a moment peering inside, allowing his eyes to adjust to the darkness of the interior.

Then he saw it. A body lying half off the bed, head hanging down. Jack looked up and down the corridor, stared hard inside, and, not seeing anyone, walked swiftly into the room. He reached the bed and saw that it was Dr. Thacker, who apparently, had been shot. Considering the amount of blood on the bed and the wall, the man was shot several times. Jack stood there, not knowing what to do first, and then he heard a low moan. Startled, he realized the man was still alive. He quickly leaned down and with much effort, managed to raise the wounded man up on the bed.

When he looked into Thacker's face, he knew immediately the man was dying. Uttering a curse, he reached for the phone but Thacker, with a superhuman effort, grabbed his arm. With blood pouring from his mouth, he spoke in a rasping whisper, "Don't bother. It's too late. You have to stop them. You have to stop them." He began coughing and blood trickled from his mouth but he managed to add, "You have to stop Solomon."

"Stop them from what?" Jack asked frantically. "Who is Solomon?"

"Stop them from . . ." Thacker's voice fell to an even lower whisper but as Jack leaned closer to listen, there was only a gurgle as one last bubble of air traveled through the bleeding throat. With one last gasp, he said weakly, "Solomon."

Then he was dead.

# 2.

---

# Chapter Two

In his Colorado office, Clay Davis was working late. As he read the report a member of his staff had prepared, he stopped and looked up at the attractive woman seated opposite his desk. "This is all pretty strange, Diane."

She shook her head in agreement. "Strange is the right word. We're not sure whether it's all just a coincidence or if it has something to do with our problem."

"Who first stumbled onto this?" "Sean. When we checked on the earth tremors that have been hitting us, he discovered that there have been some weird things going on all over the world—tremors, one serious earthquake, unusual sunspot activity, meteor storms, higher tides along the coast." She paused and added, "All very unusual, and unnatural."

Clay nodded. "Any ideas?"

Diane hesitated, then, in a slow, deliberate voice, replied, "Not really. It could just be the normal cycle of things." Then, in a hesitant voice, added, "This might sound silly, Clay, but all of these flukes began about the time we started testing the force field."

Clay's head jerked up, then he laughed. "Are you suggesting our experiments are affecting the world's weather?"

Sheepishly, she answered, "No, I just mention it because the first unusual report we received coincided with our first experiment. And remember today—immediately following your test, when you turned the force field generators off, we had that earth tremor."

Clay laughed again. "I don't think so, Angel. The force field generator may be the most powerful thing around right now, but I seriously doubt it's affecting weather cycles in any way. That wouldn't make sense."

Diane tossed her head, dismissing the subject but Clay gave her a curious look and asked, "That doesn't mean the possibility of weather tampering doesn't exist. Do you think that perhaps someone has figured out how to control Mother Nature?"

The thought was so ludicrous, he almost laughed out loud but the scientist in him was ready to accept the possibility. He knew, more than anyone in the world, with technology, anything was possible.

Diane Williams shook her head. "It's a possibility. I think someone should be keeping an eye on all this, just in case."

"All right," Clay said, "you and Sean stay on top of it. If there's anything to it, we'll find out before anyone else. In the meantime, I'll continue to have Art check the facility for structural damage. I don't think we've had a tremor big enough to affect this place, but I don't think it'll hurt to keep an eye out." He placed the report in one of the trays stacked on his desk and asked, "Is there anything else before we call it a night?"

"Yes," she answered, with a mischievous gleam in her eyes.

"You haven't told me you loved me today."

Clay laughed out loud. Standing up, he walked around the desk and stood before her. "OK, business hours are over. Let's talk about the advantages of my girl also being my top research assistant." He leaned forward, pulled her from her chair into his arms, and their lips met.

Below Clay's office, several stories deep within the bowels of the earth, Art Gibson stepped from the elevator into the basement, or lowest level, of the underground facility. The inspection was completed. As far as he could determine, neither the day's tremor nor the previous tremors of the past few weeks had affected the building in any way. Moving from floor to floor, he inspected every square inch of the facility and in his report to Dr. Davis, he could honestly say there was absolutely no structural damage. He had expected none. But Davis wanted the inspection and, like a good soldier, Art inspected. Now, as the elevator doors closed behind him, he felt more relaxed. He stopped and stood, listening—intently. Art Gibson was in his domain, and it was a world of sound. Unlike the six other levels, which were chrome and stainless steel and lighted ceilings divided into practical, functional sections, Level Seven, deep within the earth, was dimly lit, rectangularly open, filled with whirring, running machinery; and that is what Art was listening to—the sound of motors. His sensitive ears were finely tuned to each, as a doctor's ears to a stethoscope, and he could listen and detect a missed beat, an unsynchronized cycle, or an irregular rhythm.

As Art listened, he separated the symphony of sound, isolating each piece of machinery and, hearing nothing that indicated anything was amiss, he began to walk toward the rear of the basement to his office. Every piece of equipment in the room was computer controlled, and although he knew the computer would alert him to any problem, he always visually, audibly, or physically checked everything as often as possible. He had never quite been able to completely accept the computer as a reliable problem detection system. The scientists, working on the various levels above the basement, joked about his reluctance to move into the twentieth century but he ignored their good-natured gibes and simply reminded them that he, not the computer, would be fired in the event of a serious or destructive equipment failure.

The gentle, good-natured Art was a popular man in the facility. Overweight and a little rough and gruff in his manner, he was a study in contrast among the educated men he worked for. And they liked him. They especially enjoyed kidding Art about his computer resistance, but they also knew that he was a conscientiously efficient maintenance man. He was responsible for insuring that either everything worked, or if it didn't work it was repaired as quickly as possible. He did both quite well, especially when taking into consideration the fact that he, and his assistant, maintained a seven-story structure by themselves.

Few buildings, anywhere in the world, were as completely self-sustaining as this facility. Although the complex was powered primarily from outside sources, it could, with the flick of a switch and the push of a button, activate one or all of its three massive power generators. These generators were more than sufficient for the power requirements of the entire complex, including the needs of the facility's electricity-devouring scientific experiments.

A ceiling-high air conditioning and heating unit supplied all the levels with fresh, filtered, clean air, and the computer regulated the temperature of that air for each level, even each room. An innovative recycling unit, similar to those utilized aboard submarines, allowed the facility to use and reuse its own air and exhaust.

A subterranean reservoir provided water for the complex. The water was pumped up from the depths and then moved into holding tanks. Its flow into the building's hot and cold water systems was controlled and regulated by computer, based on demand and usage. Still another pumping system forced the water upwards while yet another brought it down in the form of waste or used water, which, if necessary, could be recycled, stored, and used again.

On the outside, gigantic fuel storage tanks holding millions of gallons of fuel had been buried. In the event of power failure, or even power shortages, the fuel was available for gasoline and diesel engines which, in turn, could be connected to the generators. It was all very impressive, but for what purpose?

Art could not understand, nor had anyone ever provided a satisfactory explanation, why there was a need for all the back-up systems. Whenever he raised the subject with one of the scientists upstairs, his question was either ignored or the answer provided was so blatantly vague he knew he was being given the run-around. Why, he often asked himself, was it necessary for the facility to be so independent and self sufficient? He knew the facility was listed officially as a seismic detection center, supposedly tracking earth tremors around the world. But, he also knew that very little seismic monitoring took place within the facility. Whatever the scientists were working on, Art knew it had very little to do with earthquakes. As he entered his office, he immediately dismissed the questions from his mind and, sitting down at his desk, Art began checking the messages on his computer. There was only one requiring his immediate attention. It was a request from Clay Davis, the director of the facility, to install yet another high voltage outlet inside the laboratory on Level Four.

Art shook his head in disbelief as he studied the message. The request represented the fourth such outlet he had been asked to install in less than three weeks. The request only substantiated the fact that the facility was anything but a seismic center. Whatever Davis was working on, it obviously utilized enormous amounts of electricity. Obviously, Art thought to himself, something big and mysterious was going on upstairs. The question was, what?

A loud, ear-piercing sound interrupted Art Gibson's thoughts as he sat at his desk. Immediately, his eyes darted from gauge to gauge, seeking the source of a malfunction being signaled by the computer. He quickly defined the problem. It was simply another massive power fluctuation in the generating system, the third of the day, and every time it happened the back-up generators were activated. He shook his head, turned to his computer keyboard and began entering commands. Within seconds, all systems returned to normal and he breathed a sigh of relief.

The power fluctuation had become a recurring problem and, as he learned, one not restricted to his equipment. Art knew that installations throughout the world were experiencing the same problem. The power fluctuations were not serious but they did present an irritating deviation from the norm—a situation which no one seemed able to explain.

He checked the gauges again and, seeing that the generating system was stabilized, reached for Richard Mendoza's Friday shift report. A quick glance revealed, as it usually did, that Richard had completed all the minor repair jobs assigned by Art the previous day, Thursday, and he noted that several new malfunctions had been repaired also.

The two men worked well together. They shared the work load and both took pride in maintaining the facility at top efficiency. They alternated their work days in such a manner to insure that when one was off, the other was on duty. In the vernacular of the blue-collar workingman, Art and Richard had it made. The work at times was tedious but they were not overly supervised nor did anyone badger or hound them to work faster, work harder. The two were allowed complete freedom and autonomy to work at their own pace. There were long periods when there was nothing to do because when there was no maintenance or repair work, the computer controlled all facility functions automatically and the maintenance men were left to occupy their time as they saw fit. Richard enjoyed playing cards with the security guards or watching television. Art, on the other hand, preferred to remain at his desk, on the lowest level, isolated from staff members, reading and studying his Bible.

The well-worn Bible resting, with several Bible reference books, on his desk attested to the fact that the short, powerfully built man had spent a considerable amount of time leafing through the pages of the Holy Book. He freely admitted, when asked, that he was a born-again Christian but for the most part the gentle giant was a low-profile Christian. He preferred to display his convictions by example rather than by words and although everyone upstairs sensed something different in Art—a gentleness or sweetness not usually associated with such a rough-looking man—few knew that his demeanor could be attributed to the inner peace he had achieved with his God.

So, with nothing requiring his immediate attention, Art reached for his Bible and turned to the book of Revelation.

- - - - - - - - - - - -

In New York, Adam Armstrong looked up from his work as his personal secretary entered. He smiled, and asked, "What is it, Sylvia?"

"Chris is here, Mr. Armstrong."

Adam glanced at his watch. "On time, as usual. Tell him to go on in and get ready. I'll be there in a moment." Reaching for a stack of papers, he handed them to Sylvia and said, "These need to go out first thing in the morning." He reached for another stack, and instructed her, "These also need to go but there's no rush. And this is my Los Angeles speech. Fax Michael a copy and tell him to make the revisions I've noted in the margins."

With that, Armstrong leaned back in his executive lounge chair and studied Sylvia as she gathered up the papers. She was not an attractive woman but what she lacked in beauty she more than made up for in efficiency. More importantly, he knew she was completely loyal to him and him alone. For just a moment, he was tempted to bring her into his confidence and explain what was about to take place, but he immediately knew sharing the knowledge would be a mistake. Instead, he said, "It's late, Sylvia. You'd better call it a night."

She gave him a reassuring smile and replied, "There are still a few things I have to do. No problem. I'm fine."

He watched her leave and, as the door to his office closed silently, he began clearing papers from his desk. He was tired, but he was also excited. Adam Armstrong knew it was about to happen and, being a man of vision, he was prepared. He had studied the complete blueprint and although he could not alter or stop the chain of events already in motion, he could formulate his own plan of action and prepare for the disaster he knew was sure to follow. In essence, he was prepared to pick up the pieces and put them back together to his own benefit. He raised himself from his desk and began walking toward the door leading to the study adjoining his office. Chris was ready to give him his daily massage and afterward, he had a late dinner appointment at his club with General Norman Petrie. Things were going as planned. Pleased with himself, he opened the door and entered.

"Good evening, Mr. Armstrong. I'm ready when you are, Sir" said Chris.

- - - - - - - - - - - -

In Houston, Texas, Ryan Abernathy guided the young woman through the theater doors and into the humid night air. They headed immediately toward the parking lot and Ryan's car, walking slowly, hand in hand, neither anxious for the evening to end.

"Good movie," Ryan volunteered.

Pam looked up at him, smiled, and agreed. "It was good. I'm glad we decided on seeing it instead of the other one."

"Still not too late. Want to grab a little something to eat?"

Pam shook her head. "I have a busy day tomorrow and I need to get to bed. Besides, we're going out to dinner tomorrow night." She asked mischievously, "Or have you forgotten?"

Looking down at her, Ryan answered seriously, "You have to be kidding. You're the greatest thing that ever happened to me and you think I would forget a date? No way. You're stuck with me, Pamela Richards. And don't you forget it."

She laughed. "I know it. And I love it."

As they got into Ryan's car, she leaned her head back on the neck rest and sighed. The night was so beautiful, she thought, and the evening had been perfect. Reluctantly, she knew it was time to give Ryan the bad news and she wondered how he would react.

"Ryan?"

Busy maneuvering the car through the exiting theater traffic, Ryan responded without looking at her. "What is it, Love?"

"Do you really love me?"

The question made him steal a quick glance at her. "Do I really love you? What kind of question is that? Of course, I love you. Do you have any doubts?"

"No, I was just checking."

They drove in silence for a while and, finally, she asked, "Do you remember when we first met?"

Keeping one hand on the wheel, Ryan reached over and took her hand in his. "Considering that was the most important thing that ever happened in my life, of course I remember."

Ryan loved the small, blonde-haired, blue-eyed angel sitting next to him with all his heart. He had never in his wildest dreams thought he would fall for another woman. His first marriage ended in divorce—a messy, dirty, expensive divorce—and the experience left him disillusioned and embittered. Fortunately, no children were involved but his emotional state was shattered. For months afterwards, he buried himself in his work, rejecting all social overtures from friends and acquaintances. He wanted nothing to do with any woman, and he became a workaholic. He might have spent the rest of his life working fifteen, sixteen, even eighteen hours a day, pausing only to catch a few hours of sleep and living off fast foods and frozen dinners.

Then, he met Pamela.

Ryan had always heard of, and dismissed laughingly, "love at first sight." Never again. She was transferred from Washington to General Petrie's NASA office, and the first time he saw Pamela smile, he knew he was in love. For a long time, in deference to NASA policy, which prohibited employees from fraternizing, he avoided her. But he managed to meet her—accidentally, of course, in the lounge, cafeteria, and even the parking lot. He often invented excuses to visit her office in order to flirt with her or just to see her. This went on for several months and just when Ryan thought he would go out of his mind over his one-way infatuation, she stopped him in the hall one day and said, "Ryan, I really think it's time you asked me to dinner or some thing. We can't go on like this."

Ryan and Pamela began dating and for the first time in his life, something became more important to Ryan than his work. He lived for the time he spent with Pamela and his job became something that filled the hours before he saw her again. He knew they had something special and, he believed, or hoped, she also knew they had something special.

Chuckling, Ryan offered, "What made you ask me to go out?"

With a feigned shocked look, she replied, "Me? Asked you?

All I did was state the obvious. I knew you wanted to go out and I wanted to go out with you. I just wanted to know when you were going to stop beating around the bush and ask me out."

"Well, I'm glad you did." He turned off the expressway, followed the exit ramp and then made a right turn, continuing on toward her apartment complex.

"Ryan, I may have to go away for a while."

"What? What do you mean, go away?"

"I mean, I have something personal I have to take care of. Something for my father."

Pamela never discussed her father and Ryan really had no idea what the man did. Nor was he even curious about her family. She never mentioned them, and he never brought the subject up. However, if her father's presence was going to cause an interruption in their lives, Ryan wanted to know why.

"Where are you going?"

"I'm not sure. Probably back to Washington for a while. I shouldn't be gone long and I'll call you every day, I promise."

"Maybe I can take some vacation and go with you," Ryan suggested.

"No," she said quickly. "That won't be possible." She added reassuringly, "It's not a big deal, but I have to do it. I won't even be gone long enough for you to miss me." Ryan doubted that. "When are you leaving?"

"I'm not sure about that either but I'll let you know in plenty of time so you can treat me to a magnificent going-away dinner at the most expensive restaurant in town."

Ryan laughed. "You're always thinking about your stomach. I can't figure out where a little thing like you puts all that food you eat. And I can't figure out how you keep that figure either."

She grinned. "Just be thankful, Mr. Abernathy." She moved over closer and snuggled on his shoulder. "I do love you, Ryan." She sighed and added, "I love you so much."

Ryan pulled to a stop in front of her apartment, turned off the motor and lights, turned slightly and took her in his arms.

"And I love you, Ms. Richards."

- - - - - - - - - - -

Meanwhile, back in New York, the police had questioned Jack Clayburn at length but he was unable to contribute much in connection with the murder of Dr. Floyd Thacker. Jack told them of his short conversation with Thacker in the banquet room but he carefully omitted any references to the "conspiracy" story. Nor did he tell them about the two men following him through the hotel. He told the detective he had gone to Thacker's room in hopes of continuing the interview but when he arrived, the door was open and Thacker was dead. Again, Jack omitted part of the story and did not offer any reference to Thacker's dying words. He felt he would be much better off retaining that information for himself.

Finally, the police finished their questioning, released him, and Jack returned to his room. There, he sat on his bed, in the dark, trying to comprehend all that happened. Thacker's last words referred to someone named Solomon. Jack had no idea who Solomon was or if

Solomon was even a first or last name. Picking up the phone, he dialed the network number and asked for Cindy in the research department. She was on the line in a matter of seconds.

"Cindy here."

"Little girl, this is Jack again."

She groaned. "Give me a break, Mr. Clayburn. I haven't even started on your stuff yet."

"No problem. I have something else for you to check."

He could hear her sigh but she said brightly, "OK, lay it on me, and I'll see what I can do."

"Run the name Solomon through your computer and see if you come up with anything."

There was a pause on the other end and Cindy then asked, "Is that Solomon as in King Solomon or is it Soloman?—with an 'a' ?"

"Try them both and see what you get," Jack instructed. He added, "I hate to tell you but . . . "

"I know," she interrupted. "This is a rush priority."

He thanked her, hung up, and looked at his watch. It was almost midnight. There wasn't much else that could be done. With the weekend staring him in the face, Jack knew it would be Monday morning before he could seriously begin any investigation on either Thacker, Solomon, or the so-called computer virus. He slammed his fist into his hand, mumbled a curse, and began to undress. He figured a quick shower, a little sleep, and then the following morning, Saturday, he would return to Washington. He knew once he was back in his office, he could begin searching for some answers.

# 3.

# Chapter Three

**R**yan picked up the lamp and threw it against the wall. The crash of broken glass sounded good to his ears and he briefly thought of slinging something else. Not only was he mad and frustrated, he was beginning to get very worried.

He returned to Pam's apartment after a fruitless weekend of trying to find out where she had gone. Saturday morning, when he called her from his office and received no answer, he assumed she was sleeping late. When there was no answer at noon or to his calls every fifteen minutes for several hours, he finally told his assistant to take over while he went to check on Pamela. That's when he discovered she was gone.

Fearing the worst, he let himself into her apartment with the key she had given him weeks earlier. A quick check of her apartment relieved one fear but produced another. There was no sign of violence, no sign of foul play; but there was also no sign of Pam. Everything was as it should be except her closet and bathroom. Both were empty. Her clothes were gone as were all her toilet articles and makeup. Neither was there any sign of her hair dryer or curlers. That's when Ryan realized she had packed her things and left.

But where? And why?

He sat down at her kitchen table replaying the Friday night conversation. There was nothing said on their date that provided him any clues other than the mention of her plans to help her father. Ryan didn't even know her father's name, where he lived, or where he worked. He vaguely remembered he was in the military and Ryan guessed the two had a loving but strained relationship. She never talked about her father, and any question Ryan asked about him was immediately ignored or brushed off with a smile or shake of the head. The more he thought about it, the more he realized he didn't really know very much about Pam other than that he loved her. But Ryan did know one thing. He knew she loved him too, so if she left, she must be in trouble. And he knew it must be serious trouble or she would have explained everything to him.

Acting on the theory that she was in trouble, Ryan proceeded with his own investigation. He knew if he went to the police, they would laugh. (Another girl got cold feet with her boyfriend and left.) Or, she found another man. That was their usual assumption. Ryan knew better. Pam didn't have cold feet, and he knew there was no other man.

As the Security Director for NASA, Ryan enjoyed certain privileges and he wasted no time calling any and every one on the installation who might possibly help him with the mystery of Pamela's disappearance. He spent Saturday afternoon, Saturday night, and Sunday calling everyone he knew in every government office across the country. When he received no help from any of the people Pam worked with, Ryan located and called General Whiteside. Rather, he tried to call General Whiteside. The moment the general's aide discovered whom he was and why he was calling, Ryan was told "the general is unavailable at the moment."

Ryan's fingers drummed a steady tattoo on the kitchen table. Everyone he contacted readily agreed to help and promised to get back to him as soon as possible. That wasn't quick enough for Ryan. He needed to stay busy, checking, calling, doing something. He reached for Pamela's phone and dialed his boss's office.

"Mr. Marchand, this is Ryan." He didn't ask. He simply stated a fact. "I won't be in today or tomorrow. I have a personal problem I need to take care of, and I should be back Wednesday or Thursday."

Ryan listened for several moments and then interrupted the speaker on the other end. "I'm aware of that, Sir, and I'll be back for that for sure. My staff will do just fine until then."

He listened again, impatiently drumming his fingers, and finally said, "I understand all that, Mr. Marchand, but this can't be helped. I have to take off two, maybe three days. But I'll be back in time." He added, "And thanks for your understanding." Without giving the man another chance to respond, Ryan hung up.

He sat there for a moment thinking out his next steps. Ryan fought the sense of frustration and desperation threatening to consume his thoughts and calmly weighed his options. He had friends in both the FBI and the CIA and thought they might be able to help. But, he would have to go to Washington. Once there, he could enlist some professional assistance. Ryan knew one man who might really be in a position to dig up some answers. The two had become friends over the years and though Ryan had never asked him for a favor, he knew he could count on his help. He reached for his address book, looked up the name, reached for the phone, and dialed the number. On the first ring there was an answer and Ryan said confidently, "This is Ryan Abernathy from NASA calling. I would like to speak to Jack Clayburn."

# 24 J. Carroll

The network cafeteria was never crowded on Monday mornings. Jack attributed the absence of the regulars to a long and harried weekend, or, as others suggested, a stomach too weak for Monday morning cafeteria food. Whatever the reason, he enjoyed the Monday morning privacy and as he munched on a Danish and drank coffee, he scanned the morning paper. Then, he heard his name being called. Looking up, he saw Skip Reynolds, science editor for the network, heading for his table.

Skip wasn't the most popular man on the Washington Bureau staff, and it had been rumored for several months that he was on his way out but whether he stayed or left, Jack liked him. He seriously doubted if the network would fail to renew Skip's contract because even though the opinionated reporter managed to step on more toes and egos than any other staffer, he consistently pulled high ratings. The viewing public and the critics liked his down-home, folksy style and the uncomplicated and easy-to-understand way he had of explaining even the most technical scientific news.

Skip pulled a chair out and without waiting for an invitation, sat down. Smiling at Jack, he said, "You're a hard man to catch up with. Where have you been all weekend?"

Jack grinned and answered, "Here and there but mostly around." Jack filled his coffee cup, added a half-teaspoon of sugar and stirred. "What are you working on right now?" Jack asked, more out of politeness than curiosity because he really didn't care what Skip was on.

"I'm doing a piece on the goofy things that have been going on across the world."

"Goofy things?"

Skip nodded. "A few abnormalities. Last week there were five separate earthquakes. Tides have been running higher all up and down the coast, here and around the world. And, there have been some unusual earth tremors reported where normally there is never any seismic activity."

Jack politely asked, "Any scientific explanations for all that stuff?"

Skip shrugged. "Take your pick. It's all being blamed on everything from sunspots to underground testing to acid rain. No one really knows. Just another bunch of unexplainable freaks of nature." A big grin spread across his face. "Speaking of unexplainable freaks of nature, I saw your face on the tube all weekend."

Jack looked up and said dryly, "Yeah, I know. I wanted to keep a low profile on that, but someone jumped on the story."

"Well, it was a slow weekend and you ain't exactly unknown around the country. You're news, especially when you're a witness to a murder."

Quickly Jack replied, "I wasn't a witness to anything. I just happened to find the body, that's all."

Skip's tone changed as he commented, "That's a shame about Thacker. He was a pretty decent chap. I wonder why he was murdered?"

Jack did not volunteer any theories but did ask, "Did you know him?"

"Not very well, but I knew a little about his work. He was one of the top three or four computer men in the country. Really knew his stuff. He could write his own ticket out in corporate America, but when he left Armstrong Industries he said he preferred the quiet college life to business. Guess that's why he accepted the position down at Waylanth College." "Thacker worked for Armstrong Industries? Adam Armstrong's company?"

"That's right. He was one of Armstrong's fair-haired boys until they had a falling out."

Jack digested this tidbit of information for a moment and then said, "I didn't know Armstrong was into computers."

Skip looked at him curiously. "Not computers. Software. His company is one of the governments biggest suppliers of software."

"Really?"

"Yep. Armstrong Industries provides just about all the management, inventory, and systems software for the major government departments." He laughed and, looking around to make sure no one else could hear, whispered, "Old Adam might make the front pages with all his do-gooder stuff and charity work but he's out to make a buck just like the next guy. And believe you me, he makes big bucks off Uncle Sam."

"I didn't realize Armstrong was doing that much business with the government."

Skip shook his head. "Big business." He leaned back in his chair and added, "Ironically, it was Thacker who convinced him to go after government contracts."

"Thacker?"

"Yeah. Thacker used to work with the computer whiz, Clay Davis, and when the two of them split, he quit government work and went with Armstrong. Used his connections and influence to build the software business for Armstrong Industries." He laughed. "And get this. He ends up going back to the government, as a computer consultant—all while he was on Armstrong's payroll. Thacker advised the various government agencies on which software to use which, by pure accident or coincidence, happened to be the software manufactured by his boss, Adam Armstrong. Neat arrangement, right?"

Jack nodded yes. "Very neat." Curious, he asked, "Who is this Clay Davis you mentioned?"

"Davis?" Skip smiled at Jack and answered, "Jack, you're going to have to start keeping up on things. Davis is the number one computer man in the country. He sets the pace. He writes the book. Others just kind of follow him."

Jack struggled to remember the name but finally admitted, "I swear, I've never heard his name mentioned until now."

"That's not hard to believe. He's a real low-profile kind of guy. One of those true egg-heads. Spends all his time cooped up in a laboratory inventing things for the Defense Department."

The two men continued talking for several more minutes and finally Jack said, "Skip, I've got to get upstairs and make a few calls. I'd like to get with you some time today and talk some more about Thacker. Can you spare a minute or two?"

Skip nodded. "The only thing I have is a taping session and then I'm free. Just give me a holler."

Jack threw him a salute, and walked away.

A few seconds later he was climbing the stairs, leading to the third floor. As he stepped from the stairway, he stopped at the receptionist's desk to pick up his messages and then proceeded down the long corridor to his office, waving to several people yelling out greetings. As he made his way, he noticed the handyman replacing still another name on an office door. Curious, he began to count the new names on office doors as he walked and before he reached his office he had counted six. To Jack, that was a high number. Networks were notorious for having a high personnel turnover but the six represented key positions at the network—and that was most unusual. He wondered where all the new people were coming from and, more curiously, he wondered why there had been so many changes.

Opening his office door, he walked in and promptly forgot all about network replacements. His desk top was empty. Just as he left it. The package he expected to be on his desk from Research was not there. He reached for the phone and dialed a number and when someone answered, said, "This is Jack Clayburn—I asked for some materials Friday that haven't arrived yet. Where are they?"

He listened for a moment and, in reply to a question, answered, "I wanted some background info on a Floyd Thacker and I wanted a tracer search on a man named Solomon."

He listened and then interrupted the speaker on the other end of the call. "Well, I don't know what the problem is either, but I need that information. See if you can find it and get it to me as soon as possible."

He thanked the researcher, politely, and hung up. Strange, he thought. Usually, the Research Department made few errors and was prompt but his request was lost. Nothing to do, he thought, but wait. Then, he had a sudden thought. Over the course of many years, Jack developed a nice working relationship with most of the investigative departments in Washington and occasionally, in return for a favor or in an exchange of information, he could draw on these contacts for research help. With this in mind, he picked up the phone, and called a friend with the FBI.

"Roger," he said when the phone was answered, "this is Jack Clayburn. How are you doing old buddy?"

He talked with the FBI agent for a few minutes about a variety of subjects and then casually said, "Roger I need a favor. Can you run a name through your computer and see what you can find?"

He gave Roger Grant the name "Solomon" and asked him to call as soon as he had something. They talked for several more minutes and then Jack said, "Roger, I'm going to have to run. See what you can find for me, Buddy. I appreciate you." Hanging up the phone, he turned his attention to the mail. As usual, it was a large stack; and he knew it would require a little time to sort through everything so, reluctantly, he began.

He was barely into the chore when the phone rang. To his surprise, the receptionist informed him he had a call from a Ryan Abernathy in Houston. Curious, he took the call immediately. He knew Ryan from previous assignments at NASA while covering space shots, and over the years the two had developed a good relationship. They had even become friends.

"Hi, Ryan. What's going on?" Laughing, he added, "Or should I say 'What's going up'?"

From the other end, in Houston, Ryan answered, "A lot of things going on, Jack, and I'm not referring to the big launch this week. Are you coming down for it?"

"Not this time, fellow. Someone else is covering it. Must be too big a story for me to handle. They're sending Big Al down to cover it."

Big Al was Al Walker, the network anchor, who, occasionally, left the studios of New York for an on-the-spot report of major events.

Ryan replied quickly, "Good, because I'm coming up to Washington and I'm going to need your help. I've got a problem I need you to look into."

With interest piqued, Jack asked, "What's the trouble, Ryan?"

Ryan told him of Pamela's disappearance and of his unsuccessful efforts to locate her. When he finished, he said, "Jack, I'm running into dead ends; and I'm running out of people to help me. I'm about to go out of my mind and I wouldn't ask you to do this but I'm desperate."

Patiently, Ryan explained further. "Jack, I know this woman. I'm in love with her. We were planning to get married. And now she has disappeared without a note or anything, and no one in her office is excited or disturbed about it. Does that make sense to you?" Jack thought about the disappearance for a moment and then suggested,

"Ryan, if she's on some kind of secret assignment for NASA or the military, or just helping her father with some personal problem, I'm sure it's just a temporary thing. Wouldn't it be best to just sit tight and wait for her to call?"

"Jack, we're talking about a young girl who is just a secretary. She's only been on her own for a few years and all of a sudden she disappears on some secret mission for the government? That's not the way it works and you know it. We're talking about a girl who has been trained to type, take shorthand, and make coffee. Does this make sense to you?"

As Ryan talked, Jack listened and detected the panic and frustration in Ryan's voice. When Ryan finally finished, he asked, "What can I do to help, Ryan?"

"That's no problem. I can make a few phone calls and have a few people check this out. I can't promise you anything, but I'll be happy to help. Give me Pam's full name and a little information about her."

He wrote everything down—her name, social security number, date of birth, driver's license number, the office where she worked, General Whiteside's NASA office—and, again, reassured Ryan he would help. "You call me the minute you get in." He added, "you have a place to stay? You're welcome to hang out in my apartment, if you don't mind the couch."

"No, thanks Jack, I appreciate it, but I'll get a motel room. I'm going to be pretty busy and I want to be where I can come and go in a hurry. But I do need to sit down with you." "You got it, Ryan. You call the minute you arrive, and I'll put you on the schedule downstairs so you can come right up."

"OK, Jack. I knew I could count on you. I'll see you when I get to Washington."

Jack hung up the phone, and turned to his mail. Conscious of the fact he had broken one of his own rules, he was a little disturbed. Jack never allowed anyone to lean on him with requests for personal investigative assistance but Ryan was something special. Jack liked the young NASA Security Chief and the urgency in his voice moved him to help in any way possible. After all, that's what friends are for. To help each other. So, he would help Ryan locate his girl. When he finished the mail and dictation, Jack left his office to attend several staff meetings scheduled for that morning. Fortunately, each was brief and by midday, he was back in the cafeteria, grabbing a bite of lunch. There was another staff conference at 1:00, but the meeting had barely begun when he was paged and told he had a visitor in his office.

It was Roger Grant, from the FBI.

"Hey, this is great. Didn't expect you to drive all the way over here just to deliver some information to me. How do I rate this blue-chip treatment?"

"I'm not exactly delivering, Jack. You got me in deep water."

Puzzled, Jack asked, "What do you mean?"

"Solomon. I ran the name through the computer and all I got was a visit from the CIA and the Defense Department wanting to know why I was checking up on Solomon. I had to do some fast talking to get them off my back."

"What's the big deal? How did they get in on it?"

Grant shook his head. "Evidently when I ran Solomon through the computer, the name was keyed into their security monitoring system which let them know someone was asking about highly classified material. About an hour later my boss called me into his office and these two young hotshots were there. They started asking me a lot of questions I couldn't answer."

Jack asked, "Did they tell you who Solomon was?"

"They didn't tell me anything. All they did was ask questions. They wanted to know how and why I was checking on Solomon."

"What did you tell them, Roger?"

"I just told them the name popped up in an investigation I was doing and I ran it through the computer to see if any bells would ring."

"Did any ring?"

Roger frowned and answered slowly, "In a way, yes. But the hotshots don't know that. After they left, my boss wanted to know what was going on; and I had to tell him I was doing you a favor, checking on someone named Solomon."

Jack apologized. "I'm sorry, Roger. I didn't mean to get you in hot water with your boss."

"I'm not in trouble with my boss, Jack. He didn't like the idea of me using our computer for a private citizen, but he knows you've helped us from time to time so he'll overlook that little transgression. No, I'm here because he wants to know why the CIA and Defense Department got so upset about our query. He has the feeling that something is going on that the FBI doesn't know about."

Jack studied Grant closely, wondering how much he should tell the man, and decided that nothing was better than too much.

So, he simply said, "I got a tip to check up on someone named Solomon."

Grant shook his head. "Not good enough, Jack. We think it might have something to do with the Thacker murder."

"Oh, you know about that."

Roger scowled. "Jack, of course we know about that. Is Solomon involved in the shooting?"

"What makes you think it has something to do with Thacker?"

"Because I saw your ugly mug on television all weekend and I just sort of added two and two and came up with the fact you must know something. Come on, Jack. My boss and I want to know what's going on."

"Roger, I don't know what's going on. I just want to know who Solomon is."

Reluctantly, Roger told him about Solomon. "When I ran the name through the computer, I was told that the Solomon File is available only on a NEED TO KNOW basis. Now, what really has our curiosity up is the fact that when the name popped up in our computer, it told us that Solomon had something to do with a domestic project or operation because foreign activities are never entered into the computer system by the CIA or Defense Department."

"That doesn't make any sense, Roger. If the CIA or Defense Department is doing something that they are trying to hide, all they have to do is keep the information out of the computer. Who would know?"

"They probably do that, but in this case they couldn't hide the entry."

"Why not?"

"Money," Roger answered. "Any government agency spending money within the USA that involves bids, contracts, people, supplies, or what have you, is subject to auditing by the General Accounting Office."

Grant stopped for a moment, but Jack encouraged him to continue. "Go on, I'm listening."

"The fact that Solomon popped up on our query tells us that somewhere, somehow, someone is paying money to Solomon and since the CIA and Defense Department showed so much interest it means one of them, or both, must be the sugar daddy. What we want to know is why, where, and how because it must involve a lot of money or it wouldn't be in the computer system in its own file. If it was a petty cash type thing, they could hide the amount in their normal budget." He paused again to catch his breath. "My boss wants to know what the CIA is doing that the FBI doesn't know about."

Jack smiled and said, "This is getting pretty interesting."

"Yeah, we think so too. That's why our computer boys spent the morning trying to track down Solomon." "Did they find anything?"

"That's why I'm here, Jack. My boss wants to know what you know about Solomon."

"Roger, that's all I know. I didn't know I was opening up a can of worms."

"You have, Buddy Boy." He stared at Jack hard and asked, "Are you sure you're telling me everything?"

"Positive," Jack lied. He wasn't about to tell Roger that the word "conspiracy" was used with the name "Solomon" by Thacker.

"The name Piaute Mountain mean anything to you?"

"What?"

Roger repeated the name. "Piaute Mountain."

"No. Where's that? What's that got to do with Solomon?"

Grant gave him a sly smile and replied, "Jack, I'm not going to tell you everything." He looked at his watch and said, "I've got to get out of here. If you think of anything you haven't told me, Jack, call me."

Jack assured him he would. The two men stood, looking at each other for a moment and, with a resigned shrug, Roger turned to leave. Jack stopped him. "There is one thing you might want to check, Roger."

Grant looked at him expectantly, waiting.

Jack mentally crossed his fingers and hoped what he was about to do did not come back to haunt him as he said, "I can't explain why, but run this through your computer and see what you can come up with." He pulled the notes taken during his conversation with Ryan Abernathy and rewrote them on another sheet of paper. Handing Roger the material on Pamela Richards, he said, "Now, don't ask me the connection, just check it out and let me know what you come up with. I'm not really sure how this young lady fits into the scheme of things."

He knew, even as he handed Roger Pam's name, social security number, driver's license number, and other facts that the young woman had nothing to do with Solomon; but if Roger didn't know that, he would check it out. Jack doubted he would honor another request to "check on something."

Roger studied the sheet of paper for a moment and said, "All right, Jack, I'll have this checked out. But at some point you're going to have to tell me everything you know."

Guiltily, Jack watched Roger leave; afterwards, even as the door was closing, he reached for the phone. He dialed the network Research Department and the moment a researcher was on the line, said, "This is Jack Clayburn. I need you to check on something for me. See if you can find out anything on a place called Piaute Mountain."

As he hung up the phone, he decided to hedge his bet, or call. Considering how slow Research was answering his requests for information, Jack decided to enlist some more research help. He dialed Skip Reynolds' office and when the science reporter was on the line, asked, "Skip, do you have anything in your files on a place called Piaute Mountain? I don't have any idea where it is or what it is."

There was a long pause on the other end but finally Skip spoke, "Piaute Mountain. Jack, that name is familiar; but I can't place it. Let me look it up and see what I can find. I'll get back to you."

Jack thanked him, and hung up the phone. Looking at his watch, he realized it was time to call it a day. He began clearing his desk, getting ready to leave and running the events of the day through his mind. He was not completely unhappy with his progress, but he felt a sense of urgency and a need to move faster toward identifying the man called Solomon. However, there was nothing he could do until he had more information. Sighing, he turned off his desk lamp, and walked out. Perhaps Tuesday would be more productive.

# 4.

# Chapter Four

It required two lies, a little charm, and some innocent flattery; but Ryan obtained the general's home address. As he sat huddled in his rental car, he shook his head at how lax a supposedly security-minded organization could be. Explaining to the young secretary that he needed to send the general a wedding invitation and did not want to send it through the normal channels, the woman assumed that since the request came from NASA's security director, it was all right. So, she gave him the address.

A visit to the Government Motor Pool, a few cups of coffee and a little small talk with the dispatcher provided him with the general's schedule. Ryan knew exactly what time the army limousine would arrive to pick up the general and carry him to his office in the Pentagon. All he had to do was wait. When the general walked from his house, Ryan would confront him and ask where Pamela was. The plan was simple. So simple, Ryan thought, it might work.

He looked at his watch. From the dispatcher, Ryan knew the driver arrived every morning at 8:30 sharp. Only a few minutes remained before he arrived and Ryan fought the nervousness building within his tired body. Unable to sleep the preceding night, after arriving on the flight from Houston, Ryan spent most of his time calling friends, checking to see if they had discovered any news or leads on Pamela. The visit to the Pentagon offices and motor pool took up the rest of his time. He was tired but not sleepy. He was nervous but not scared. He knew the general could get him fired, but Ryan wasn't concerned with that. All he was interested in was finding Pamela. And General Matthew Whiteside knew where she was.

Ryan was positive of this. Pamela worked in Whiteside's Houston office and to disappear, without a trace, without a ripple, meant that only someone with a lot of weight, a lot of pull, had to be responsible. Whiteside had the necessary clout. Even more curious to Ryan was the fact that although Pamela worked in the general's office, her disappearance did not disturb anyone.

Ryan straightened up. A long, black automobile bearing the flag of a four-star general was rolling to a stop in front of the greystone mansion. It was the general's car, right on time. Ryan slipped out of the car and walked rapidly toward the front gate. As he crossed the street, he saw the front door open and the general, accompanied by his aide, stepped out. Timing his arrival to coincide with the general's arrival at the limousine, Ryan approached.

"General Whiteside."

The tall, erect figure turned to look in Ryan's direction. "General Whiteside," Ryan continued, "we've met before, Sir. I'm Ryan Abernathy, Security Director at NASA, in Houston."

"You're a long way from home, Mr. Abernathy."

"General, I'm looking for Pamela Richards. I need to know where she is."

The general studied Ryan for a moment and then turned to his aide, motioning him to open the car door. As the aide pulled the rear door open, Ryan stepped forward. "General, I need to know, and I think you know where I can find her."

"Young man, in the middle of the street is not a place I discuss things. Call my office and make an appointment."

"I've tried that, General. You won't accept my calls."

Ryan stepped forward, blocking the general's entrance into the car and repeated, "I need to know where to find Pamela."

Impatiently, the general looked at his aide and nodded.

Almost immediately, Ryan felt the hard steel barrel of a .45 pushing against his side. "OK, Mr. NASA, the general is finished talking to you. You now have a decision to make. What's it going to be?" Ryan backed slowly away, holding his hands in front of him, "All right, but I'll find her, General. And if she has been hurt in any way, I'll be coming for you."

The general looked at him, smiled, and said, "I don't think you understand what's going on here, Mr. Abernathy. But maybe you can understand this. Don't jump into water you can't swim out of." With that, General Whiteside slipped into his car, the aide followed him, and as the door closed, the long black limo pulled away, leaving a seething Ryan in its wake.

- - - - - - - - - - - - -

The overcast clouds finally fulfilled their promise and unleashed a torrential rain just as Jack arrived for work Tuesday morning. Wet, irritated, and late, his normally cheerful mood bordered on the aggressive as he reached his office. Hanging his wet sports jacket on a hook to dry, he sat down at his desk and was surprised to see a large brown envelope lying on his desk, marked URGENT! FROM RESEARCH DEPARTMENT. He ripped open the envelope and extracted a thin packet of papers.

Reading swiftly, he scanned the summary of Thacker's life.

Primarily, the report contained biographical information, vital statistics, and honors earned by the late doctor. Only two items grabbed Jack's attention, and he read both entries several times. Dr. Thacker was employed for seven years by Armstrong Industries. While in the employ of Armstrong Industries, prior to accepting the presidency of Waylanth College, he served as a special advisor and consultant to the Piaute Mountain project.

There it was again, Piaute Mountain and Armstrong's name. Jack swiveled his chair around and stared out the window, watching the rain beat a steady tattoo against the glass pane. Mentally, he ran what he had through his mind, checking off the few possibilities. He realized he needed more information and the only way to get it was by digging. He turned to his desk, reached for the Network News Contact Telephone Directory, looked up the number for Armstrong Industries.

When the call was answered, Jack identified himself and asked to speak to Adam Armstrong. He was not surprised when the call was transferred to another secretary, but he was mildly shocked when she advised him to hold one moment while she checked to see if he was in. Chief executive officers of large corporations usually required appointments, so Jack was prepared to play the game and, he hoped, have his call returned. He got another shock.

"Hello, this is Adam Armstrong."

There was no mistaking the deep, melodious voice. It was him, no doubt about it. A flustered Jack stuttered for a moment before he regained his composure and he said, "Mr. Armstrong, this is Jack Clayburn. I'm a newsman. . . "

Armstrong interrupted him. "I know you, Mr. Clayburn. I am very familiar with your excellent work on the network. What can I do for you?"

Mildly pleased that a man of Armstrong's stature knew him, Jack continued, "Sir, I apologize for calling without an appointment, but I'm working on a feature story and I'm looking for a little help."

"I'll be happy to help you any way I can, Jack. What's the story about?"

"It deals with computer viruses. We've had several tips that there is a possibility some of the government and business computers may be subject to a virus infection. Would you care to comment on that?"

"I'm afraid I can't help you with that, Jack. We are, of course, very involved in computers, but I think it might be better for you to talk to one of my computer people. I can have someone call you who can provide more information than I could."

Jack didn't want the conversation to end, but he said, "That would be great, Mr. Armstrong. I would appreciate that." Thinking rapidly, he blurted out, "While I have you on the phone, I'm sure you know about Dr. Thacker's death. Unfortunately, I was the one who discovered him. Would you care to comment on his death?"

"I have no comment at all, other than to state I am extremely sorry it happened. Dr. Thacker was at one time a very close friend of mine and a valuable employee of this company."

"Yes, I understand that. When he worked for you, he was assigned to the Piaute Mountain project. What was his function on that project?"

There was a slight pause on the other end before Armstrong replied, "I'm afraid I can't recall that project. I have no idea what he did."

"Do you recall a Dr. Solomon working with Dr. Thacker on that project?"

There was another pause. Jack had the impression Armstrong was choosing his words very carefully. "I don't think I know a Dr. Solomon. He certainly doesn't work for us. And since I don't remember the Piaute Mountain project, I certainly would not remember who worked on it, would I?"

Jack laughed. "No, I guess not. I just thought you might know of the gentleman. You don't know a Dr. Solomon then?"

"No, I don't know a Dr. Solomon." Then Armstrong said, "I thought you were working on a computer virus story. What does a virus story have to do with Dr. Thacker? Or this Dr. Solomon you mentioned?" He added, "Or with Piaute Mountain."

"I have no idea, Mr. Armstrong. I'm just running down names, trying to fit pieces of a puzzle together."

The voice on the other end of the line became lower and in a more confidential tone, Armstrong said quietly, "Jack, I like your work; and from what I've seen, I would probably like you. I'm not at liberty to discuss any of these questions; but on a personal note, please take some advice from a friend who admires you. Be very careful with your investigation. Some things are best left alone."

Jack's attention immediately went into the alert mode. "I'm not sure I understand what you're saying, Mr. Armstrong."

There was an even longer pause this time and then, "Jack, a lot of things go on, and some things need to be checked by the news media. However, one has to remember that personal safety must always be maintained. All I'm saying is that I suggest you exercise a great deal of caution if you pursue this line of questioning with others. You might find yourself stepping on some highly classified and top-secret toes. That could be very dangerous for you."

Jack felt the adrenalin begin to race through his veins. "Mr. Armstrong, I appreciate your concern, but I'm just checking out a story. Is there something I should know that you could tell me?"

Armstrong chuckled, changing the tone of the conversation. "No, Jack, I'm not at liberty to discuss anything. Look at it this way. If what you want to know is classified Top-secret, I can't discuss it. And if it's classified Top-secret, I don't know about it anyway. Right?"

Jack knew the man was being purposely evasive. "Sort of a Catch 22 situation."

"Exactly. Now, is there anything else I can help you with?"

"No, Sir, but I do appreciate your time this morning. And your suggestions." He added, "You've been more help than you realize."

"You're quite welcome. But remember, be very careful. I am very sincere in what I'm telling you."

"I appreciate that, Mr. Armstrong." He said goodbye, placed the phone back on the cradle, and smiled. Jack had the feeling his story was about to explode wide open. He could smell it happening.

- - - - - - - - - - - -

At precisely the moment Jack Clayburn was talking to Adam Armstrong, a slender, elderly woman stood patiently in front of the receptionist's desk, waiting for the young lady to acknowledge her presence. Finally, the wide-eyed receptionist hung up her telephone and breathlessly announced, "I'm sorry to keep you waiting. May I help you?"

The well-dressed woman, in her late fifties or early sixties, asked in a low but firm voice, "I need the name of the reporter who was mentioned on the news last week in connection with a shooting in New York."

The young receptionist's voice fell open and all she could do was stare, open-mouthed, at the woman.

"Did I say something wrong?" the attractive woman asked.

Flustered, the young receptionist replied quickly, "No, of course not. It's just that working down here I never get to watch the news or anything. I have no idea who you mean."

The security guard, standing near her desk, leaned forward and asked, "Are you referring to the newsman who discovered the body in the New York hotel?"

"Yes. I think so."

"That's Jack Clayburn, Maggie."

"Yes, that is his name," the woman said. She continued, "I would like to see him."

Shaking her head, the receptionist asked, "Do you have an appointment, ma'am?"

"Of course not. If I had an appointment, I would not be asking you for his name nor would I be asking to see him."

"Well," the young receptionist said defiantly, "you can't see him without an appointment. We have very strict instructions about that. You must have an appointment to see on-the-air personnel."

The woman frowned. The disappointment, or irritation, showed in her face. But she was obviously prepared for the possibility of not seeing the reporter because she opened her purse and pulled out a white envelope. "Then, would you see that he gets this?" As she spoke, she picked up the pen lying on the desk and wrote on the front of the envelope: JACK CLAYBURN. PERSONAL AND CONFIDENTIAL! Handing the envelope to the girl, she added, "This is very important." The young lady was accustomed to accepting notes from lonely, infatuated women who created fantasies in their minds with the various network personalities, so she smiled and said cheerfully, "I'll see to it personally and I can assure you that Mr. Clayburn will be very happy to receive your note."

Sensing the condescending tone of the girl's voice, the woman straightened up and said with a harsh bite, "Young lady, this is not what your little mind imagines. This is important. Mr. Clayburn will want to see this. And I suggest you give it to him immediately."

With that, she wheeled around and began walking toward the front door, leaving in her wake a surprised young receptionist.

The young girl shrugged and, placing the envelope into the box marked INTERNAL MAIL, watched the woman exit the lobby.

- - - - - - - - - - - -

Following the daily round of staff meetings, Jack returned to his office. He was sitting at his desk, trying to determine his next call, when there was a knock on his door. He looked up and saw Skip.

"Are you going to be around for a while?"

Jack looked at his watch and answered, "Yeah, I'll be tied up here for a bit longer. I'm waiting for a call, and I still have some things to check out."

"I need to run pick up something, and my car is in the shop. Mind if I borrow yours for about a half hour?"

"No problem, Skip." Jack fished the keys from his pocket and threw them to the science reporter.

As he caught the keys, he said, "I have something for you on Piaute Mountain. You want it now?"

Jack's eyes brightened. "You bet I do. Tell me what you have."

Skip sat down opposite Jack and began. "It's not much but maybe it will help you. I have to begin way back. Is that all right?"

"Fire away," Jack encouraged.

Skip took a deep breath and began. "Piaute Mountain is an elevation on the western border of Nevada, about halfway between Reno and Las Vegas. There was a small cave in the base of the mountain which in the olden days was used by the Piaute Indians.

That's how it got its name. Well, back in the 1860s, sometime around the Comstock Lode discovery, in Carson City, Nevada, prospectors found the cave and sunk several shafts, looking for gold or silver. They didn't find any.

"About a hundred years later, in 1961, the Atomic Energy Commission acquired the cave, sank deep shafts in the floor, and installed seismic equipment to monitor and measure underground nuclear tests being conducted at the Nevada Test Site, which is located about a hundred miles to the southeast. In the late sixties, however, the AEC abandoned the facility and turned it over to the army."

"What did they do with it?"

Skip grinned. "Officially, it's still listed as a seismic detection center. But get this. It's the only Top-secret classified seismic detection center in the world. No reporters allowed. No visitors allowed. No questions allowed. No nothing."

Jack said slowly, "Which suggests the facility might be something more than a place to measure earthquakes."

"Could be." Giving Jack a curious look, he asked, "What are you onto, Jack?"

"What makes you think I'm onto something?"

Skip rolled his eyes, smiled, and said, "Because by strange coincidence, I found a little news clip from several years ago concerning an appointment to that facility."

"And?"

"It was Dr. Floyd Thacker, who at the time was General Matthew Whiteside's chief computer consultant. The facility was, and is as far as I know, under his command."

Jack drummed his fingers on the desk top, looking deep into Skip's eyes, thinking. "Now, what would a top computer expert have to do with a seismic center?"

"Good question. Maybe he was checking out their computers or something." "Sure," Jack said skeptically. "the army sends one of its top computer boys out to the boondocks to make sure the equipment works. No. It has to be something else. But what?"

"Yeah, but what?" echoed Skip, standing up. "I've got to run if I'm going to get your car back to you on time. I'll do some more checking tomorrow. Now, you have me curious." He opened the door, just as Jack's phone rang, paused, and asked, "Do you need me to pick up anything for you?"

Jack nodded no, waved a goodbye, and answered his telephone. "Jack Clayburn."

"Hi, Jack. Ryan here."

"Hi, fellow. Where are you?"

"I'm in town. I've been doing a little checking on my own but not having much luck. Have you been able to come up with anything?"

"Not yet, Ryan," Jack said apologetically. "I have someone working on it but they haven't given me anything yet." Reassuringly, he added, "But don't give up on me. If my contact doesn't come through, I have several more I might enlist to help us."

"I appreciate it, Jack. My best lead sort of fizzled out today. I wasn't able to find out anything. I keep running into either blind alleys, dead ends, or closed mouths. No one will talk to me."

"Well, we'll hang in there together. Something will break. Knock on enough doors and something will happen." Then, he asked, "Where are you staying?"

"At the Farmington House Hotel."

"Yeah, I know where it is. Wanna get together for dinner and a few drinks tonight? We can put our heads together and see if we are overlooking something."

"Sounds good to me. What time and where?"

"How about 7:00 tonight? At the Blue Onion Restaurant? That's close to where you're staying."

"OK, I'll find it, and I'll be there at seven." There was a pause and then Ryan said, "Jack, I appreciate this. You don't know how much, but I do."

"No problem, Ryan. I haven't helped yet, but I'm glad to lend you a hand. And don't worry. We'll get the answers, and it will turn out to be something easily explained. I'm sure your girl is all right."

"I hope you're right. Well, I'll see you tonight."

Jack hung up the phone and reached for the government telephone directory, a thick volume which listed the names and phone numbers of every department and office in Washington. Suddenly, he heard a dull thud from the outside, toward the rear of the building. It startled him—the first thing he thought of was Vietnam. The sound resembled something he had never become accustomed to while covering the Vietnam War as a correspondent for the network—a distant mortar shell exploding. He smiled grimly and continued scanning the government telephone directory, looking for names of people he might contact.

Perhaps five, maybe ten minutes went by when his concentration was interrupted by they sound of excited voices coming from the corridor. He arose from his desk to close the door to his office, but before he reached it, his doorway was suddenly crowded with people staring at him and all talking at once.

"What's going on?" Jack asked.

Melvin Blakely, the bureau news director, stared at Jack with wide and disbelieving eyes. "You're here," he exclaimed.

"Of course, I'm here. Where else would I be?"

Another voice asked, "Then who was in your car?"

Jack scowled at the crowd standing in his doorway and in a voice stinging with irritation, asked, "What's going on, Melvin?"

"Was someone using your car?"

Patiently, Jack explained. "Yes, someone is using my car. Skip Reynolds needed to borrow it."

There was a sudden hush and one of the girls in the rear began to sob uncontrollably.

"What is going on?" Jack demanded again.

Blakely's shoulders sagged and with a pained expression said, "Jack, we've just come from downstairs. Your car was destroyed by a bomb."

Jack went numb.

Blakely continued. "There is a body inside the car and we all assumed it was you." Jack's face went pale and he felt a knot begin to grow in his stomach. Fear gripped him as he slowly realized he had missed death only because a friend borrowed his car. In a strange, hoarse whisper, he said aloud, "My God, Skip is dead."

For almost an hour several detectives talked to Jack, in his office, asking questions, probing, trying to determine if he had any idea why he was a target for some car bomber. Patiently, Jack answered all questions with a simple, "I have no idea. I don't know." One of the detectives even tried to tie the Thacker killing to the car bombing, suggesting that perhaps Jack had seen the killer and the killer was attempting to eliminate a witness. Again, Jack replied, "I have no idea. I don't know."

In truth, Jack didn't know. He did know, or at least guessed, the two incidents were connected, but he honestly had no idea how they were related. Finally, the officers ran out of questions—or patience—and advised Jack to be careful and to call them the moment he could volunteer any information that might shed more light on the incident. Jack assured them he would call, and as they left, he sat down to figure out his next move.

That's when he realized he had no car. He had no transportation and somebody in the nation's capital was trying to kill him. First, he had to get home. There, he could at least retrieve the small handgun he kept in his safe. Also, he felt he needed to get away from the network offices. He called Melvin and requested transportation home, which was quickly arranged, and he immediately left his office. Ordinarily, Jack would have left by the rear exit but considering that's where someone had tried to kill him, Jack elected to leave by the front door. As he stepped from the elevator into the lobby, the receptionist spotted him and called his name.

"Mr. Clayburn."

Jack looked in her direction, and warily walked to her desk. "Yes?"

"A woman left this envelope for you and I promised her I would see that you received it."

Jack took the long white envelope from her, examined it a moment, shrugged, stuck it in his coat pocket, and promptly forgot about it. He was quite used to receiving notes from women and he had no reason to expect this latest to be anything other than another invitation to dinner—or even more.

Thanking her, Jack walked to the entrance and, spotting the network shuttle car, walked outside to his ride.

# 5.

# Chapter Five

**R**oger Grant was seated before the computer in his office. Normally, by late evening, Grant was at home enjoying his family, but on this Tuesday night he informed his wife he would be late—very late. He was absorbed with the challenge of tracking down information related to the can of worms opened by Jack Clayburn. He and his chief, upon hearing of the attempt on Jack's life earlier in the day, had decided to devote every effort to determine what, if anything, was going on.

He made a list of all known factors. Entering into the computer the names Thacker, Piaute Mountain, Armstrong Industries, Waylanth College, and Pamela Richards. The computer was searching every available government data base, collecting, collating, and comparing information. Roger was looking for any parallel or connecting thread which would link any or all of the names. It was a time-consuming job but he was a patient man. He knew eventually something would click. All he needed was one common denominator between any of the names and he would be off and running.

Patiently he watched the screen. Several hours went by and then suddenly, a pattern began to emerge. One single reference number began to appear as a match with each of the names entered. He watched carefully as the computer searched, and entered the same number opposite each of the names he entered. Anxiously, he awaited a scan on the last name. If the number appeared next to the name of Pamela Richards, Roger knew he would be onto something. Seconds ticked by, and after an agonizingly long period of time, it popped up—REF: 445/10/Z17. The number matched each of the names entered by Grant.

Smiling triumphantly, he entered a query command in an effort to define the project or file for Item 445/10/Z17. The computer answered the query with NEED TO KNOW BASIS ONLY.

Bingo!

Smiling triumphantly, Roger entered the FBI search code and sent the computer searching for the originator or authority of entry number

445/10/Z17. Grant knew that if he could find the originating point of the NEED TO KNOW BASIS command, he might then be able to crack the access code or even obtain the access code through normal channels. He smiled confidently and continued to watch as the marvelous computer continued its search. Finally, the message appeared.

After sifting through millions of bytes of information, the computer screen came alive with a single, one-line notation:

ORIGINATING AUTHORITY:  GENERAL MATTHEW WHITESIDE, USA!

- - - - - - - - - - -

In his apartment, Jack calmly made a pot of coffee, sat at his kitchen bar, and contemplated his near demise. Jack was no coward. His courage was tested time and time again during the Vietnam War, and on each occasion his Scotch Irish ancestry rose to the challenge. However, it was one thing to face danger openly and knowingly; it was quite another to have danger approach from his blind side. And, at that moment, Jack was blind; he had no idea who was trying to kill him, which made it all the more imperative to get a handle on everything happening.

As he drank his coffee, he realized he needed to call Skip's wife, but when he tried to reach her, there was no answer. He entertained, briefly, the idea of driving to her home; but he suddenly remembered he had no car, and he knew she would not want to see him. Neither did he want to see her. He could not answer any questions she asked, and he knew she would ask. Skip's wife would have to wait. He had other things to consider. Jack looked at his watch and suddenly remembered he had an appointment to meet Ryan Abernathy at 7:00. He grabbed the telephone book, looked up the numbers for The Farmington House Hotel and the Blue Onion Restaurant. Then, picking up the phone, he dialed the hotel first. He asked for Ryan Abernathy's room and as he heard the phone ringing, he silently prayed his friend was still there. He was.

"Hello!"

"Ryan, this is Jack."

"I was just getting ready to go out the door. You still going to make it?"

"I don't know if I should, Ryan. I have a slight problem."

Jack then explained the earlier car bombing, Skip's death, and the fact that he was without an automobile.

Ryan listened without interrupting; but when Jack finished, he immediately said, "Jack, you have to get out of your apartment. I don't want to scare you to death, but you're a sitting duck if someone is trying to get you. Sitting there alone is an open invitation for some nut to try again. Now, listen to me. I know what I'm doing here. Will you do what I tell you?"

Jack, recognizing that Ryan did know what he was doing, answered, "OK, what should I do?"

"I'm going to call a cab and send it to your address. In the meantime, I'll be parked somewhere near you, keeping an eye open. When the cab arrives, you get in, go to the restaurant we agreed on earlier. I'll be right behind you to make sure no one follows you." He paused and continued. "Now, this is important. If someone is following you, I'll arrange to have a little fender-bender with whomever it is. That will slow them down, and once you get to the restaurant, if I'm not there immediately, leave the restaurant, go to my hotel, and wait for me. Got it?"

"I've got it, Ryan. We'll do it your way. It makes sense. I'll be ready when the cab gets here."

"I'll wait until I'm near your apartment before I call the cab. Give me your address."

Jack gave him the address, assured Ryan he would be ready, and hung up. He figured he had thirty to forty-five minutes to kill before the taxi arrived so he went into the bedroom, undressed, showered, shaved, and slipped into clean clothes. He grabbed an extra clean shirt, change of underwear and socks, and stuffed them into his attaché case. Then, deliberately, he walked to a small safe, spun the combination, opened the door and pulled out a 9mm Berreta pistol. Checking the clip, he grabbed a handful of shells. Jack threw the shells into his case but the pistol was shoved into his waistband to rest snugly against the small of his back. At least he was now armed in case something happened.

He returned to the kitchen, poured another cup of coffee, and sat down to wait. That's when he happened to see the envelope laying on the counter where he had emptied his pockets. Jack almost threw it away. A hand-delivered note from an admiring female was not an unusual incident. It happened all the time, but Jack always threw them, unanswered, into the trash. For some reason, he felt compelled to read this one. For one reason, groupie notes, as they were called, usually arrived in pink or light blue envelopes. The envelope on the counter was a simple, white, legal one with the word URGENT written across the front.

He reached for it, slit the envelope open, and as he read, a look of amazement spread across his face. After the second reading, he reached for the phone and dialed the network offices and asked for the home phone number of the daytime receptionist. After the guard supplied the number, Jack dialed her and when she answered, said,

"This is Jack Clayburn. I have an envelope here that someone left for me today. Do you remember who left it?"

There was a pause before the young woman, flustered because he had called, giggled and replied, "Just a woman, she came in, asked if she could see you, and when I told her no, she left the envelope."

"Did she leave a name?"

"Oh, an interesting one, huh?" she giggled again.

"I asked if she left a name," Jack said impatiently.

"No Sir, she didn't," the girl responded, a little more professionally.

Jack thanked her and hung up and immediately reached for his telephone directory. He found the number he wanted and dialed. After several rings, Roger Grant answered. "Hello." "Roger, you're working late. Good. I need some quick information. Have you ever heard of a place called Hinterwald, up in Maryland, just outside of town?"

There was a big sigh on the other end of the line. Finally, Roger answered, "Jack, what are you into?"

"Come on, Roger, I don't have much time. Do you know of it?"

Wearily, but curiously, Roger said, "Yes, we know about the place. It's a country estate owned by retired general Aaron Wheeler, who is on the president's staff. But the place is more than just a farm. It's a school, used to train security and bodyguards for overseas corporate executives who fear reprisals or attacks from terrorists. To spell it out for you, Jack, the place is an armed fort."

"Thanks, Roger, I just wanted to know what it was."

"Jack, what have you found out? Is this place connected in any way to what we're working on?"

"I don't know yet; but if I find out anything, you'll be the first to know." Jack could hear a horn outside and assumed that the taxi had arrived. He said impatiently, "Roger, I have to run. Talk to you later." He hung up, grabbed his briefcase, looked around the apartment, turned the lights off, and walked out. It was time to play cops and robbers.

Thirty minutes later Jack and Ryan were seated in the Blue Onion Restaurant. "Ryan, thanks for following me here."

Ryan grinned and replied, "Hey, I enjoyed it. Gave me a chance to put all that stuff I learned to work. At least, we know no one was watching your house, and no one followed you here."

Jack looked at his watch. "Ryan, I said we'd have dinner, but something has come up and I have to go somewhere. What do you know so far?"

"Well, not much of anything. The only positive note is the fact that you're helping me."

"And I'm not doing too well at that," Jack volunteered. "But my contact is checking on your girlfriend and maybe he'll have something tomorrow."

Ryan shook his head. "If you find out anything, you'll have to call me in Houston. I've got to head back tonight."

He explained, "The big launch is tomorrow and I really should be there."

Jack nodded understandingly.

Ryan continued. "I did get face to face with Pamela's boss, General Whiteside. But he wouldn't tell me anything. He knows something, though. I know he does. In fact, he gave me some advice when I told him I was going to find Pamela, with or without his help."

"What advice?"

"He more or less told me I was in water over my head." "That in itself says something, doesn't it?"

Jack looked at his watch again. "Ryan, I'm going to have to get out of here, or I'm going to be late." On a sudden impulse, he asked, "Ryan, in your position down in Houston, have you ever heard of a place called Piaute Mountain?"

Ryan stared at him and said, "Sure. It's a place out in Nevada. The Security Director used to be my assistant. Why?"

"Do you have any idea what they do over there?"

Ryan thought a moment and answered, "All I know is they have quite a group of scientists working there but I don't know what they do. James Butterly is my friend, and I don't think he knows either."

"Could you ask your friend if a Mr. Solomon works there?"

"That's no problem. I can ask him tomorrow when I get back."

Jack took out a note pad and wrote down a number. Handing the sheet of paper to Ryan, he said, "Here's my pager number. The minute you talk to your friend about Solomon, give me a call and I'll get back with you right away. Can you do that?"

"Sure, Jack, glad to help."

"Now, I need one more favor."

"You name it."

"I need you to drive me to a car rental agency. I have to get some wheels."

"All right, let's do it now; and you'll be on your way. I can head for the airport and get out of this town." The two men stood up and walked out together.

- - - - - - - - - - - -

Two hours later Jack Clayburn was lying, hidden in bushes, watching a large, rambling, ranch-style house nestled under the towering, centuries old oak trees. When Ryan dropped him off at the rental agency, he rented a car, drove up from the capital, following Interstate 270 until he reached Maryland Highway 27. Turning east, he followed the narrow state road to Cedar Grove and, six miles up the road, just as the note had instructed, he found the house. He drove past the house, slowly, continued up the road for another two miles until he found a spot to pull off the road where he could hide his rented car. Jack left the car and keeping off the road, he walked through the woods until he found a spot in the trees where he could observe the house without fear of detection.

He had no idea what to expect, but Jack had come prepared. Once he rented the automobile, he returned to his apartment; and now round his neck hung a pair of high-powered binoculars; and lying on his jacket, fully loaded with the fastest film available, was a 35mm camera with a large telescopic lens. Lying next to the camera, also fully loaded, was the dull, grey 9mm Berreta pistol. Jack was by no means any kind of marksman but he was not without a small measure of proficiency with small arms; and after what had happened the previous day, he was not about to take any chances—especially when he was planted in a spot he knew he shouldn't be.

The house was quiet, and in an effort to make the time pass, he reached into his pocket to retrieve the mysterious note. For what seemed like the hundredth time, he read it again:

"Mr. Clayburn:

I would caution you to be extremely careful about your health and well-being. You have stumbled into a situation that might prove to be very dangerous for you. However, you have stumbled into a situation that needs to be brought to the attention of the American public— even the world. I do not know exactly what is going on, but I do know that something drastic and terrible is planned. That, however, is not why I am contacting you. I have in my possession certain facts that should interest you. If I told you the story, you would not believe me. But I can offer a token of my good faith. To prove I am not just another crazy old woman, I will tell you where to find the man responsible for Dr. Floyd Thacker's death.

There is a meeting scheduled for Wednesday evening at ten p.m. Take I-270 north to State Road 27. Go east on 27 eight miles to Cedar Grove. In Cedar Grove you will see a post office mail box in front of the small feed and seed store. Continue on for exactly 6.2 miles and you will see the entrance to a large house, identifiable by the sign hanging on the gate which reads "Hinterwald." I would suggest you exercise extreme caution and not be seen.

I will contact you within the next few days, at which time I will share the information I have concerning the OTHER story, which concerns a major figure in this country."

The note was unsigned and he had no idea if it was genuine or if he was on a wild goose chase. But it was the only good lead he had. Stretched out on the ground, peering over the small rise from which he could see every automobile enter or leave, the estate did look like an armed fort. He spotted several armed guards. One, wearing a light blue suit and tie, was located at the gate. Another, wearing a battle fatigue jacket held a position up the road several hundred feet and stood in a clump of bushes on the side of the road. Several others stood nonchalantly near the house; yet another guard walked the grounds, holding a guard dog on a tight leash. What really garnered his attention, however, was the automatic weapon slung casually over each sentry's shoulder.

Jack's legs began to stiffen and cramp from lying in one position for so long. He carefully moved backward out of possible view. He stood and stretched for a few moments until he felt the blood begin to circulate again. Then, he crawled slowly back to his observation post and continued to peer through the small opening in the bush. Time seemed to drag, but Jack occupied himself checking his equipment. The outside floodlights provided a beautifully illuminated view of the porch and front door.

Jack checked his *f*-stop to insure that it was set at the absolute maximum lens opening and then removed the lens cover. Peering through the view finder, he focused the lens until the porch jumped into view. He smiled to himself. According to the built-in light meter, there was more than enough light from the porch and floodlights to filter through the lens. He knew he would be able to get detailed close-ups from where he was hidden, and all he needed were the subjects to be photographed—and their cooperation in looking at his lens. Once developed, he would have a photo gallery of everyone attending the meeting. But what was the purpose of the meeting?

Jack assumed it had something to do with the conspiracy since the note suggested it was related to Thacker's death. All he could do from his vantage point would be to at least, he hoped, identify those attending the meeting. That would be more than he had at the moment. As he thought about it, all he really had were two dead men, Skip and Thacker, a note from an unidentified woman, a hint or two from Roger, and a mysterious government facility somewhere out in Colorado. Jack knew if he carried what he had to his boss and told him he was on a story, he would laugh.

His body stiffened in anticipation. An automobile had turned into the driveway and, following the armed sentry's waving arm, proceeded slowly along the drive toward the lighted house. Jack immediately glued his eye to the camera's view-finder and watched as the car stopped. Both rear doors opened and three men stepped out. It was Aaron Wheeler, the retired army general who served on the president's staff as the National Security Advisor. Jack pressed the shutter release button, the camera made a clicking noise followed by the whirring noise of the film advance mechanism and in a split second he was ready to take another shot. Again, he pressed the shutter release. As the camera clicked, he placed a name with the face he photographed. He recognized the man as General Norman Petrie, a high-ranking army officer and, getting out on the other side, was General Matthew Whiteside.

As the three men entered the house, a second car turned into the driveway and proceeded to the house. When it stopped, one man stepped out; and Jack photographed him as he leaned forward to retrieve an attaché case. Jack blinked his eyes several times to make sure the night glare wasn't playing tricks on him. It was William Winnington, president of Jack's own network.

Cars began arriving regularly from that moment on. Some of the occupants Jack recognized; but whether he recognized them or not, he photographed them. Still, as they arrived, he could not help but feel astonished—and puzzled—at the assortment of high-level personalities arriving for the meeting. In addition to the generals, cabinet member, and Jack's own network president, automobiles continued to arrive, discharging passengers he recognized, including two more network presidents, the CEO of a news wire service, the president of a large cable service, several navy admirals, and at least a half dozen ranking officials from Middle Eastern and European countries. There were many he did not recognize, however, and he wondered if any of them was named Solomon.

Within thirty minutes the caravan of arriving automobiles and limousines ceased. All were inside; Jack knew he would give a month's salary to be in there with them, listening, taking notes. He contented himself with the fact that at least he had the pictures.

Jack was uncomfortable from lying in the same position for so long. He tried to twist his body into a different position. Then, it happened. His foot pressed against a stick wedged between two roots, and as he pushed against the stick, it snapped. In the quiet night air, the crack of the stick sounded like a gunshot. Jack's body stiffened and he immediately trained his camera on the sentries. They appeared unruffled or unconcerned and Jack assumed they did not hear the sound. But, as he scanned the yard he saw that although the guards had not heard anything, the guard dog had. It stood frozen, on point, looking in Jack's direction. The sentry, realizing that something had captured the dog's attention, leaned forward and strained to see into the darkness.

If Jack had remained perfectly still, he might have gone undetected; but unfortunately, he moved and when he did there was a slight rustle of the bushes. The guard dog went into a frenzy, and the sentry yelled out, "There's someone out there."

The sentry reached down and unleashed the dog who began running at breakneck speed, straight for the spot where Jack was concealed. The sentries were running in his direction with guns raised. Jack knew he was in deep trouble.

# 6.

# Chapter Six

**S**entries began running after the fierce-looking Doberman. The dog was closing in on Jack's position and the gate sentry was close enough to present an equally immediate threat. Jack didn't hesitate. He raised to a crouch, assumed the firing position, balancing his right arm with his left arm, aimed near the sentry in order to fire a warning shot and squeezed the trigger. The gunfire had the desired effect. The guard threw himself to the ground unsure where the shot was from. To add to the confusion, Jack swung his arm around and fired three quick rounds near the remaining guards. They also threw themselves to the ground.

For the moment, they ceased to be a threat; but the dog galloping toward him was cause for urgent concern. Jack had no choice. He steadied his arm, aimed carefully, and as the dog reached the bushes, he fired at point-blank range. With a yelp, the dog fell to the ground—dead.

"He shot the dog," one sentry screamed out.

Another voice yelled, "He's in those trees across the road."

Gunfire from a half dozen automatic weapons raked through the bushes, but Jack, holding the camera close to his chest, rolled down the embankment to safety. His only advantage was that they knew he had a gun, and they would be hesitant to rush him. Also, they had no idea in which direction he would flee. But Jack realized these were only temporary advantages. He needed to retreat—and fast.

Crouching low to the ground, he ran through the trees, giving thanks he had spent so much time walking up and down stairs instead of riding elevators. When he stopped, he was breathing hard but not exhausted. Listening carefully, he tried to determine where his pursuers were; and as he stood in the darkness catching his breath, he checked his location. He knew his car was still more than a mile ahead which meant he had to cover a lot of ground in a hurry if he was going to get out of this mess.

Then he heard it. Someone was following him and he was very, very close. Jack crouched behind a tree, trying to see through the darkness. He suddenly remembered the sentry who had positioned himself beyond the gate. The guard had obviously crossed the road during the confusion and, not threatened by Jack's warning fire, had reached the clump of trees before anyone else. With his head start, he was now on Jack's heels.

Jack had never shot anyone, and he briefly wondered what he would do if he had to shoot. He didn't have to wait very long to find out because the man was suddenly standing in front of the very spot where Jack was concealed. He stopped and stood very still, straining to pick up any sound that might disclose Jack's position. Jack knew he could not allow the guard to continue on and get between him and his car. Nor did it seem prudent to merely sit and wait for the other guards to catch up. He took a deep breath and said quietly, "If you move, you're a dead man. Drop the gun and put your hands behind your head."

The guard stiffened but did as he was told. He let the automatic weapon slip to the ground and raised his hands up behind his head as Jack stepped from behind the tree. "All right, move away from the gun." The guard took several steps and Jack moved forward, leaned down, picked up the weapon by the strap and slung it over his shoulder.

"You're not going to get out of here, Mister. My friends will be here any second. Why don't you just give me your gun and you can get out of this alive."

"Shut up," Jack snapped. The guard was right about one thing. His friends would be on top of them in a matter of seconds. Jack had to get moving, get to his car, and get away. As he stood there, trying to figure out his next move, a small animal suddenly darted out of the bushes. This startled Jack. As he instinctively turned his head, the guard took advantage of the diversion and moved. Quick as a cat, the guard leaped toward Jack, while reaching for the gun. Jack didn't think. He simply raised his pistol and fired. The slug slammed into the guard's body with enough force to turn him completely around. He dropped to his knees clutching his shoulder.

Jack quickly stepped over to the man, shocked by the fact he had pulled the trigger but not overly concerned about it either—he knew the guard would have killed him. He stuck the pistol barrel into the man's neck and said, "I think you had better remain perfectly still."

The guard looked up, hate spewing from his eyes as Jack held the pistol with his left hand and pulled the man's shirt open with his other. He could see that the bullet had penetrated the man's shoulder and he would live. Jack knew he could waste no more time.

Behind him he could hear voices yelling again and he knew the gunshot served as a homing beacon for his location. He also knew the minute he left, the wounded guard would begin yelling his head off. So, without a moment's hesitation, Jack raised the pistol and smashed it down on the man's head. Without a sound, he slumped to the ground, unconscious, and Jack resumed his dash to the car. He knew it would be only a minute or two before the others found their companion, but a minute or two head start was all he needed. He settled into a loping, groundcovering jog, angling down the side of the hill as he ran in order to reach the road where he could find his car. The automatic weapon he had taken from the guard hung like a dead weight so he threw it into the bushes. The heavy camera was bouncing around on his chest but he wasn't about to discard it. He knew those pictures would shed a lot of light on everything. At least, he prayed they would. He continued holding the camera close to his chest, protectively.

Far to his rear, he heard a voice yell out, "Over here," and knew they had found the unconscious guard. It would be only a matter of seconds before they resumed their chase. By now even an idiot would have figured out he was heading for a car stashed up the road, and they would abandon the woods for the road and the easier running—which is what Jack decided he needed to do. He did not break stride as he jumped the ditch onto the pavement. The smooth surface was much easier to travel, but Jack couldn't quicken his pace because his breath was beginning to come in labored gasps. He was beginning to wonder if he was going to make it to the car when suddenly he saw the little dirt road. Slowing down, he headed into the dark grove and heaved a sigh of relief when he saw the car sitting there as he had left it.

He leaned across the hood for a moment, trying to regain his breath. After a few seconds he straightened up, opened the door, slipped behind the wheel, and turned on the ignition. With a quiet roar, the engine came to life. He slipped it into gear, accelerated, and pulled out of the grove onto the road. Leaving the lights off and avoiding the brake pedal so the rear stop lights would not come on, Jack turned east and sped down the road as fast as he could without any headlights to guide him.

Jack knew he could not return to his apartment nor to his office. Someone was still out there trying to kill him. With a smile, he realized there was one place he would be safe. Turning on the lights, Jack pushed on the accelerator and sped through the Maryland darkness, heading back to Washington.

- - - - - - - - - - - -

Jack awoke with a start. Then, remembering he was at Roger Grant's house, relaxed and glanced at his watch. The three-hour nap would have to suffice. He rose from the couch, sneaked a peek through the drapes at the early morning sun, and strolled in the direction of the coffee aroma.

Roger Grant, sitting at the breakfast table covered with photographs, looked up. "I was going to let you sleep a little longer."

"It's eight in the morning and time I was moving about," Jack said, pouring a cup of coffee.

"When you came in this morning, you didn't tell me how you managed to get these pictures developed so fast."

Jack shrugged and replied, "There's a free-lance photographer I use occasionally and he works out of his home. I woke him up about midnight and he developed them for me."

"You want a refill?" Jack asked, watching Roger study the photographs.

"No thanks, I've had a full pot already. My kidneys are floating in coffee." He laid his magnifying glass down and asked, "Do you have any idea what this is all about?"

Jack took a deep breath and decided it was time to take Roger into his confidence. Not only was the agent a good friend, he also had the means to provide invaluable assistance which Jack knew he was going to need if he hoped to get to the bottom of everything.

He sat down at the kitchen table and began to fill Roger in on what he knew. He told of his meeting in the hotel with Thacker and how the man had hit the panic button when asked about a conspiracy; how the two security guards followed both of them from the auditorium; and he told Roger of Thacker's dying words.

"Why didn't you tell me all this before?" Roger wanted to know.

"I didn't know what I was talking about. I still don't know what I'm talking about; but when somebody blows up your car and guys start shooting at you, it's time to get a little professional help."

Jack stood up again, walked to the coffee pot, and, as he poured another cup, asked, "Do you have any idea or theories on any of this?"

Roger didn't say anything. He reached down, retrieved a folder from his open attache case, opened the folder, and said, "After we found out about the attempt on your life, my boss put a few extra men on some of the questions you've been asking." He paused for a second and said quietly, "Now, Jack, you're a good friend but there are limits to what I'm can tell you. But, I think in view of these pictures you've brought to me, my boss would authorize me to have a friendly, unofficial exchange of information. I emphasize exchange, Jack. I want everything you know or suspect. Agree?"

Jack nodded. "All right. Where do we begin?"

"Who is the girl?"

Jack looked at him, a puzzled expression on his face. "What girl?"

"What girl?" he asks. "The girl you asked me to run a check on. Pamela Richards."

Jack grinned sheepishly. "Forget her. She's not tied into this thing. I was trying to find out a little about her for a friend."

"Who was the friend?"

"Ryan Abernathy, the Director of Security down at NASA, in Houston."

Roger shook his head. "Now we have NASA involved."

"NASA?" Jack looked at him curiously. "What are you talking about? NASA hasn't been mentioned in the Thacker thing at all."

"Pamela Richards, right?"

Jack nodded.

"Works for General Whiteside's office at NASA."

"But I don't have her tied in with this."

"Then why is she working at Piaute Mountain? The very place we think Solomon is working."

Stunned, Jack sat down at the table. "Working at Piaute Mountain?"

"That's right. Jack, you need to stop playing games with me or, friend or not, I'm going to haul you downtown and let the boss ask all the questions."

"Roger, I swear to you. I had no idea she was connected to this."

Roger studied his friend for a moment and then commented, "I believe you." He went on. "We have reason to suspect that Pamela Richards was transferred to Piaute Mountain over the weekend. And I think it was probably on the direct orders of General Matthew Whiteside."

"Exactly what is Piaute Mountain?"

Roger shook his head in exasperation. "We're not sure. We had a man from Los Angeles slip up there yesterday and look around, but when he checked in last night he couldn't tell us what was going on. However, it's definitely not just a seismic center for measuring earth tremors. We ran a license check on the cars in the parking lot and came up with some pretty interesting names." He added, "And some interesting occupations."

"Anybody I would recognize?"

Roger pulled a list from the folder and began to read: "Dr. Karl Liederman, a laser physicist; Dr. Diane Williams, physicist and computer analyst; Dr. Chuck Valens, physicist specializing in laser technology; Dr. Sean MacTavish, an expert in laser transmission; James Butterly, a G-12 rated security guard which means he is probably the facility's security chief; Dr. Clay Davis, a physicist and computer man; Art. . ."

"What's that name again?"

Roger looked back at his list. "Which one?"

"Davis," Jack replied. "I've heard that name mentioned. What do you know about him?"

"He's big time, Jack. He's on the president's National Science Advisory Commission and on a dozen other committees."

He hesitated and then added, "We have a notation in our files that your Dr. Thacker worked for him on a special project, and there was a rumor the two of them were designing a new type of super computer."

Jack shrugged. "Who else is there?"

Roger looked at his list. "That's all we have at the moment. Any of the names ring a bell?"

"Just the Davis name. What does he do?"

"He does just about whatever he wants to do. From what we can understand he's the army's resident genius, especially in the weapons development sector." He smiled and asked, "And guess who heads up the weapons development department for the army? General Matthew Whiteside."

"His name does keep popping up, doesn't it?"

Pointing to one of the photographs, Roger said pointedly, "And now his picture has popped up." Thumbing through the photographs, Roger wondered aloud, "What are these people up to? I might be inclined to think it was just a high-level poker game or stag party out in the boondocks. But what about these gentlemen?"

He pointed to several photographs.

"Here we have three treasury officials from foreign governments; here's the Military Attaché from a Mideast nation; over in that stack we have two more foreign money guys; and here's a general or two from other countries." He looked up at Jack.

"I'm beginning to get very, very nervous."

Jack pointed at the five photographs off to the side. "The clue might be there," he suggested.

Roger frowned. "Some network presidents, a wire-service executive, and a cable television president? You'll have to explain those to me, Jack."

Taking a deep breath, almost afraid to suggest what he was thinking, Jack said tentatively, "Roger, if you were going to overthrow a government, what would be one of your first priorities?"

Roger thought a moment and then let loose a long, high whistle. "Grab the communications."

"Right. We suspect a conspiracy, based on Thacker's tip, and here we have the major communications executives in the country meeting with a bunch of power-hungry military men and people from foreign governments."

Roger studied the photographs for a second and then said, "All right, suppose there is a conspiracy to overthrow the government and all these people are somehow involved. Who is the head man? Is it Solomon? And if it is, who is he? Solomon has to be a code name because there is no one named Solomon at this high a level. We have to assume that whoever he is he would be equal to or above all these guys in rank or office. And how does Piaute Mountain figure in all this?"

"Or does it figure into it at all?" Jack asked.

Answering his own question, he said, "I think it does. We're just going to have to figure out how. And I have a feeling we don't have much time." He pointed to the photographs. "This gathering has all the appearances of a final briefing before some kind of action. How else do you explain the fact that all these guys sneaked out to a lonely farmhouse for a secret meeting?"

"It wasn't too secret," Roger suggested.

"What do you mean?"

"Well, someone told you about it."

Jack drummed his fingers on one of the photographs. "You're right. Someone else knew about this—a woman. I need to find that woman."

"And I need to get this up to my boss," Roger said, gathering up the pictures and stuffing them into his briefcase. "What are you going to do today?"

"I'm going to find that little old lady somehow," Jack answered. "And then I'm leaving town."

"Leaving town?"

"Yep, I'm heading west."

"West! What for?" Roger wanted to know.

"Because if there is a conspiracy to overthrow the government, they have to start with the president. He's on vacation in Los Angeles and that's only two hundred miles from Piaute Mountain." He paused, and added, "I think Piaute Mountain is the key to all this, and that's where I'm headed—after I find the mystery lady."

- - - - - - - - - - - -

As was his custom, Art Gibson was up before daylight. Although he lived with his family in nearby Basalt, there were times when it was necessary for him to remain overnight in the facility. His sleeping quarters occupied a small corner of the basement and provided him with all the necessary—though cramped—comforts he needed. He showered, shaved, dressed, and started a pot of coffee brewing. Another twelve hours remained before his shift was over, but he knew his day would be anything but boring. There was always a project requiring his attention—either the facility's or his own—but with the facility running smoothly, as it always did, he knew he could get in several hours of Bible study before breakfast was ready in the combination lounge-kitchenette upstairs.

With a cup of hot, fresh coffee, he seated himself before the computer, ready to begin where he left off the night before. For the past few weeks, Art had been struggling through the book of Revelation, or more correctly, the Revelation [of Saint John the Divine]. He began his study fully aware that many scholars considered the book to be a literary masterpiece—and he began with the knowledge that it was an extremely difficult book to comprehend.

He understood the history connected with the writing of Revelation. Art's problem dealt with understanding the relationship of the book to his own Christian life. He had discussed, or tried to discuss, the contents with several pastors but quickly discovered that they were even less informed and less knowledgeable than he. Consequently, armed with several reference books and commentaries, he continued to plod through the complex maze of names and numbers, stars and angels, Satanic beasts and unimaginable creatures—all of which dazzled his mind and frustrated his consciousness—leaving him confused.

Again, as on the previous night, Art reached for his Bible, turned to Chapter thirteen, and then placed the open Bible to one side as he inserted a diskette into his computer. It was still hard for him to accept or cope with the idea that the entire Bible could be reproduced on the small diskettes he held in his hand, and it was even harder for him to adjust to or accept reading the Bible on a computer screen. However, although the monitor was much less personal than the thin pages of his Bible, he readily admitted the computerized text was much easier to work with. A quick entry on the keyboard and he could retrieve any verse in any chapter of any book. The functions amazed him.

The computerized text had been a gift from the facility director. Art learned of the availability of the software program and asked the director if the program would work on the maintenance room computer. Assured it would, Art began considering making the purchase. Several hours later, however, the director made one of his rare visits to the basement and presented Art with the computerized text and program—just like that, a gift. Art was astounded and thoroughly confused over how the director managed to obtain the program so quickly. Also, Gibson was reluctant to accept the expensive gift, but the director insisted. Art couldn't help thinking he would never be able to figure out that man.

- - - - - - - - - - - -

Several hours later, as Art was finishing up his morning study of the Bible, upstairs on another level, Diane watched Mary Beth put three sugars in her coffee and shook her head. "Mary Beth, you're going to gain ten pounds with every cup of coffee if you keep that up."

Mary Beth laughed and reached over for a donut. "I don't care. This morning I have a sweet tooth. Need to satisfy it or I won't get any work done."

"I don't see how you get any work done anyway," Kathryn chimed in. "You're always on the telephone."

"That's not my fault," Mary Beth defended herself. "It's our boss who keeps me on the telephone. If I'm not tracking something down he needs for the lab, I'm answering calls from every general in the U.S. Army. And they seem to call every five minutes." She turned to Diane. "What are you guys working on that's so darn important?"

Diane smiled but didn't answer. Instead, she said, "You be nice to the generals, Mary Beth. Without them, we wouldn't have any money."

"Any of them single?" Kathryn wanted to know.

All three girls laughed. Diane stood up and walked to the coffee pot for another cup. "Anyone?" she asked, holding the pot in the air. Both girls shook their heads. She put the pot back on the warmer and returned to the small table.

Life in the facility, outside the lab, had become more enjoyable with the addition of Kathryn and Mary Beth to the staff. After only several days, both girls, hired to fill newly created administrative positions, captured the hearts of everyone in the facility. Diane particularly enjoyed their company and looked forward to the little coffee sessions every morning before work. The conversations were light, funny, and a welcome respite from the seriousness of the lab. She genuinely liked both girls.

With her mouth full of donut, Kathryn tried to speak, nearly choked, and as she coughed, Mary Beth began pounding her on the back. Signaling for her to stop, Kathryn tried to catch her breath, tears in her eyes from coughing and then laughing.

"You trying to kill me, Mary Beth?"

Mary Beth just grinned.

"Never try to talk with food in your mouth, dear," Diane said sternly.

"OK, Mom," Kathryn said, taking another sip of coffee in an effort to wash the donut down her throat. Finally, catching her breath, she said, "Seriously, what are you all working on down there, Diane? Everything is so hush-hush around here. You lab people walk around whispering to each other. Boss walks around like the nutty absent-minded professor . . ."

Mary Beth kicked Kathryn under the table. "Hush, you're talking about Diane's fellow."

Kathryn made a face. "He may be Diane's fellow but he's my boss and one of the privileges of having a boss is getting to talk about him, right?"

"Aw, he's not so bad," suggested Mary Beth. "Diane must think he's all right." She leaned forward and whispered, "When are the two of you getting married?"

Diane leaned forward to meet her and whispered back, "Whenever he gets up enough nerve to ask me."

They all laughed together.

"How did you guys meet, Diane?" Kathryn asked.

"I was teaching at Waylanth College, and the head of my department recommended me for a job in Washington. I went up, interviewed for the position, and he hired me as his lab assistant." She leaned toward the girls and again whispered, "I didn't like him at first." She added, "But he sort of grows on you."

"Well, I liked him the first time I met him," Kathryn said defensively."

"You like any man the first time you meet him," chided Mary Beth. Turning to Diane, she asked, "How come a good-looking hunk with his brains and money hasn't already been snatched up?" Diane shrugged. "He nearly married once. But it didn't work out. The girl married another man, and then she died, or committed suicide. I don't think he ever got over it." She added brightly, "Until he met me."

"Do you think he'll ask you soon?" asked Kathryn. "To marry you, I mean."

Diane smiled. "He'd better soon. I'm starting to feel like an old maid."

"Well, you don't look like an old maid, Diane," Mary Beth offered. "I should look as good as you when I reach . . ." Her hand flew over her mouth as she realized what she said. "I didn't mean . . . I mean. . . that's not what I meant."

Diane laughed and patted her on the hand. "Don't worry about it. I am getting along. More years than I care to admit. But I'm not dead yet."

"Diane, you're not getting along. You're only a little older than us. How old are you? 27? 29?"

Diane pouted and answered, "Close. I'm thirty-one."

"Well, you don't look it. I wish I had your skin. It's as smooth as a baby's," Kathryn observed.

"I stay out of the sun," Diane said. "That's the secret." She thought a moment and added, "And work for a boss who likes to work eighteen hours a day. That keeps you out of the sun."

"You really can't tell us what you guys are working on down there?" asked Mary Beth. "It must be pretty important the way these army people keep calling."

Diane shrugged her shoulders. "A lot of times they're not calling about what we're working on. "Many times they need to have our computer help their computer."

"Our computer help their computer?" Kathryn asked curiously. "What do you mean by that? Do we have some sort of super computer down there?"

Diane laughed and said, "You mean he hasn't bragged to you about. . ." She stopped, as she realized she shouldn't be telling the girls anything about the lab. She looked at her watch and said, "Gracious, it's almost 9:00. And I've got to get back to the lab," Diane said. "You girls have a good day and I'll see you later."

Art Gibson was stepping out of the elevator as she left the lounge, and she yelled for him to hold the door open. "Thanks, Art."

"Good morning, Dr. Williams. Coffee fresh?"

"Made it just for you, Art. Sorry I can't stay and have a cup with you, but I've got to get down to the temple before you know who has a heart attack waiting on me."

Art grinned and waved a salute as the elevator doors closed. Turning, he walked into the lounge, saw the two girls sitting at one of the tables and gave both a large smile. They were both new to the facility; but he like each instantly, probably, he thought, because they reminded him of his own two daughters. He particularly enjoyed Mary Beth's nonsense and clowning around. As he retrieved a cup of coffee and joined them at the small table, he could easily understand why more than just a few of the security guards had begun finding excuses to visit the administrative offices or lounge whenever either was present.

Unlike the tall, graceful, and formal-looking Diane, the two girls were petite, bouncy, and always bubbling with excitement and expectations. Mary Beth was the more hyper of the two; Kathryn was the more patient and calm. Both smiled a greeting to him. Mary Beth said dramatically, "I'm depressed. Begin cheering me up by telling me how wonderful and how beautiful I am."

Art chuckled. "I'll tell you I fixed your light switch today. Will that help?"

Her eyes sparkled and she gave him a broad smile. "Oh, that does help. Thank you. Now I can walk into my bathroom and see myself in the mirror. I really appreciate it, Mr. Gibson."

Art puffed on his cigar, exhaled, and said, "Don't mention it." He took his cigar out, flipped the ashes in the ashtray, and said with a groan, "I think the days just get longer and longer around here."

Kathryn agreed. "You know what gets me? You can't see the sun, you can't see the moon. The only way to tell if it's daylight or dark is to look at your watch. That's the hardest part of working here. Do you ever get used to it?"

"Not really," Art answered. "It's a little different for those of us who don't live here at the facility. For us, it's like working in a big building. We come to work, we leave, and we get to see the sun and moon once in a while. That helps. For those of you who have living quarters here, I can understand what you mean. You don't know if the sun is shining, if it's raining, or what. I'd go nuts if I didn't get out of here every day."

"How are things in the big city, Mr. G.?"

Art chuckled. Mary Beth was kidding him about Basalt, the small town just down the road from the complex. It was a small town—only six hundred people—and he lived on a small ranch with his wife and youngest daughter.

"Big doins' this weekend, girls. Old Charlie Burnside is putting in a new septic tank, so we're all going to drive over and watch the back-hoe dig it out. Wanna come?"

Mary Beth gave him one of her serious looks. "Wow, that sounds like fun, Mr. G., but I better hang around here. The boss might need me." She laughed. "A septic tank?"

Art's deep chuckle broke out again. "Well, things are a little slow this weekend around Basalt, Mary Beth."

"Mr. G., you've been here since the very beginning, haven't you?"

"From the very first day. Actually, I was working here while they were building this place. When the contractor finished, they hired me to stick around and take care of the maintenance. It's a good job. Beats having to drive into Carson City or Hawthorne every day."

"Have you always lived around here?"

"I was born about sixty miles from here. A little town over in California. Bishop. Nice place. But we moved here about four years ago, when they opened this place. We like it all right. We get to watch people dig out their septic tanks."

"Who hired you? Dr. Davis?"

"No. He doesn't hire anybody. All the hiring is done by somebody out of Washington. Isn't that who hired you?"

Both girls nodded.

"Well, we're glad they hired you. Both of you sort of help the morale around this place. I've never been around so many somber people in all my life. I wonder if all scientists are this serious?"

"I wouldn't be surprised." Mary Beth fiddled with her soda can for a moment and then asked, "Mr. G., I know I'm not supposed to ask, but are they nearly finished with all their experiments down there?"

Art thought a moment. "I'm not supposed to talk about anything they do down there, Mary Beth. I can tell you this much, though. Day before yesterday they were all whooping it up and yelling and slapping each other on the back. You can draw your own conclusions."

"Somebody told me Dr. Davis invented an invisible wall that can't be penetrated. That sounds like something out of a *Star Trek* movie," Kathryn volunteered.

"Lemme tell you something, Davis is out of a *Star Trek* movie. The man is an absolute marvel."

Mary Beth asked, "What about this invisible wall he's built? Is it really an invisible wall?" "Mary Beth, I can't talk about that. I really don't know. They just call me when they need to hook up their portable generators." He thought a moment and then added, "I can tell you this much. They use enough electricity down there to light up the city of Reno. . . ."

Art's pager began to beep. "Oooops. Somebody wants me. Gotta run, girls. Hold down the fort. I'll be back to finish my coffee."

Art stubbed his cigar out in the ashtray and walked briskly from the lounge in the direction of the elevator. Mary Beth and Kathryn watched the man walk away. They exchanged looks and then both followed him. "I guess we need to go to work, Mary Beth."

"I suppose you're right. Probably be another busy day."

Within a few minutes, both girls had returned to their offices. One immediately began filing the previous day's paperwork; the other also had filing but instead of beginning her work, she picked up the telephone, dialed nine for an out side line and at the dial tone, paged the long distance operator. When a voice responded, she said, "Operator I want to call New York, person to person to. . . ."

# 7.

# Chapter Seven

**W**hen James Butterly received his discharge from the U.S. Air Force, he promptly interviewed for a law enforcement position with several east Texas police departments and just as promptly rejected every job offer he received. The pay scale did not come up to his expectations. Anxious to remain in the security field in some capacity, especially in the area of electronic security, he applied for a job at NASA, in Houston, for a security guard position. Once accepted, he immediately enrolled in the University of Houston and began attending college by night while working by day.

His dedication and initiative attracted the attention of the Security Director who took the young military veteran under his wing as a protégé and, as the opportunity presented itself, moved Butterly into positions of ever increasing responsibility. Eventually, due to promotions, normal attrition, transfers, and his own talents, James Butterly was promoted to the position of Assistant Security Director. As Ryan Abernathy's assistant, James Butterly observed, studied, learned his profession; and when the department received a memo from Washington advising of an opening for Chief of Security, at a remote research facility in Nevada, James applied for the job. Thanks in part to Ryan's glowing recommendation, James was hired.

At the time he enjoyed the idea of being the facility's Chief of Security but after two years his enthusiasm diminished. His days were occupied with scheduling, answering the phone, checking deliveries, and—only occasionally—confronting an intruder or trespasser who invariably turned out to be a lost or inquisitive backpacker, hiker, or tourist. He often longed for the good old days at NASA when a scheduled launch had everyone's adrenalin flowing, and people appreciated a thorough and competent security system. In his present position, security men were sometimes looked upon as readily available messenger boys.

Perhaps it was because there were so many of them. James spent half his time trying to figure out what to do with the men in his department and to compound his scheduling problem, ten new officers were recently added to his staff. Sometimes he had the feeling he was director of a small army preparing for war instead of maintaining security at a government facility. He sought an explanation from the director on why so many security guards were needed, but he simply shrugged and said, "James, just prepare for the worst and keep your men alert."

He laughed but his answer confused James. Alert for what?

James looked around his office, checking to insure that each of the twelve surveillance monitors was properly focused and functioning, and then reached for the telephone. He dialed Ryan's office number and after a few rings, a man's voice answered.

"NASA Security. May I help you?"

Recognizing Ryan Abernathy's voice, James put his hand over the telephone mouthpiece, lowered his voice and, speaking in a foreign accent, said, "I can't make it to work tonight. All my uniforms turned pink in the wash."

It was a personal joke that went back to the first week James worked for Ryan. He had washed all his khaki uniforms with a new red beach towel and it had faded, coloring his uniforms.

"You nut. I was going to call you today. What are you doing?"

James laughed. "Hi, good buddy. I've been so busy this morning, I thought I would just make myself take a break and phone someone I knew wasn't doing anything. Lo and behold, your name came to mind."

"Busy my rear end. What happened? You have to turn the television off and make coffee? Or did the Indians attack and you had to run them off?"

"Much worse than that, Captain. I had to go into the wilderness and arrest a rabbit that got caught in the intruder alarm system. Talk about a fight till the death. It's too horrible to discuss."

Laughing, Ryan asked, "How are things up in the mountains? Cool? Cold? Hot? Quiet?"

"All those things. Cool in the morning, cold at night, hot in the daytime. How I miss some good old polluted humidity."

He waited a moment and then asked, "How was your trip to Washington? Did you find out anything?"

At the other end, he could sense the frustration Ryan felt.

"No, not a thing. I called or saw everyone I knew. All I can do now is wait and see if anything comes up."

"I thought you were going to take some time off, Ryan?"

"I was," he replied. "But when nothing developed on the Washington trip, I decided to come on in to work and save the vacation time till I really needed it. Not much I can do until I find out what happened or where she went." He added, "Besides, I needed to be here for the launch."

"Well, I guess it's best for you to stay busy." He added, "And I imagine you're pretty busy right now."

"We were. You talk about everyone hoppin' around. This place is buzzin' and crawling with reporters, TV people, VIPs, everybody—here to watch them send up those two launches. First time we've ever done that—sent up a manned satellite and a space shuttle. But everything went off like clockwork. The shuttle and satellite are in orbit right now."

"How come two? The paper says some kind of experiment is going to take place, and the shuttle is going to put a pod on the moon. Is that right?"

"That's right. I don't know what the experiment is. Someone told one of my boys they were going to be up there measuring light or sound waves or something. They're being pretty secretive about the whole thing. All I know is it's over for us—till they start back, of course. Then we'll sew this place up again."

"Come on, you must know something," James urged.

There was a slight hesitation and then Ryan said, "Well, just between you and me, its got something to do with the military. They have so much brass in the control room we had to turn all the magnets off. And more brass is on the way. I heard a minute ago that the top dog is coming down—General Whiteside. I have a feeling, just a feeling, that its got something to do with the research from the Star Wars program. I know they're keeping an open line to the president, an open line to the head of the Joint Chiefs of Staff, and an open line to the Senate Armed Forces Committee Chairman. So, it's something big." He added, "You wouldn't believe how tight security is."

"Tighter than usual?"

Ryan answered, "Much tighter."

"Lucky devil. I wish I was there," James said enviously.

"Listen, if you were here, you'd be working instead of sitting in that comfortable little office of yours. What do you guys do up there, anyway? I thought all the facility did was measure earthquakes or something. What's the big secrecy deal?"

"Who knows? We have all these brains running around in a fog working on something real hush-hush."

"Now, who's being vague?" Ryan asked.

"I'm not being vague intentionally, Ryan. I really don't know. It's got something to do with invisible walls or something like that. These guys don't talk much. They're not like the fellows at NASA. They would at least give you a friendly hint about what's going on. These fellows won't even give you the time of the day."

"Real nerds, huh?"

"Ah, not all of them. Davis can be a real jerk sometimes. Half the time I don't know what he's up to."

"What do you mean by that?

"Well, the other day, I was checking my monitors and I saw Dr. Davis down in the lounge. Now, that's not unusual, but I swear I saw him take something out of his pocket and put it in the bowl of sugar. You explain that to me."

Ryan sounded puzzled. "Maybe he's just making the sugar sweeter."

"Sure! And maybe he's conducting some kind of government experiment. Remember when they used to give LSD to soldiers but wouldn't tell them what it was?"

"I've heard that. Maybe you just imagined he put something in the sugar." "I'm telling you I saw it, Ryan. He opened a little bottle and sprinkled whatever it was on the sugar. There's no telling what he was putting in that sugar. I reported it to General Whiteside, but he just blew it off. Told me it was no big deal." He thought about it for a second and added, "I know one thing. I ain't going to use any of that stuff in my coffee."

"I don't blame you, pal." He laughed. "It might be some kind of truth serum and he'll be in there asking you questions about your social life and you'll have to admit you ain't got none."

James laughed. "There ain't much social stuff going on in this part of Nevada, let me tell you." James had a sudden thought. "Speaking of social life, I may have an idea about Pamela."

"What's that?" Ryan asked expectantly.

"Maybe I can talk Dr. Davis into helping you find her with that computer of his. That thing is awesome."

"How can he help sitting out there under some mountain? I've got every professional I know trying to find her. They use computers too, but they haven't come up with anything."

James said softly, "Davis' computer is a little different, Ryan."

"What do you mean, different?"

James thought about it for a moment and then answered, "You remember that fire I had in my house?"

"Yeah."

"I lost all my papers. My important stuff. Everything was lost. Most of it I could replace, like insurance policies, things like that. But it burned up all my income tax returns and information, and I was facing an audit."

"An audit? From the tax people?"

"Right. And I didn't have any back-up receipts or anything. Maybe it wasn't a big deal, but I mentioned it to Dr. Davis; he took me downstairs with him. Anyway, to make a long story short, he put my name and social security number into his computer and that thing kicked out all my tax records for the last four years."

On the other end, Ryan couldn't quite understand what James was telling him. "So, what's the big deal about that? Computers are supposed to retrieve information."

"You don't understand, Ryan. Davis was in a pretty good mood, and I think he was showing his baby off a little. He also retrieved my complete military records, insurance file, bank records, driving records, military records, everything. Are you reading me?"

"I'm reading you, but he would have to enter the Defense Department computers to locate Pam."

"Look, I'm not supposed to know this but he also entered the IRS Data Bank somehow and removed my name from the audit list. I saw him do it. He just deleted my name; I haven't heard from them since."

"Wow!"

"Exactly. I've never been around any computer that could do something like that."

"Probably. But there's more. Ryan, that big baby can solve just about any problem you come up with. Did you know the NASA people use it all the time?"

"I knew we had a hookup to you guys, but I didn't know it was to the computer."

"It's for the computer. When NASA gets in a bind, they call Dr. Davis. In fact, NASA was on-line all night long, tied into the computer."

"Hold on a second, James," Ryan said—his voice muffled by a hand over the telephone. He was obviously talking to someone on his intercom system. In a moment, he was back on the line and said, "James, I've gotta run. I'll get back to you a little later."

"All right, old buddy. Call me when you can. I'll be here." He hung up the phone, checked his monitors again, and then, sighing, reached for a magazine. Another boring shift, James thought. Another day at Piaute Mountain—where nothing ever happened.

- - - - - - - - - - - -

Several hours after leaving Roger's house, Jack was speeding south on U.S. Highway 95, heading for Ashland, Virginia and Waylanth College—a few miles north of Richmond. After telling Roger he was on his way to find the mystery lady, Jack realized he had no place to start. Reluctant to visit his office, because as far as he knew someone was still trying to eliminate him, he had virtually no research tools available except the telephone. Then he remembered the network receptionist's description of the woman delivering the message about Hinterwald: "She was an elderly woman." Thacker was an elderly man. Was it possible a disgruntled widow had pointed him in the right direction? He also remembered the woman's promise from the note: "I will contact you within the next few days."

From a roadside coin telephone, Jack called his office, dialed in his personal message retrieving code, and listened to the messages awaiting him. There were several unimportant calls, one from Roger Grant, and two from his boss, Melvin Blakely, telling him to call the office as soon as possible, but there was no message from his mystery woman. He ignored all the messages, hung up, and dialed his home phone number. His answering machine answered the call. After entering the message retrieval code number, he listened as the calls were played back. Again, nothing important. Another call from Roger and a call from Melvin, advising him to call the office immediately and several personal calls from friends.

Suddenly, he stiffened, as an unfamiliar voice reached his ears. "Mr. Clayburn, I found your number in my husband's desk. I'm assuming you received the note I left at your office. I hope you enjoyed your country drive; and if you would like to discuss this further, call me."

Grabbing a pen from his pocket, Jack quickly wrote the number down. She left no name but she did leave her number. Hanging up the phone, he next dialed the operator and asked for the city where the area code and prefix she provided him was located. He waited and then smiled as the operator answered, "Sir, that number is for Ashland, Virginia." Her mention of finding his number in her husband's desk was the tip-off. He was right.

His next phone call was to the number. After several rings, a feminine voice answered.

Jack, fearful that her line might be tapped, said cryptically, "Hi, Mrs. Thacker. I wanted to call and say I got your note the other day and followed your advice. It was a real eye-opener. Thank you very much."

Mrs. Thacker, realizing what Jack was doing, replied, "I'm glad you enjoyed it. We must get together real soon."

"And when would that be convenient?"

"Oh," she answered casually, "anytime would be fine. The quicker the better."

"I'll see you later. Again, thanks and I look forward to seeing you."

He hung up the phone.

Ashland was a one-hour drive south of Washington. Once he was out of the capital's traffic, he made excellent time. And shortly before noon, Jack drove slowly by the Thackers' brown English colonial-style home. He had obtained the address from the telephone directory and a few requests for directions enabled him to find the home, adjacent to the college campus, without any problem.

There was another problem, however. A few hundred feet north of the Thacker home, a late model sedan with two men seated inside was parked. As Jack drove by, he turned his head so the men would not get a clear view of his face, but the fact that they showed more than just a casual interest in his car made him overly cautious. They might simply be innocently parked, waiting on a friend; yet, they could well be watching Mrs. Thacker's house.

Jack decided not to take any chances. Driving slowly, he threaded his way through the narrow streets, making a trip around the block until he was opposite the back of the Thacker home. Parking his car, he walked through the adjoining yard, pushed his way through the hedge separating the two properties and walked swiftly to the Thacker back entrance. He knocked on the door and waited. Presently, a voice from the other side asked softly, "Who is it?"

"It's Jack Clayburn, Mrs. Thacker. From the network."

There was a long silence, then the sound of the door opening. Through the crack, Jack could see her, pointing a small pistol at him. The picture of the small, elegantly dressed grey-haired woman holding the pistol was incongruous; but Jack somehow had the feeling she knew how to use the weapon. Involuntarily, he stepped back "Whoa, Mrs. Thacker. It's me. The man you sent the note to. I'm Jack Clayburn."

She studied his face for a moment, and, recognizing him, opened the door wider. "Come in, Mr. Clayburn. I've been expecting you."

Jack walked into what had obviously been a porch until it was enclosed. The room was now an airy, comfortable looking indoor patio with plants scattered throughout the room on the wall and in buckets and planters on the floor. He stood for a moment, uncertainty on his face, until she motioned for him to take a seat on one of the many cushion-seated white wrought iron chairs.

He sat and said immediately, "I appreciate you taking the time to see me, Mrs. Thacker. I realize what you must be going . . ."

She interrupted him and said, "Let's not talk about that, Mr. Clayburn. I appreciate the fact that you were the last one to see my husband alive but I don't want any of the details. I just want to get even with those responsible. May I offer you some tea? Coffee? Or a soft drink?"

Jack shook his head. "No thank you, ma'am. I just want to know what's going on."

Mrs. Thacker walked elegantly to another chair opposite Jack, sat, and said, "I'll tell you what I know. It isn't much, but I'm sure it's more than you know now."

Jack admitted he knew very little.

"My husband and I were married forty-eight years, Mr. Clayburn. Jack nodded.

"He was a good man. A man of character and a man of ethics. And he was a brilliant man. But he made a mistake. He allowed himself to be dragged into something for which he had no stomach. It caused his death."

"What was he involved in, Mrs. Thacker?"

She studied him for a moment before answering. "I would like to think that Floyd was not actually involved in what is going on. I believe he was unknowingly part of it. When he found out what was transpiring, he tried to extricate himself. Obviously, he didn't. No, Mr. Clayburn, my husband was not killed because he was involved in something. I think he was murdered because he knew too much. And being a man of character, I think the people involved knew he would eventually tell what he knew." Her lips quivered and, with a gasp, unable to control herself any longer, she broke, and began to cry. "I'm sorry, I . . . "

Patiently, Jack asked, "What did Dr. Thacker know, Mrs. Thacker?"

Twisting the small handkerchief in her hands, the teary eyed woman leaned back and deliberately, very slowly, began to tell Jack the story. "I'm going to tell you about Solomon. And I'm going to tell you about someone else. Someone who is very, very dangerous."

An hour later, a white-faced Jack Clayburn stood to leave.

He took Mrs. Thacker's hand and said, "Thank you, Mrs. Thacker. You've made a lot of things more clear for me and I can assure you that what you've told me will be passed along to the right people."

She looked up into his eyes and said quietly, "I believe you, Mr. Clayburn. Do what you can to bring my husband's murderers to justice."

He promised her he would, and thanking her again, left. As he walked through the backyard, retracing his earlier steps, out of the corner of his eye he saw a man standing near the kitchen window. Taking no chances, Jack pulled the pistol hidden in his waistband, wheeled around, and aimed the gun at the man. "You, what are you doing?" Jack yelled out. Spinning around, the man saw Jack, turned and threw something through the window; then, he began running away.

For just a split second, Jack's mind fought to understand what was happening. Then, it hit him. Screaming, he ran toward the house, but it was too late. The bomb exploded with a thunderous roar, followed closely by another explosion, and then a fireball mushroomed skyward. The impact threw him to the ground, and he shielded himself from the falling debris with his arms. Finally, raising up, he saw there was nothing he could do. The house was a blazing inferno. He knew Mrs. Thacker could not have survived.

Turning, he sprinted for his car. Pushing through the hedge, he ran into a woman coming from the other house. She screamed out, saw the gun in Jack's hand, and screamed again. He didn't stop to explain. He continued running. Jack knew he had to get away before the man, and his accomplice, came after him. As he ran, he could hear the woman still screaming and yelling, "Stop him. Somebody stop him!"

Two hours later Jack was back in Washington. He parked the rental car behind a small restaurant, went in, ordered a sandwich and glass of milk, and while his order was being prepared, stepped to the pay phone at the rear of the dining room. He dialed Roger Grant's office, and within a few seconds his friend was on the line.

"Roger, we have to meet."

"I'll second that. Where are you now?"

"I'm back in Washington. I know all about Solomon, but I don't want to talk on the telephone."

"Jack, I'm getting ready to leave for a meeting. I have no idea when it will end. Can you give me a clue?"

"No, not over the telephone. It's too big, Roger." Jack thought for a moment and then said, "No way you can get out of your meeting and get with me?"

"Absolutely not. Can it wait until tomorrow?"

"I don't know," Jack answered. "I guess it will have to."

Roger gave him instructions. "OK, meet me tomorrow morning at The Silver Pan restaurant on Miracle Drive for breakfast. How about 7:00?"

"All right, will do."

"And, Jack. Be careful."

"Don't worry, buddy. You can't imagine how careful I'm going to be." He hung up the phone, fished another quarter from his pocket and dialed the network office. When the receptionist answered, Jack said, "Give me Melvin Blakely. This is Jack Clayburn."

Within seconds, Melvin was on the phone. "Jack, where are you?"

"I'm in Washington, Melvin. Where do you think I am?"

"No, I mean where are you exactly? I'll send a car to pick you up." He added, "We need to talk."

"To tell you the truth, Melvin, I'm a little reluctant to come in there. You'll remember the last time I was at my office, someone tried to kill me."

"That's why we need to talk. We're giving you another assignment. One that will get you out of the city and away from whatever you've gotten yourself into."

"I don't want another assignment, Melvin. I'm working on a story right now—a good one. It might be the biggest story I've ever worked."

"Not any more. I have instructions to pull you off the virus story and re-assign you."

A warning bell rang in Jack's head. Cautiously, he asked, "Who gave you those instructions, Mel?"

"They came from the top, Jack. You have no choice but to get off the story, come on in to the office, give me any notes you have, and take the new assignment."

"I'm not giving anyone my notes," Jack replied. "If I give them to anyone, they're going to be to Roger Grant with the FBI."

There was a pause on the other end and finally Melvin said,

"Jack, I think you're into something too deep here. All I know is that your reassignment came down from the New York offices. Not the News Department but THE offices. Somebody at the top passed the word to pull you. I have no choice."

Jack thought for a moment. He knew what he was about to do would probably cost him his job, but there was no backing out now. "I'm sorry, Melvin. I'm staying on this story. It's bigger than you can imagine. I'm not quitting now."

Another pause. Then, "Jack, there's another reason you have to come in."

Puzzled, he asked, "And what's the other reason, Melvin?"

"Were you in Virginia today?"

"Why?" Jack asked slowly.

"Because you've been identified as a suspect in a murder." He added dramatically, "Jack, the police are looking for you for the murder of Floyd Thacker's wife. They now suspect that you're the one who killed Floyd Thacker."

Stunned, Jack hung up the phone.

# 8.

# Chapter Eight

**P**aul Marchand looked at his watch and, seeing that he was slightly behind schedule, closed his notebook. He looked around the room and said, "Ladies and Gentlemen, that concludes this NASA update." He paused a moment, and added, "As you leave the room, Major Powell will provide you with the current schedule of activities for the astronauts in both ships. Thank you."

With a smile and a final wave, he turned from the podium and, ignoring the inevitable clamor of voices shouting last minute questions at his back, left the room. Walking briskly down the hall to the elevator that would return him to his office and desk in Mission Control, he wondered if his children were watching the televised news conference. He doubted it. They would be busy getting ready for school and he knew his wife seldom turned on the television set until they left. They would have to catch him on the evening news. He thought perhaps seeing their dad as a celebrity might compensate for his continued absence from home over the past few months. He promised that as soon as the mission was completed, he was going to arrange to spend more time with his family.

Stepping into the elevator, he pushed the button marked *B2*. As the doors closed and the elevator began its slow descent to Mission Control Center, his thoughts turned to the press conference just adjourned. As Mission Director, he was not unaccustomed to presiding over these necessary functions; but he never became completely comfortable with them. However, he felt he did well—particularly well, he thought, since there were certain aspects of the dual launch that had to be guarded from the press and public.

It was not, of course, unusual for NASA to have two spacecraft in orbit simultaneously; but it was unusual for the space agency to launch two craft on the same day. Members of the press were told that the event was simply an effort to illustrate America's launch capability, and that the two craft, were independent of each other. It was explained that the manned space satellite would conduct communications experiments. The space shuttle, however, carrying a two-man Lunar Landing Craft, was scheduled to direct a landing on the moon surface to retrieve previously implanted crystals and space-monitoring equipment. For the most part, the questions from the reporters had dealt with the astronauts aboard the spacecraft and only a few newsmen seemed interested in the scheduled experiments. They knew that a general fact sheet and press release concerning the technical side of the launch would be provided to them at the con-clusion of the meeting. There was one moment, however, when Paul became inwardly apprehensive and nervous. One Houston newspaper reporter asked if the dual mission was in any way connected to the military Star Wars program. Paul laughed the question off by answer-ing, "If there was a connection it would be so Top-secret I wouldn't be up here talking to you and since I'm up here talking to you, it can't be Top-secret. Next question."

He knew by the look on the reporter's face the answer was not satisfactory but Paul ignored him for the remainder of the news conference. He did not know if the question was just routine or if the resourceful newsman picked up a hint on the launch's real, but extremely secret, purpose. It didn't matter. No one could tell what was going on in space and with a little luck no one, other than those involved, would discover what was scheduled to occur in space within the next twelve hours.

The elevator stopped, the doors opened, and Paul Marchand stepped into a technological and computerized marvel, Mission Con-trol Center. He walked immediately to his desk and control console where, before seating himself, he paused for a quick look at the men and machines under his supervision. The murmur of soft voices and the casual air of those working in the center told him everything was under control. There was nothing to worry about because everything was proceeding as planned.

- - - - - - - - - - -

Jack Clayburn drove by The Silver Pan restaurant several times, checking carefully to insure no suspicious people were watching. He had no idea who or what to look for but seeing nothing out of the ordinary, he relaxed, parked his car behind the restaurant, entered, and sat to wait on Roger. He was early for their appointment but, he knew Roger was always prompt and there would be no long wait. Meanwhile, he ordered coffee, and leaned back to wait.

Five minutes later, Roger walked through the front door, looked around, saw Jack, and headed toward his booth. "Good morning, Jack," he greeted, as he slipped behind the table. "You look terrible. Where in the world did you spend the night?"

"In the back seat of my car at a rest stop on the Interstate. I didn't want to check into a motel or anything. Someone might have recognized me."

"I don't blame you. You're in real deep and very hot water. What's the deal on Mrs. Thacker?"

"You know about that?"

Roger shook his head and said sarcastically, "We're a law enforcement agency, Jack. We know about these things. At the moment, you're a wanted man." Jack looked at him cautiously. "Are you going to try to take me in, Roger?"

Roger smiled. "I talked it over with my boss. See those two men who just came in?"

Jack nodded nervously.

"Well, my boss sent them along with me. If I don't like what you tell me or if I think you're pulling a fast one or holding out on us, those two gentlemen are going to pick you up and carry you back to 'ol Virginy.'" He paused, then asked, "What happened down in Ashland?"

Jack took a deep breath and began his story. When he got to the part about the man throwing a bomb through the window, Roger stopped him. "Could you identify him if you saw him again?"

"Probably. He was only fifteen or twenty yards away."

"We may want you to look at some pictures."

Curious, Jack asked, "How did the police know I was there?"

"From what we understand, they had an anonymous tip, and when they showed your picture to the next door neighbor, she identified you."

"The lady in the hedge?"

"The hedge?"

"I ran into a woman coming though the hedge as I was leaving."

Roger dismissed the observation and continued. "All we know is a woman saw a man leaving the scene of the bombing and the man was you."

"Well, I can tell you this, Roger. The guy who threw the bomb through the window was a cold-blooded sucker. He wasn't content to throw one. He threw two."

"What did you learn from Mrs. Thacker, Jack?"

Jack took a deep breath and then repeated what the woman told him.

"About five years ago, when Thacker was still working for Armstrong Industries, he went in and told Adam Armstrong he had learned something the company needed to look into. Thacker was a good friend of Clay Davis, the computer whiz, and Davis told Floyd that he had developed something entirely new. Something that would revolutionize the computer industry. As Thacker explained to Adam, it had something to do with what Davis called a 'Looping Chip.'

"Now, I'm not sure what the Looping Chip could do but according to Mrs. Thacker, Adam Armstrong became very excited, called in several top army experts, and the next thing Floyd Thacker knew, he was sent to Piaute Mountain to work with Clay Davis.

"As it turned out, Davis' invention opened the door for the development of a new super computer."

Roger interrupted. "I've never heard of it."

"Nor has anyone else because for the past few years they've kept the lid on it. As far as most people know, the computer is just an advanced sophisticated piece of machinery that is very fast and able to verify and check data almost instantly. All government agencies such as the IRS, Defense Department, NASA, Census Bureau, use the computer to verify and authenticate information."

"Sounds innocent enough to me, Jack. Get to the point."

Jack considered his next statements carefully, selecting his words slowly. "According to Mrs. Thacker, Davis and her husband fell out because they disagreed on how the computer was being utilized. The army, which was in charge of the project, insisted on expanding the computer's capability to such an extent that the computer ceased to be a piece of machinery. It became a power base."

"What do you mean?"

"Information and control are power, Roger. That computer is loaded with everything imaginable. That's power." He added, "And as Mrs. Thacker pointed out, power has the capability of changing history, controlling history, controlling events."

"This sounds more like a sci-fi movie script, Jack."

"That it does but if what she told me is true, it's a fact. The computer at Piaute Mountain is the most powerful and most dangerous thing in the world."

"All right. You have my attention. Explain what it can do."

Slowly, Jack listed the super computer's capability. "According to Mrs. Thacker, Davis' computer can steal information from any computer in the world without detection. In other words, it can access a computer's data base, copy everything in it, leave, and no one is the wiser. The computer can change bank accounts, transfer money, change records. It can actually manipulate and operate other computers. And if it's ordered to do so, it can ruin other computers by accessing them, depositing a virus that will eventually destroy the computer's hard drive and files, and leave without being detected."

Jack paused. "But here's the scary part. Davis' computer can start a nuclear war because it can enter and control any computerized missile site in the world."

Roger's mouth fell open as he listened. He now reached for his coffee and suggested, "We have only her word that this thing can do all that. What if she's just trying to get someone excited enough to check into it and maybe stumble across her husband's killer?"

"Well, I had trouble believing everything she said until she told me the computer's name."

"And?"

"Davis' computer is known as SOLOMON."

Roger whistled. "And Solomon, according to what Thacker told you before he died, is the key to a conspiracy." Reflectively, he said aloud, "Which brings us to the big question. What is the conspiracy? And who is involved?"

"I think someone is trying to overthrow the government and is going to use Solomon in some way to pull it off." He stopped, thinking for a second before continuing. "As to who is involved, I can't answer that. I'm tempted to believe that somewhere in all this General Matthew Whiteside's name figures in some way, but how I don't know. That's what I'm going to find out. Davis, the computer whiz at Piaute Mountain, is surely involved someway because it's his baby. And I think we can throw in all the people I photographed at the Maryland house, including my bosses at the network."

"Well, if ever there was a perfect time for an attempted overthrow of the government, now is the time. The economy is all messed up, the vice president has everyone yelling for his head, the president has the lowest popularity of any president in history, and public trust in the entire administration has bottomed out."

Roger started to say something else but Jack stopped him with a wave of his hand. "Roger, how many men do you have with you?"

"Just those two, why?"

"There are two men standing outside, looking through the window at us. In fact, they're coming in. Are they your people?"

Roger turned, took a quick look, then, turning back to Jack said, "Ahhh, it's just a couple of customers looking for breakfast." He started to say something else, but Jack screamed out.

"Roger, look out! They've got guns."

The FBI agent hesitated a split second. The hesitancy probably cost him his life. One gunman sprayed a volley of shots down the counter, catching the two FBI men off guard, wounding one and killing the other before they knew what was happening. The other gunman directed his fire toward the booth where Roger and Jack sat. The first splatter caught Roger Grant in the back, straightening him up, before he collapsed dead. Jack threw himself under the booth table, pulled the 9mm pistol from his waistband and squeezed off several quick shots.

He didn't aim; he just pointed the weapon in the general direction and squeezed the trigger. He sneaked a look around the corner and, to his surprise, saw one gunman clutching his throat, blood pouring through his fingers. Jack's shot scored a hit.

The second gunman, realizing he was now alone, began backing slowly out of the restaurant, spraying a shower of bullets across the dining room. Jack squeezed off two more shots but missed and then the gunman was gone. There was silence. Then, a low moan from a wounded customer. Jack stood up cautiously, checked Roger's pulse, then cursed. His friend was dead. He could see the other two agents sprawled across the floor; and from their positions, he knew they too were dead.

A dazed cook stood in the kitchen doorway, clutching his blood-stained arm, staring in disbelief at the wrecked and body littered dining room. Jack walked cautiously to the front door, peered out, and saw a car pulling away rapidly. Turning, he addressed the cook and screamed, "Call the police and tell them what happened. Tell them ambulances are needed."

The cook just looked at him.

He repeated his instructions and when the cook still failed to offer any sign of understanding, Jack walked over to him, shook him gently by the shoulders and said, "Call the police. Tell them what has happened here."

Shaking his head, the cook walked slowly in the direction of the telephone, still clutching his arm as blood poured from the gunshot wound.

Jack left. Scrambling through the door, he dashed to his car, looking left, right, and all around, for anyone who might pose a threat, opened the door, and, for a split second, gritted his teeth and prayed a quick prayer as he turned the ignition key. He half expected the car to explode, but to his relief, the engine roared to life. Jack threw it into gear, slammed his foot on the accelerator and squealed out of the parking lot, leaving a trail of skid marks. Within seconds, he was moving swiftly away from the scene, heading again for the safety of the open road.

How did anyone know he and Grant had a meeting? Obviously, Grant's phone was tapped, or someone in his office had sold out, or maybe they had followed Grant from his home hoping he would lead them to Jack. It no longer mattered. What mattered was getting to the bottom of the conspiracy as soon as possible. Jack still had the nagging feeling that whatever was going to happen was scheduled to happen soon. If so, the logical place to be was Piaute Mountain.

With that thought, Jack headed for the Interstate leading to New York. He knew the airports in Washington would be on the alert for him so it made sense to catch a plane for Nevada out of New York. He remembered Skip telling him that the facility was somewhere between Reno and Las Vegas. If he could make it to one of those cities, he could rent a car and drive to the secret government facility. Jack knew that's where the answers were—at Piaute Mountain.

- - - - - - - - - - - -

The president's California home, nestled into the side of Springer Mountain, near the Stone Canyon Reservoir in Beverly Hills, was bustling with activity when the long, black limousine carrying Adam Armstrong and Michael O'Conner arrived. Two military staff cars were parked in the driveway in front of the main entrance and several limousines were parked downhill from the house, along the horseshoe drive, indicating that other presidential advisers were already present.

Armstrong looked at his watch and heaved an impatient sigh as he realized the unexpected summons from the president was crunching his schedule. He was scheduled to deliver a speech that evening but planned to spend the afternoon touring his California computer manufacturing company. He had no way of knowing how long the visit with the president might last but he feared the worst. Armstrong looked at his aide and said, "Michael, it appears you are going to need to revamp today's itinerary."

Unhappily, Michael agreed. "After the speech tonight, Sir, do you want to return to Washington or spend the night and visit the plant tomorrow morning?"

"No, we'll proceed as planned. I have to be back in Washington tomorrow. We'll inspect the plant some other time."

The car pulled to a stop and a secret service agent greeted Armstrong as he stepped from the limousine. "The president is expecting you, Mr. Armstrong. Go right in."

Armstrong thanked him, and as he and Michael entered the house, they were met by a second agent who proceeded to escort them to the president's study. There, a third agent opened the door, allowing them to walk right in.

As they entered the large, spacious room, the president promptly jumped to his feet, walked over to meet them and said, "Adam, I'm so glad you could make it on such short notice."

"Happy to be here, Mr. President," Armstrong said, shaking the president's hand.

"I believe you know everyone, Adam, so just take a seat and we'll get started."

Armstrong looked quickly around the room, smiling at each man in the room. In addition to the president's immediate staff, General Kenneth Curry, from General Petrie's office, and Colonel Walter Nix, a member of General Whiteside's staff, were also present. Sitting in the far corner, drinking a cup of coffee, were Aaron Wheeler, National Security Adviser, and Brandon Miles, Assistant Deputy Defense Director. Armstrong was not happy to see him. He and Miles had sustained a long-running feud over defense budgets and, on more than one occasion, participated in some heated debates with one another. Neither professed any love or respect for the other.

Nodding politely at Miles, who unenthusiastically returned the greeting, Armstrong took a seat near the president's desk. Warren Boyd offered him a cup of coffee and as Armstrong balanced the cup and saucer in his hand, said, "I take it you've reached a decision, Mr. President?"

Wearily, the president nodded. "Yes, Adam, I have." He toyed with the paperweight on his desk and continued. "I hoped this entire thing would slowly die away but the media will not turn loose. As all of you know, I am not the most popular man in the country because of this. What's my rating now, Warren?"

Warren frowned and answered, "It's at an all-time low, Mr. President. The public lacks faith in the present administration."

"And all because my vice president gets caught coming out of some woman's bedroom at three o'clock in the morning." He sighed, "The problems go with the territory. The vice president has an adulterous affair and I take the heat." He leaned back in his chair and said strongly, "But no more. I've asked the vice president for his resignation and this afternoon I plan to announce that I've appointed Adam Armstrong the new vice president of the United States. Will you accept, Adam?"

Adam showed no emotion at the announcement or question. Inwardly, however, his heart swelled with excitement. Not even his most grandiose plans included this development—vice president? The enormity of the possibilities were immediately apparent. Smiling, he looked at the president and asked, innocently, "Why me, Mr. President?"

The president stood up, paced the width of the room, turned and looked at Adam. "You know why, Adam. You're certainly capable and qualified. But to be candid, you might be the most trusted man in the country right now and putting you next to my office isn't going to hurt this administration one bit.

Plus, I won't have any trouble getting you confirmed by Congress."

Adam already had that figured. "There's the little problem of conflict of interests. My companies do an enormous amount of business with the government."

The president waved his hand nonchalantly. "That's no problem. We've already thought of that. All you have to do is relinquish your active control of the companies, announce that you have put your stock in trust, turn the stock over to a trustee, and everyone will be satisfied."

"When would you want to make the announcement, Mr. President?"

"Does that mean you'll accept?" the president asked excitedly. Smiling broadly, he walked over to Adam, grabbed his hand and, shaking it vigorously, said, "Adam, this may be the smartest thing you've ever done. You won't regret it, I promise you." Adam smiled.

- - - - - - - - - - - -

When he reached New York, the first thing Jack did, after dropping his car off at the rental agency and purchasing his ticket to Las Vegas, was head for the airport barber shop. There, he lowered himself into the chair and instructed the barber to give him the works. Shampoo, haircut, shave, and facial. Sitting in the chair, his face covered with hot, steamy towels, Jack allowed his body and mind to completely relax for the first time in many days.

When the barber finally tapped him on the shoulder, indicating he was through, Jack did not want to move. But he did. He paid the barber, gave him a generous tip, wandered back out into the concourse of the airport, and began looking for a gift shop. When he found one, he entered, purchased a baseball hat and pair of sunglasses. He tried them on and nodded his head appreciatively. He was no longer easily recognizable. Next, Jack walked slowly toward his departure gate. He still had an hour to kill before boarding, but he wasn't hungry and was too keyed up to read a magazine. So, he decided to kill time, walking.

Somewhere between Gates 11 and 16, Jack suddenly remembered he owed Ryan Abernathy a call. At the next bank of pay phones, he inserted his telephone credit card and placed a call to Houston. While the phone was ringing, he remembered the space launch and wondered if he could reach the Security Chief. When someone finally answered and he asked for Ryan Abernathy, he was on hold so long he considered hanging up and trying later. Maybe from Las Vegas. But then, Ryan answered his phone.

"Security Office. Ryan Abernathy speaking."

"Ryan, this is Jack Clayburn."

Ryan's voice immediately became less businesslike. "Jack. Where are you? Are you in town?"

"No, I'm not in Houston." "You sound like you're right around the corner. Thought you were calling to get an admission pass or something. What's on your mind? Do you have some good news for me?"

"Well, I don't know whether it's good, but I do have some news for you. I think I know where your girl is."

Jack heard the deep breath on the other end and then heard Ryan ask, "Where is she, Jack?"

"This is from one of my contacts, Ryan. I don't know for sure but he told me Pamela Richards was transferred to Piaute Mountain, in Colorado."

Ryan interrupted. "I know where it is. But are you sure? I have a good friend working there and he's even trying to help me find her. If she was assigned there, he would have told me."

Jack dismissed that quickly. "I don't care what he told you, Ryan. Pamela Richards works at the Piaute Mountain Facility for Dr. Clay Davis. Believe me, that's a fact."

There was a long silence at the other end. Finally, Ryan wondered aloud, "Why would Butterly lie to me? That doesn't make any sense."

Jack agreed. "The fact remains that she works there." He paused and then said, "Now, you can help me, Ryan. Who did Pamela work for at NASA?"

Ryan answered immediately. "She worked in the Military Liaison Office that coordinates NASA and Pentagon projects."

"Who heads up that office?"

"General Petrie is in charge but he answers to General Whiteside. I really don't know how they work it. I just know that Pamela works directly for Whiteside."

"Does NASA have much to do with the Piaute Facility?"

"That I know. Remember, I told you we use their computer all the time."

"Have they used it recently? Would you know that?"

"Yes. Just before the launch."

Jack continued his questioning. "What do you know about Dr. Clay Davis?"

"I'm not sure, Ryan But if Pamela is working for him, she might be in some serious trouble."

"What do you mean? What are you talking about? Is she in some kind of danger?"

"I don't know, Ryan. But let me ask you something. Is it possible that Pamela is mixed up in something she shouldn't be involved in and kept it a secret from you?"

Ryan cursed. "What are you trying to say, Clayburn?"

"I'm not trying to say anything. I'm just asking. Is it possible that Pamela is involved in some kind of," he searched for the right words, "some kind of covert operation?"

"I don't know what you're trying to suggest, but I can tell you this. Pamela probably doesn't even know the meaning of the word covert." Suspiciously, he added, "You're obviously not telling me everything you know, Jack. Is my girl in some kind of danger? Or trouble?"

"I don't know, Ryan. I really don't know."

There was a pause and then Ryan said, "I'm going out there. I want to see Pamela and find out what's going on. And I want to find out why Butterly lied to me."

"How are you going to manage that? You're in the middle of a big space shot."

Ryan laughed. "Well, I can feel myself getting real sick; I'll just have to leave. I can't manage security if I'm sick." He added seriously,

"Well, if you're determined to go, we need to meet up with each other in Hawthorne.  I'll be there also.  Why don't you arrange to be near the local post office on every even hour until we catch each other."

"That makes sense to me, Jack.  Every even hour I'll check for you.  I'll see you in Hawthorne."

# 9.

# Chapter Nine

The NASA Mission Control Center, constructed in the style of an amphitheater, was arranged in such a manner that Paul Marchand's vantage point was at the top of the semi-circular auditorium, providing him with a sweeping view of the entire complex. To his left and his right, at descending levels, computer terminal consoles were arranged in orderly fashion. There were fourteen on each of the four tiers—seven on either side of the sloping walkway leading from his station desk to the base of the room—a total of fifty-six work stations and each station was manned by two NASA technicians. They were responsible for the programming and monitoring of various functions and responses for spacecraft and their crew members.

At the base of the auditorium three large screens or monitors stretched the full width and height of the room, covering the entire back wall. The large screens furnished the NASA engineers with continuous visual coverage of the mission and on this mission, the flanking monitors were reserved for video reception from the cameras on-board each spacecraft. The center screen provided the NASA engineers with a space map, or grid, on which the two orbiting spacecraft were tracked and depicted by flashing cursors, or blips, illustrating their positions, in space, in relationship to the moon and earth.

It was the center screen that commanded Paul Marchand's attention as he seated himself at his console. The flashing blips immediately indicated that the space shuttle had positioned itself for a launching of the Lunar Landing Craft when the appropriate time was reached. He could see, however, that the manned satellite needed to make several more orbits before reaching the designated holding point from which it would conduct the secret experiment.

As he studied the grid, one of his assistants handed him the latest computer readout sheets. Paul only casually glanced at them before placing the papers on the side of his desk. If there was a problem, he knew one of the specialists in the room would sound an alarm. He had complete faith in his crew and their ability to do their respective jobs. As Mission Director, he had very little to do between the launch, orbit, reentry, and retrieval. Primarily, he served as a silent supervisor who was needed only if an emergency developed. During the mission, computers—monitored closely by everyone—did all the work.

A quiet voice behind him disturbed his concentration. "We have several hours to go, Paul. Why don't you go upstairs and try to catch a couple of winks."

Recognizing the voice of Mark Huffman, the Mission Systems Analyst, Paul did not turn around but continued to watch the flashing blips on the screen. "I'm so keyed up and so full of coffee, I couldn't sleep. I'll just stay down here and keep an eye on things till they push the button."

"I can understand that. I'm a little keyed up myself."

"Where's the third blip right now?"

Mark took a note pad from his pocket, consulted it, and said, "Right about now it should be coming up on the top side of the screen. If you want to see it, though, you'll have to change the configuration of the grid."

"That's not necessary. We know it's there. And we know it'll be there when the time comes."

Returning the note pad to his pocket, Mark said with a sigh, "I need to go up and check on the big brass. See you in a little while."

He headed for the VIP viewing room, a glassed-in enclosure which allowed guests to view the entire proceedings in luxurious comfort. The room was tastefully decorated with leather lounge chairs, mahogany end tables, and the walls were covered with color photographs of memorable space accomplishments. It was a comfortable room, designed to cater to the whims and wishes of Congressmen, Senators, generals, admirals, and high-ranking public and business figures. It was a room designed to foster good relations and, on more than one occasion, a future budget hearing before the Congress had been influenced by the good will established in the VIP room.

- - - - - - - - - - - -

Three generals were seated comfortably in their deep leather chairs talking while three aides hovered nearby, anxiously trying to anticipate each general's need. Brig. Gen. Samuel Snyder, the military liaison at NASA, was explaining the scene on the big screen to his immediate superior, General of the Army Matthew Whiteside. Listening intently to the conversation was a third general, from the Air Force, Lt. Gen. Norman Petrie.

"The flashing blip at the bottom left of the screen is the manned satellite. As you can see, it's moving and will soon be off the screen, orbiting the earth in a maneuver that will eventually position it where it should be to safely conduct the experiment."

General Snyder continued. "The blip in the center of the screen is the space shuttle and it is stationary because it has already reached a holding point for the second experiment. On the screen to the left, you can see the astronauts preparing the LLC for the moon landing but they won't actually launch until they get the go signal from here."

"Where is the target satellite?" General Whiteside asked.

"I don't see it on the screen right now, General, so I assume that it is on the other side of the earth and it should be coming up shortly. When it does, it will be a flashing blip on the far right of the screen, orbiting the earth. And it won't be up there long because it will pass through the grid rather rapidly."

General Whiteside nodded his head in understanding. "So, I guess all we do now is wait." He looked over at General Petrie. "Norm, feel like going for a bite to eat, or do you want to stick around?"

"Ah, let's go get a bite to eat. If anything happens, they can come get us. What do we have now? About two, three hours?"

"Just a little over three hours, General," Mark Huffman said.

Changing the subject, Whiteside asked, "Well, Gentlemen, what do you think of the president's announcement?"

"About Armstrong?" Petrie asked.

"It's hard to picture Armstrong and the president working smoothly, hand in hand." Laughing, General Whiteside added, "Well, you'll have to admit, it was a stroke of genius on the president's part. Selecting Armstrong as his vice president will help his image."

"Too bad the move is a little late," Petrie said.

Whiteside shrugged. "Yeah, it is, isn't it? It does strengthen our position, though, doesn't it?" He winked at Petrie and said, "Does offer some interesting possibilities, doesn't it?"

Petrie nodded. "Yes it does. A bit of luck we did not anticipate."

Mark could not figure out what the generals were talking about but, then, sometimes he had trouble figuring out generals anyway. So, he volunteered, "I just wanted to check and make sure you gentlemen had everything you needed."

"We're fine, Mark," General Whiteside replied. "Are we still on schedule?"

"In the green, Sir. So far, so good." Mark turned to leave and as he stood in the doorway, he added, "If anything comes up, we'll let you know."

As Mark left the room, General Snyder asked, "Does he know about the experiment?"

Whiteside nodded. "He knows about part of the experiment. He knows what everybody else knows and that's all."

Snyder volunteered, "I talked to Clay Davis a little while ago. He wished us well but still pushed for a change in our plans."

Petrie snorted. "He doesn't give up, does he?"

Whiteside laughed. "No. He's still pushing his Force Field. He thinks we're wasting our time."

"I wonder what he would say if he knew what was really going on?" Petrie asked. Whiteside shrugged. "I think as long as nothing affects his research money, he could care less about what happens."

"Yeah," agreed Petrie. "But we need to remember that with Solomon, he can make or break us; we need to watch him carefully. Especially since he's been going through his attitude change. The last six months or so, he's gotten a little moralistic."

"Speaking of someone who can make or break us, what's the word on Jack Clayburn? Have they found him yet?"

"No, but it's only a matter of time. We've got every angle covered and the moment he shows his face . . . "

Snyder interrupted Petrie and said, pointing to the monitor, "There's our guinea pig."

The three men directed their attention to a small, flashing blip appearing on the right-hand side of the monitor screen and moving slowly down the grid. They watched the blip for a moment and General Whiteside finally said, "The president's little blip has a date with history in just a few hours, doesn't it?"

Smiling wryly, Petrie said, "I almost feel sorry for him. If he only knew what was about to happen." All three nodded and watched in silence as the flashing blip descended through the grid. As it disappeared from sight, Whiteside observed, "Well, the president has only himself to blame. If he'd listened to me in the first place, none of this would be happening."

- - - - - - - - - - - -

As he moved along the mountain trail, a path beaten down by his own weeks and months of daily journeys up and down the mountain, the solitary runner quickly passed the scattered clumps of grey-green rabbit brush and the isolated patches of Bethlehems with their delicate, creamy pink stars. Moving at an easy, relaxed gait, he ran through the last stand of nutpines and into the openness of the upper elevation, barren except for an occasional Joshua tree or a struggling desert lily.

Within a matter of minutes he had reached the summit of the small mountain and, as always, he sat and drank in the panoramic view before him. To the west, in distant California, he could see the snow-capped peaks of the Inyo National Forest; to the south, clearly visible in the evening grey, was the highest elevation in Nevada, the thirteen thousand feet high Boundary Peak; to the north, some four thousand feet smaller but still impressive, was Powell Mountain; and to the east, he could see the edge of the great salt marsh, which stretched for miles to the desert beyond.

As usual, upon reaching the top of the mountain on his daily run, he was awed by the immense vastness of the cinematic scene spanning before him from horizon to horizon. His arrival each day—when his schedule permitted—was always a humbling experience.   His presence in the middle of so much splendor only served to remind him of just how small, how feeble, how insignificant man really was.  On top of Piaute Mountain, he was but a speck of life surrounded by the very essence of infinity.

Sitting on the edge of the precipice, his back resting against a small boulder, he knew that what his eyes saw had remained virtually unchanged, untouched, for countless centuries; and he felt a heady sense of euphoria knowing that he might well be only one of a very few—perhaps even the only one—who ever viewed the magnificence before him.

At this altitude, there was an almost reverent stillness surrounding him.  A calm silence slowly engulfed every fiber of his body, relaxing his taut muscles, slowing his heartbeat, and erasing all thoughts from his head.  His body and mind joined in a state of spiritual weightlessness, and he allowed his very being to succumb to a rare moment of complete, harmonious existence.

Clay Davis was not often able to indulge himself in such luxurious peacefulness.  For most of his thirty-five years he had been an intense individual, competing aggressively not with his peers but with himself. He had grown accustomed to pushing himself in an effort to reach beyond his physical and mental capabilities.  Although it was well recognized that he was a genius in his field, he was so driven in the pursuit of excellence that he often stepped on the toes of those with whom he worked.   There were some who considered him to be a relentlessly ambitious workaholic and there were others who thought him to be a tyrant.  Yet, his staff, and those who knew him well, appreciated the fact that he was neither.

He was simply a man who believed strongly in the protestant work ethic, and lived by his standard of values and morals.  He was also a man whose vision was so far reaching, and whose grasp of what could be was so incisive, he appeared at times to be working on a plane far above natural man.  His staff loved him; his peers envied but respected him; and those who had occasion to work fleetingly in his presence were, more often than not, frightened and intimidated by him.

He was by nature a sensitive and reserved man, but he would not tolerate sloppy thinking or work, and the slightest evidence of either by a subordinate or associate drove him to a fury. He expected the best anyone had to offer and never settled for anything less.  Clay had learned how to reach within himself and go beyond his limitations and he expected those around him also to rise above their comfort zones. It was a quality, or strength of character, he learned from his father.

Clay rolled over on his stomach, rested his chin on a crossed arm, and stared out into the valley below.  A deep sigh escaped from his lungs as he lay stretched out on top of the mountain.  He loved, and looked forward to, the precious moments of solitude and the unsurpassed beauty that were his and his alone but, he hoped, not his alone for long. He had special plans following his dinner date. Clay planned to ask Diane to marry him that evening.

He laughed out loud. Within a few hours, Clay Davis was going to be engaged to be married. A fitting end to a good day. As he watched the soft light of a fading sun slowly melt into the darkness of night, he allowed the events of the day to race through his mind. The latest and final test of his laser induced force field was successful. He knew the Defense Department was eager to examine his latest in a long line of advanced weapons systems and he felt the force field was, indeed, his most exciting breakthrough—second only to his primary pet and labor of love, the computer sitting on the fourth level of the Piaute Mountain Facility.

The force field was a major scientific breakthrough, representing not only the attainment of a new level of laser research but the means to achieve, at long last, man's dream of worldwide peaceful coexistence. The Force Field possessed the potential of making wars obsolete because of its ability to literally neutralize or negate all weapons. It was the ultimate weapons system or, as Clay preferred, the ultimate defense system.

His staff was already whispering about a Nobel Prize. Clay smiled at the thought. It was ironic. His other weapon, discovered years earlier, was so classified few people even knew it existed. Consequently, he was compelled to enjoy its potential and capabilities without the luxury of bragging about it to other scientists or associates. Even Diane was not completely aware of the capabilities of Solomon. In the final analysis, Clay knew his computer system was far more powerful, more deadly, than the force field. Together, the two accomplishments possessed unheard of power.

Clay idly wondered what Adam Armstrong thought of the new force field. The thought of Armstrong darkened Clay's mood for a moment. Listening to the news, prior to his daily run, he heard the announcement that Armstrong was the president's choice to replace the resigning vice president. Clay was not pleased. He did not like Adam Armstrong, and he knew Armstrong carried no love for him.

The two men, whose careers had paralleled and crossed for years, were always at odds with each other. Clay believed in defense through strength; Armstrong believed in defense through diplomatic channels. Despite the force field's obvious peaceful potential, he expected the powerful Armstrong to twist its introduction into something that would appear obscene or dangerous. Now, as vice president, Davis knew Armstrong's power of influence was expanded.

Clay sighed and dismissed Armstrong from his mind, refusing to allow his old nemesis to ruin the evening. He turned his thoughts to a more pleasant subject, Diane. He wondered if she suspected their dinner date was to be a memorable one for them both. He knew he had postponed the inevitable for too long. He loved Diane and wanted to marry her. Finally, Clay raised up and took one last look at the dark and shadowy skyline, illuminated only by the light of a full moon beginning to appear on the horizon. He stood there, on the edge of the precipice, a tall, lean man, silhouetted against the moon. A shock of blond hair, brown from the sweat of his brow, hung down over steel-blue eyes, which always seemed more blue because they were accented by fair, almost albino, eyebrows. He had the shoulders of a swimmer, broad and tapering into a muscular back and slimmed hips; a handsome man with the tanned face and sleek body of a long distance runner.

With a final look, Clay turned to head back down the mountain trail but something in the sky caught his attention. Jerking his head around, he stared at a dark spot just to the right and far above the moon. He watched in pleasured amazement at the sight visible in the distant sky. A meteor shower, one of the few he had ever viewed, was taking place. What seemed to be literally hundreds of meteors were obviously entering the atmosphere simultaneously, creating a Fourth of July fireworks spectacular.

He watched, spellbound, fascinated by the fiery Roman candle display taking place thousands of miles away, in space. He remembered there had been more than a dozen such displays reported over the past few days but this was his first and he found the view to be spectacular. Clay knew the recent sightings corresponded with the numerous reports of radio transmissions and unusual reports of magnetic force deviations. Obviously, something was causing more than just a few irregulairties in the normal scheme of space laws.

He had other things to think about, however, so he turned and headed back down the mountain. He knew he had just enough time to reach the facility, shower, dress, and be ready for his dinner date with Diane, the future Mrs. Clay Davis.

- - - - - - - - - - - - - -

Two hundred miles southwest of Piaute Mountain, in downtown Los Angeles, a long, black limousine left Harbor Freeway, turned off Olympic Boulevard, and began inching its way down Figueroa Street toward the Convention Center. The lone passenger, totally oblivious to the heavy traffic, was absorbed in making last minute changes to the speech he was scheduled to present that evening to the two thousand members of the National Society of Editors and Publishers.

Adam Armstrong was satisfied with the speech. The events of the day dictated immediate changes to his subject matter, and he felt, as he looked over his notes, he covered everything quite well. He knew his audience would expect him to announce his plans or intentions as the new vice president. The president's announcement concerning the appointment of Adam Armstrong to the vice presidential position and the press conference following the announcement went smoothly and without incident. Adam knew it would. The press loved him. And he knew the audience he was addressing shortly loved him also. Adam Armstrong was a much-loved man.

He maintained an extremely high profile serving on the president's Foreign Relations Committee and as the Chairman of the National Science Council. In addition to his public service activities, work, and support in behalf of more than a dozen charitable causes, Armstrong served as president and chief executive of Armstrong Industries, a huge conglomerate of diverse operations. His largest corporation, International Research Laboratories, specialized in the development and manufacture of not only computer software for the government but electronic sensing devices as well.

The company was particularly noted for its pioneer work in the field of micro-transmitters and the development of a micro transmitter chip known commercially as THIS, an acronym for Tracking and Homing Integrated Signal. THIS, which could be easily implanted in animals, birds, and fish, transmitted a coded signal, enabling a radio receiver and computer to maintain constant monitoring of vital signs and location. Farmers and stockmen utilized the system to keep track of livestock and conservationists used the chip to monitor the migration and movement of wildlife and fish. The system was so reliable and efficient that someone once jokingly remarked that it "was ideally suited for use on humans, especially errant husbands whose activities needed to be monitored by suspicious wives." Armstrong merely smiled at the suggestion. He was aware of the potential misuse that could be applied to the transmitter chip. In fact, Armstrong secretly initiated experiments utilizing the chip in ways that would shock civil libertarians; and his research indicated the chip was "ideally suited for use on humans." However, he resisted all efforts by the military and government to expand the chip's use. Armstrong felt the potential power of the chip was far too dangerous to be entrusted to the hands of incompetent government and military bureaucrats. If the chip was ever to be used, Adam Armstrong would insure he was the one to control its distribution.

He was brought back to the reality of the moment as he felt the big car slow and make a sweeping turn. Glancing out the window, he noticed they were approaching the rear entrance of the Convention Center. Startled, he looked again. A large crowd, obviously learning of his arrival, had gathered to greet him. He spotted signs reading NOT NUMBER 2—NUMBER 1; NUMBER 2 NOW—NUMBER 1 TOMORROW. The crowd appreciated his appointment to the vice presidential post.

He felt a wave of anxiety sweep through his body. More of a wave of anticipation. It was a sensation becoming more and more familiar—a foreign sense of nervousness, even hesitation. He knew something was stirring within him—an inner force signalling he was on the verge of fulfilling his dream, a moment he welcomed with anticipation. Yet, it was disconcerting for him to realize he still had many things to do before he was totally prepared.

The limousine pulled up to the rear entrance, parked, and the chauffeur jumped from behind the wheel to open the door for his illustrious passenger. Armstrong gathered up his papers, closed the briefcase, and as he stepped from the limo, immediately handed it to his aide standing and shielding his boss from the pressing and adoring crowd.

"Thank you, Michael. Quite a crowd."

"Yes, Sir. As soon as the announcement was made and people heard you were speaking here tonight, they started gathering." He added, "And now you have, in addition to our own people, secret service agents guarding you."

Armstrong smiled. "We'll have to get used to this, I'm afraid. The price of fame, Michael."

Michael nodded and began clearing a path through the well wishers and adoring fans. Within seconds, thanks to the Secret Service clearing the way, Armstrong was in a small waiting room where he immediately sat in one of the two brown leather chairs to await Michael's signal to prepare for his stage entrance. He looked at his watch and estimated he had only a few minutes remaining before they called him.

For security reasons, he did not explain to Michael that as they sat there in the Los Angeles Convention Center, a manned spaceship was orbiting earth preparing to conduct an experiment he vehemently opposed. He had warned the president of the dangers and possible international repercussions that would follow the experiment. He fought a losing battle. The president was convinced the launch would serve as a rallying point to the restoration of his popularity. Adam knew he was wrong. Even Clay Davis, the perpetual thorn in Armstrong's side, agreed. The experiment was obviously proceeding as scheduled.

"Dr. Armstrong." Michael's voice interrupted his concentration. "It's time, Sir."

"Well," Armstrong said, "Let's get this over with. Remember, Michael, get me away from here as soon as the speech is over. We have a plane to catch."

"Don't worry about a thing, Sir. I'll have us on that plane and back to the capital no matter what happens."

The two men walked over to the small flight of stairs leading to the stage, crossed the stage wing, and stood hidden from the audience by the curtain. The emcee was in the midst of his introductory remarks and Armstrong listened inattentively, waiting for his cue. He was planning his next moves following the space experiment. Adam Armstrong never allowed a day or night to pass that he didn't calculate

every move in his life.  He knew his most important moves were just
beginning.

# 10.

# Chapter Ten

At precisely the moment Adam Armstrong was stepping onto the stage in Los Angeles, Clay Davis and Diane Williams were leaving the Piaute Mountain complex. As they entered the main level, leading to the tunnel exit, James Butterly, Security Director for the facility, was working on a small television camera that monitored the tunnel passageway.

"A problem, James?"

"Not really, Doc. Just cleaning the lens a little. When the outside doors open, the wind blows in dust that settles on the lens."

Clay grinned and observed, "All this technology and Mother Nature can goof it up with just a little bit of dust."

Clay waved a goodnight to James and, reaching for Diane's arm, guided her to the passageway. Inserting their security access cards at the main exit, they waited for the retina scanner to confirm their identities and then the two scientists walked through the tunnel, passed through the main entrance, and onto the parking lot. As they walked, Clay felt in his jacket pocket, reassuring himself that he had the small velvet jewelry box containing the engagement ring. The ring was a special order, designed as per Clay's instructions by a Las Vegas jeweler. It was a wide gold band with a single, half-carat emerald-cut diamond solitaire mounted in a gold setting. On each side of the stone, a small delicate cross was carved through the band, creating an unusual see-through effect. The ring was delivered earlier in the day and Clay planned to offer it to Diane right after dinner.

As they reached the dark gray Mercedes-Benz, Clay reached around Diane, opened the door, and she slipped into the seat. He walked to the other side, opened the door, and seated himself behind the wheel and inserted the key. But before switching on the ignition, he leaned over and kissed Diane on the cheek.

She feigned indignation and exclaimed, "Sir, I think the proper procedure is to feed me first and then you get to kiss me."

He laughed. "Listen, Lady, if I'm going to take a girl out and blow four or five bucks on a gourmet meal at Sally's Truck Stop, I want to make sure beforehand that the investment is worth it."

"Four or five bucks, huh? That much. Gosh, little ole me is not used to such worldly extravagance. A big spender like you doesn't come around very often. I'd better be extra nice."

She leaned forward, reached gently behind his neck with her left hand and pulled him forward. Their faces met, gently caressing each other with their lips before settling into a long, lingering kiss. Her slender, delicate fingers tenderly stroked the outline of his cheek and neck while the fingers of his left hand gently traced the delicate profile of her face. Finally parting, breathless, he looked into her eyes and whispered, "I love you."

She returned his look, love brimming from her laughing eyes, and asked, "Does this mean I can have dessert with my dinner?"

Laughing, and pushing her away, he started the car, backed out of his parking space, changed gears, and headed out of the parking lot, saying, "Diane Williams, you are just too, too much."

Clay followed the long, winding drive down Piaute Mountain until it merged into a secondary road. Turning right, he headed east for several miles until he reached Basalt and Highway 360, where he turned again, left, and headed north to pick up Highway 95, which would carry them into Hawthorne.

It was a typically beautiful Nevada night. The stars were shining brightly in the clear western sky and the moon, full and bright, hung suspended, a huge lantern lighting the entire countryside. It was so bright Clay knew he could, if he desired, maneuver the winding mountain highway by the light of the moon. He was so engrossed with the view, he didn't notice the automobile to his rear that had emerged from a clump of trees by the side of the road, near the facility entrance and was now maintaining a discreet but constant distance—as if following the couple.

Diane and Clay spoke very little as they sped along, preferring, obviously, to simply enjoy the rare opportunity of spending private time together. Her hand rested on his leg and as they drove, he would reach down occasionally to gently caress her long, slender fingers with his own. He particularly fondled the delicate finger that would, tomorrow, be wearing the ring he carried in his coat pocket. He remembered reading somewhere that an engagement ring and wedding ring were worn on the second finger of the left hand because the ancient Greeks believed a nerve extended through that finger, running straight to the heart. The ring supposedly controlled those feelings of love for an eternity, or as long as the ring was worn.

Clay was excited. Feelings of desire flooded his body as he guided the car around the ever-changing curves and twists of the mountain highway. Often, when he looked at Diane, he felt the urge to pinch himself to see if he was awake or dreaming. He found it hard to believe a woman so lovely, so intelligent, could really, actually be in love with him. He knew his moments of insecurity were normal and unfounded because he knew Diane did love him.

From the corner of his eye, he could see Diane by the light of the moon. She had a radiant beauty about her on this night. Her face, as if softly chiseled from fine stone, faced upward, her head leaning on the head-rest of the seat. Her lips, he knew, were colored ever so slightly with a delicate shade of wet pink, accenting the tan of her face. Her eyes were closed and she appeared asleep but he knew by the gentle pressure he felt from her hand on his leg that she was awake.

Only once did Diane interrupt the pleasant silence of their twenty-five minute drive. When he stopped the car at the Highway 95 intersection, before he could make his turn, she leaned over and kissed him softly on the ear, asking, "Did I tell you how sexy you are, Dr. Davis?" He smiled at her as he eased the powerful Mercedes onto the main road for the final leg of their trip.

As a town, Hawthorne barely qualified. It could boast a population of less than five thousand and this included, some joked, all the jackrabbits, mule deer, and bears in a ten-mile radius. The town depended primarily on the presence of a military contingency assigned to maintain and operate an ammunition supply depot. Moreover, only one mine was in operation, a ski resort opened during the winter months, and nearby Walker Lake, famous for its fishing, swimming, and boating attracted people from all over the state during the summer months. There was, of course, gambling available but unlike Reno, to the north, and Las Vegas, to the south, there were no fancy, opulent casinos. Hawthorne was simply a stop in the middle of the mountains.

There were several places to eat but the main gathering place was Sally's Truck Stop and it was to the rambling, shingled family restaurant that Clay was headed. He pulled into the parking lot and eased into one of the few open spaces near the front entrance.

As soon as Clay and Diane entered the front door, the owner of the restaurant rushed over and greeted them. "Dr. Davis. Diane. It's so good to see you."

"Hello, Mr. Sally, how are you tonight?"

"Just great. Just the two of you tonight?"

"Just the two of us," Clay answered.

The restaurant owner guided Clay and Diane to a booth, seated them, and rushed off to find a waitress to take their order. Clay reached for the menu, though there was no need to read it. Sally's Truck Stop served only one thing worth ordering: steaks! And when the waitress arrived, Clay ordered for both. "Bring us two rib eyes, both medium rare, baked potato with sour cream and butter, salad with French dressing on both, one coffee, one tea, and," he said laughing, looking at Diane, "I owe the lady some dessert, so bring her a piece of your deep-dish apple pie."

As the waitress walked away, Diane grinned at him. "I'm glad you pay your debts, Sir, but don't think you're going to get any additional rewards just because you're buying my dinner."

"Ma'am, you're tough. You don't give a man any slack, do you?"

Clay stretched his arms and arched his back, and heaved a big sigh.

"Tired, Dr. Davis?" she asked.

"A little. Seems like I spent more time than usual hunched over my desk today. I hate paperwork. I remember people used to tell me that computers would provide us with a paperless society. I don't think that day will ever come. The more computers we get, the more paperwork we have. Why's that?"

Diane laughed. "Why don't you invent a computer that does nothing but take care of paperwork?"

Thoughtfully, Clay replied, "That's not a bad idea. A robot paper pusher. Possibilities, Dr. Williams. I'll think about it. And we can fix it so it can make coffee at the same time."

As if on cue, the waitress arrived with coffee for Clay and tea for Diane.

Clay reached over, squeezed the wedge of lemon into the tall glass and added a packet of sweetener. "You'll have to stir it yourself," he said, adding sugar to his coffee.

"Thank you, kind Sir. Chivalry is not yet dead. Or is it? Do you have ulterior motives?"

"Of course, I have ulterior motives. Why do you think I'm buying your dinner?"

Diane wrinkled her nose and, with a feeling of weakness rushing through her body, said: "Well, if you keep playing your cards right . . ."

Clay raised his hand to catch the waitress's attention. When she came over to their booth, he said, "Listen, I forgot to tell you. Take your time bringing our food. We're kind of winding down after a long day and I don't want to be rushed.

"You've got it, Dr. D.," the waitress said cheerfully.

As the girl returned to the kitchen, Diane smiled.

"What are you smiling about?" Clay wanted to know.

"You've changed. I can remember when you would be crawling the walls by now because you didn't have your food. You're more patient than you used to be."

"Was I impatient?"

She laughed. "Were you impatient? Oh, I can't believe you asked that. You, the man who threw books across the room when somebody didn't turn on a switch fast enough to suit you. You, the man who once left his car and me in the middle of traffic and ran to his office because he got tired waiting for the traffic to move. Impatient? You were more than impatient. You were ridiculous."

Clay lowered his head self-consciously. "I guess I did occasionally get a little upset."

"Occasionally? All the time is more like it." She thought about it for a moment and added, "But the new Clay Davis is a pretty nice guy."

"Why thank you. I guess you can take all the credit."

"No, I don't think so. I may have calmed you down a bit, but you have a quieter sense about you, a more gentle spirit."

She thought a moment and added, "I think you're at peace with yourself now and you know why."

He nodded, agreeing. "Yeah, I guess I do. I know I wasn't the easiest guy to get along with. That was before I learned to put everything, in its proper perspective."

"It makes a difference, doesn't it?"

"Well, you know as well as I do, it does. You were the one who brought me around."

"It wasn't me."

"I know."

"I think we love each other more, now," Diane said in a soft tone.

"No doubt about it. I know I love me more."

They both laughed. Then Clay's voice became serious and he asked her, "Where do you think we'll be two, three, even five years from now? Think we'll still be at Piaute Mountain?"

"That's up to you, Clay. You know they'll let you go anywhere you want to go and let you do what you want to do. They like your little toys." She hesitated for a moment and asked, "Are you thinking of leaving the project now that everything is nearly finished?"

"Not only leaving the project but maybe just getting away for a while—maybe for good. I feel like my brain is drained. I don't have any new ideas floating around up there."

He paused, took a deep breath, and said, "I think I really would enjoy getting away for a year or two. Lately, I've had the feeling it's time to slow down and start living like a normal human being. I think I just need to get away from laboratories, generals, paperwork, everything."

"Everything?" Diane asked with a slight tilt of her head.

"Yeah. What do you think I should do?" Diane hesitated for a moment. She was not sure how she wanted to answer the question. There was a growing feeling in the pit of her stomach she didn't like. The thought of not working with Clay in the laboratory never occurred to her. "I think," she said cautiously, "that if you feel you need to get away from everything for a while, maybe you should. Where would you go?"

"I don't know. I haven't given that much thought. Maybe a place on the ocean. Maybe down in Mexico. Perhaps right here in the Colorado mountains. It doesn't really matter. Just somewhere quiet. A place where I can think, work a little, goof off a lot. I've never done that before."

The feeling in Diane's stomach continued to grow. Clay was serious. He was serious about leaving, and he obviously did not include her in his plans. She didn't want him to see the hurt and pain she was beginning to feel, so she looked away as she said, "When do you plan to do all this?"

"Well, General Whiteside is coming out next week to look over the force field, and I wanted to mention it to him then." She forced a smile. "Do you really want someone else playing with Solomon?"

Impatiently, Clay replied. "Not really. I'm concerned about someone other than myself having full access and control of Solomon."

Puzzled, Diane said, "Clay, six of us have full access and control of Solomon now. True, you're always there, but we know how to operate Solomon."

Clay shook his head. "No, Diane, I've never explained everything about Solomon."

"What do you mean?"

Clay sighed, hesitated for a moment as he collected his thoughts, and then began in a very low voice. "Everyone on the staff knows that Solomon is an extremely advanced computer, but none of you realize that Solomon is even more advanced than it seems. When General Whiteside and I discussed the idea of Solomon, the military at that time was concerned with what would happen if there was a nuclear war and Washington was destroyed. If that event ever became a reality, our governing machinery would be destroyed. There would be utter chaos and confusion, and the military feared the government might never recover.

"They felt an alternative standby government was needed. Perhaps a central control system from which the nation could be governed by the military until the country stabilized and civilian control restored. What they wanted was a computer system that could serve as a data control center, functioning as both the executive and legislative branches of government."

Clay paused, trying to figure out a way to explain a very complicated theory in simple terms. He continued, "What it boils down to is that if one computer system contained in its files all the information stored by all the individual government and civilian computer systems, then there would be no disruption of services or control in the event any or all the other systems were destroyed in a nuclear attack. Do you understand what I'm saying?"

Diane, with a puzzled expression on her face, said, "I'm not sure. What you're saying is that Solomon could act as a central computer system and the nation could be governed and run from Piaute Mountain?"

Clay smiled. "Not could be. It is the central computer. Right this moment, everything stored on every major computer and computer network in the nation is stored within our system and that includes all the files from the CIA, FBI, Treasury department, military, Census Bureau, banks, insurance, medical, State Department ...you name it and Solomon has it, is in the process of getting it, or could go retrieve it at a moment's notice."

Still puzzled, Diane asked, "Are you saying that Solomon has been retrieving and storing information all along? Does that include files on individuals?"

"Yes. It includes everything."

Curious, and in an attempt to understand Clay more clearly, she asked, "Am I in Solomon somewhere?"

Clay smiled smugly. "I could punch your name into Solomon and in just a few seconds it would tell me everything I wanted to know about you. It would give me your birth certificate, school records, tax records, employment history, health status, credit reports, checking and savings records—everything."

A sudden sense of understanding flooded Diane. "So, that's what Top-secret LCF function is. We wondered why you were the only one with access to that? We just thought it had something to do with payrolls or budgets or some military stuff."

Clay nodded. "That is the LCF function. It retrieves information from other computers and stores the data."

With a note of irritation in her voice, Diane said, "I think you're exaggerating a little. I know the Internal Revenue Service is not going to allow anyone to access their files, and I know my bank isn't going to give you anything without a court order. People just can't turn over information like that because your little generals want it."

Clay grinned. "That's the beauty of Solomon. No one knows what it can do because Solomon does its thing without anyone being aware of what's happening."

Confused, Diane asked, "Are you suggesting that Solomon can access other computers without anyone's knowledge or authorization?"

"Exactly. Solomon can not only access a computer, it can gain control of a computer after obtaining access."

"Isn't all this a little bit illegal? Maybe even a smack of 'Big Brotherism'?"

"It's a safeguard measure, Diane. If all other systems were destroyed, all records would be on file in Solomon's system."

"Why haven't you ever told me about this? I thought I was a trusted employee. A trusted aide. A trusted girlfriend."

Clay shrugged. "I've wanted to, many times. But I'm not supposed to discuss it with anyone except the very highest authorities. The program is so Top-secret it doesn't even exist. Only a handful of people know about it."

"Can you tell me how it works?"

Lowering his voice even more, Clay answered, "It's done with something I invented about the time you came to work for me. I call it the 'Looping Chip.' The chip allows Solomon to confuse other computers and trick them into allowing access to their files and computer banks." He laughed, "It's a computer company's nightmare because it is virtually impossible to establish or maintain any measure of security against Solomon's probes and raids."

"I don't think I like what you're saying, Clay. Something like this could be very dangerous if it fell into the wrong hands."

"It's not in the wrong hands, Diane. It's in the hands of the military, which is part of our government."

"When you say Solomon can access other computers, can it access the computers controlling our nuclear arsenal?"

In a boastful tone, Clay admitted it could. "I do it all the time. General Whiteside has me access our defense system to insure everything is on ready-alert. And we go visit the Russians to check their status. Maybe borrow some of their classified information." He smiled, and added, "We also borrow a little money from them from time to time."

"You what?"

"Borrow a little money. I can transfer money right out of the Soviet Union into a foreign bank and have it sent to a special account in Switzerland or England, and then transfer it to another special account here in this country." He laughed. "Ironically, even though they don't know it, the Russians pay for much of our research and experiments at Piaute Mountain."

"Clay, are you stealing money from the Russians?"

"I don't call it stealing, Diane. It's more like borrowing."

"You can call it what you want. It's stealing." She thought about this for a moment and then asked another question. "A moment ago you mentioned you could access the defense systems of both the U.S. and Russia. Does that include the nuclear systems also?"

Smiling, Clay answered, "Yes it does. If I wanted to, I could enter both United States and Russian computers and neutralize all nuclear arsenals and missile systems."

"Could you activate them?"

Clay laughed. "I'm not going to activate them, Diane."

"Yes, but someone else could, right?"

Irritated, he responded. "Believe me, I'm the only one who can control that function."

Anger was building up within Diane as she listened to the man she loved. She was mad, not so much at what he permitted with Solomon, but mad at his obvious childlike naiveness. She tried to reason with him, to explain the danger of such a powerful tool in the hands of the wrong person, but Clay was convinced Solomon had more than enough fail-safe programming stop-gaps to eliminate that possibility. They argued throughout their dinner, which quickly became an unenjoyable experience, taxing the patience of each.

Finally, she looked at him and said, "I'm disappointed in you, Clay. In fact, I'm angry with you. Don't you understand what you've created? What you've done? You provided an instrument capable of destroying not only this country but other countries as well."

Clay, realizing he was seeing a side of Diane he was not aware of, tried to placate her. "Diane, you have to understand that . . ." Before he could finish, he saw James Butterly enter the dining room.

The Security Director paused at the entrance, looked around and for a moment Clay thought he was only trying to find a booth, but then he spied Clay and walked toward the booth.

"Must be trouble," Clay said under his breath.

Diane, who couldn't see who was heading for their booth, asked, "What?"

"I said there must be trouble. Butterly is coming over. Something must be wrong back at the facility."

Butterly stopped, leaned over, and said quietly, "Doc, I hate to butt in and disturb your dinner, but you and Dr. Williams are needed back at the facility."

"What's the problem, James?"

"I don't know, Sir. All I know is that the president's office has been trying to reach you. General Snyder down at NASA has called a half-dozen times for you. And the Secretary of Defense is calling. Our switchboard looks like a video game."

Clay thought a moment. The key was Snyder. If he was calling from NASA, it meant a space problem. That might suggest something went wrong with the satellite experiment—either a problem with the experiment itself or with one of the spaceships. Whatever the problem, he assumed Solomon was needed. But why was the president calling?

"All right, James. We'll leave right away." He and Diane stood up, Clay threw a bill on the table to cover the check and tip, and the three of them walked out of the restaurant.

"We'll see you back at the mountain," Clay yelled over to Butterly. He opened the car door for Diane, then walked around to the driver's side and slipped in behind the wheel. As they drove back to the facility, in silence, Clay could feel her anger and he thought of giving her the ring in the hope it would improve her disposition. However, he realized it was not the time or place to propose marriage, and he decided to wait for a more pleasant opportunity. Neither exchanged a word on the long drive back to Piaute Mountain. Clay's plans had not included this type of ending for the evening.

When Clay and Diane left the restaurant, neither paid any attention to the man seated at the counter near the door, eating dinner. But Sally, the restaurant owner, noticed him. In fact, he couldn't take his eyes off the customer. Finally, curiosity overcame him and he walked over to the gentleman and said, "Anyone ever tell you that you look exactly like that guy on the network? The one who does the news for . . ."

The man shook his head, swallowing as he did so. "All the time. Everywhere I go. Gets to be a pain after a while."

Sally laughed. "Man, you look enough like him to be his twin." Continuing the conversation, he asked, "You just passing through?"

"Yeah, but I may spend the night here." Casually, the man asked, "Who were those folks that just left in such a hurry?"

"Oh, them. That's a couple of scientists from up at the government place on the mountain. Dr. Davis and Dr. Williams. That was their Security Director who left with them. He said he had to get the doctors because they had some kind of emergency." He leaned closer and said confidentially, "I don't know what they do up there, but they have tighter security than the ammo dump does. Guards all over the place up there."

"Is that a fact?" the man asked, trying to look disinterested.

Sally, hearing his name called from the kitchen, walked away. Jack Clayburn signaled his waitress to bring more coffee. He figured he would have another cup and then return to his motel to figure out his next step.

# 11.

# Chapter Eleven

**F**rom where he was seated, Paul Marchand's attention alternated between the lights and gauges of his command console and the three massive viewing monitors spanning the rear wall from ceiling to floor directly in front of him, in NASA's Mission Control Center. He paid only cursory consideration to the screens mounted on the left and right, displaying a televised view of the capsule and shuttle interiors; instead, he concentrated attention on the center screen, displaying a computer enhanced grid map of the section of space occupied by the capsule, shuttle, moon, and, not yet visible on the grid, the no-longer-functional and expendable satellite.

His concentration was interrupted by frequent, quick looks at the large, rectangular chronometer board, suspended from the ceiling near the screens, providing a digital display of both Houston and countdown time. The rapidly numerical insets provided an instant time reference for everyone in the tiered center and, at that moment, Paul, along with everyone in the center cast quick glances at the countdown display flashing the time remaining—in seconds—until Zero-Hour.

A sense of nervous tension and excitement crackled across the large room, increasing with every descending tick of the clock. Paul Marchand, as Mission Director, especially felt the stress of the occasion; perhaps more so than others because, for the moment, he had less to do than anyone. Technically, he was in charge of the mission, responsible for every second, every function, every action by humans and machines. In actuality, he was merely an observer watching clocks, monitors, gauges, and lights because at that point in the mission, with both the capsule and shuttle in position, the entire operation was being controlled by computers.

Sitting on the edge of his desk, behind and slightly to the right of Paul, Brig. Gen. Samuel Snyder was also beginning to feel the effects of prolonged inactivity. He stood up, stretched, walked the few steps to Paul's console and said, "I guess it's the waiting that really gets to you."

Paul looked up and shook his head affirmatively. "That, and the waiting for something to go wrong."

Snyder laughed. "What a pessimist you are. We've checked this computer program a hundred times; we've got two back-up programs; and if all the systems fall apart, we've got an automatic abort system and that, too, has a back-up. If all else fails, we can still cancel the mission manually by just pushing a button." He paused. "You just need to relax."

Paul leaned back in his chair. "Well, you're probably right. Except I have seen systems break down for absolutely no reason and from what I've been told about this one, we don't need any mistakes up there."

"Hey, it's been smooth as silk so far. And look, we only have a few minutes to go."

They both looked at the clock and countdown timer, which indicated only three hundred seconds remained. From the speakers mounted in Paul's console, both men could hear the astronauts talking to the mission specialist, and to each other.

Paul glanced at his console and then swiveled his chair around to face Snyder. "Sam, I know basically what this experiment is all about but what makes this so hush-hush? I know the capsule is carrying a new kind of weapon; I know it's going to take a shot at a useless satellite; and I know the shuttle is up there to photograph and examine the debris. But I don't know what's so Top-Secret about all this."

Snyder thought a moment and then replied. "You know how the army is. Everything is hush-hush and top-secret from the erasers to the rockets. This new weapons system is totally different from anything we have. If it works, and all tests indicate it will, Star Wars capability becomes a reality."

"But how? I thought we were still a long way from any Star Wars weapons."

"We were. But then one of Whiteside's bright boys figured out a way to combine a bomb explosion with a laser beam and that's basically what we have up there right now."

"I don't think I understand," Paul said.

"Let me see if I can explain it." He leaned forward, over Paul's console, and with a pencil began to draw a diagram on the pad resting on the desk top.

Drawing a cone-shaped funnel on the paper, he explained: "If we were to pour a liquid into this funnel, the cone would quickly fill up and the liquid's own weight would force it through the tube of the funnel, or the apex. Now, if we apply pressure on the liquid, it's forced out of the tube's opening at a faster rate because we are forcing the liquid through a smaller opening or outlet."

He continued. "Now, instead of a liquid, imagine an explosion within this cone, or the large part of the funnel. And, rather than allowing all that released energy from the explosion to expand in all directions at once, we force the energy to escape through the small tube. The energy is focused in a straight line or toward one spot, the end of that tube. So, when the energy is concentrated in a straight line, forced to travel through a small conduit, when it escapes at the end of the tube leading from the cone, the impact area is hundreds of times more explosive. What we achieve, basically, is a concentrated explosion." "How do you get a tube long enough to stretch from the capsule to the target, or that orbiting satellite?" Paul asked.

Snyder replied, "The bright boys figured out a way to attach a laser beam to the end of the funnel. When the released energy from the explosion reaches the end of the funnel, it travels down the laser beam until its progress is impeded or stopped by a solid mass. In this case, an orbiting satellite. When the progress is stopped, an impact area is created and the concentrated energy is focused at the end of that laser beam. Bang. We get a second explosion. The mass disintegrates."

Paul thought about that for a moment. "That must be one heckuva explosion."

Snyder ginned. "It is. It's generated by nuclear fission."

Paul was stunned. "A nuclear device? In space? That's against international law. It's illegal to conduct atomic experiments anywhere in space."

"True, but there are loopholes in every law and the powers-that-be decided in this case we'd just have to do it not only to see if it works but to let the rest of the world know we can do it."

Paul asked, "Do the fellows up there in the capsule and shuttle know that a nuclear fission is going to take place?"

"They know. They've been in on all the experiments and know exactly what to expect." Snyder tried to reassure him. "Hey, nothing can go wrong." Their conversation was interrupted suddenly by a low-pitched electronic beeping sound, signaling the countdown had moved into its final stage. Instantly, Paul focused his attention on the space grid map displayed on the large screen. He reached over and flipped a switch, activating the center's sound system so all communications between Mission Control and the orbiting spacecraft could be heard by everyone.

The center was immediately flooded with the calm voice of Lt. Col. David Hendry, the capsule commander and pilot: "Mission Control, this is Space One and we are now activating voice scrambler and Buck Rogers."

Buck Rogers, as everyone knew, was the code name for the Star Wars firing device—a name derived from the old comic strip space hero. The voice scrambler was intended to distort all transmissions so that only Mission Control could understand the message transmitted.

General Snyder, standing behind Paul, spoke softly as if to himself, "They're inserting the fission core into the device."

Commander Greg Cook, pilot of the shuttle, spoke. "Control, this is Space Two. Gilbert and Cannon are beginning their descent to the moon in LLC-1. Our voice scramble is also activated."

Paul Marchand spoke into his microphone. "Roger, Space One and Two. We understand." He paused to glance at the clock and then said, "We are now at 300 seconds and counting." Flipping the intercom monitor switch, he spoke to the radar specialist, several levels away, "Radar, let's get a blip for the Lunar Landing Craft on the screen as soon as possible."

Immediately, a third flashing blip appeared on the screen and the radar technician's voice confirmed, "Blip's on the screen."

Commander Cook's voice broke in. "LLC-1 is away and headed for the moon."

"Roger, Space Two. Space One, your status please?"

"Control, the core is set. Major North is activating the laser."

"Roger, Space One. Space Two, did you copy?"

"Affirmative, Control," answered Commander Cook in the Lunar Landing Craft. As an afterthought, he added, "Make sure you guys point that thing in the right direction."

Another voice from within Mission Control spoke, "Orbiting target should be appearing in ten seconds."

"Control, this is Space One. Laser is activated. We are holding our position steady. Firing time is three minutes, thirty-two seconds."

"That's a roger, Space One," Paul answered. Looking at General Snyder, he asked, "Anybody up in the VIP lounge with the brass?"

Snyder looked in the direction of the VIP viewing room and saw Huffman talking to the two generals, Whiteside and Petrie. "Mark's doing his job."

The radar desk reported, "Target blip now on the screen." Everyone looked at the monitor where a fourth flashing blip could be seen. The target was moving into position.

The capsule commander's voice reported, "We have target on radar and computer is programming."

Paul knew that the computer was identifying, locking on to the target, and automatically activating the capsule's firing system.

From the medical desk, a voice advised quietly, "Increased heart beat and respiratory rate from all crew members."

The report caused no concern because everyone knew that as the countdown neared its zero mark, it was only natural that those aboard the capsule and the shuttle enjoy a preliminary surge of adrenalin brought on by the upcoming event.

Colonel Hendry spoke from the capsule. "Firing mechanism activated. Laser activated. All systems are go. We have one hundred twenty seconds until Mission time."

Paul answered quickly. "Roger, Space One. You have two minutes till firing. Space Two, LLC-1 approaching the surface of the moon. Landing in one minute forty-five seconds."

"Roger, Control, I have them on radar."

"Control, this is Space One. Final programming sequence has been activated by the computer. Are we GO?"

Paul looked at General Snyder. Final authority to continue with the mission was his responsibility. The point of no return had been reached. The mission was either abort or go. Snyder returned Paul's look and receiving no negative reaction said, "Mission is go. Advise all personnel."

Paul repeated the command. "Mission is go!"

All eyes riveted on the three large screens. There was nothing anyone could do except monitor the sequence of events. With the computer in control of all functions, an intrusion by anyone was completely limited to the Mission Director. Only Paul had the capability to override the computer, which he could do merely by pushing the Emergency Abort Button, thereby initiating a new programming sequence in the computer. In the event the first Fail-Safe System failed to function, a second, even a third, programming sequence could be activated. However, as smooth as the mission had been up to that point, it did not appear there was a chance of any problem developing.

On the screen, the flashing target blip slowly approached the point that would intercept the preprogrammed trajectory of the capsule's firing position. Only seconds remained before the computer fired the laser. A millisecond later, the fission process would begin, a nuclear reaction would take place and the resulting released energy would be funneled into, and along, the laser beam until it struck the satellite with incredible force.

Suddenly, Paul tensed. The picture depicting the interior of the capsule, Space One, began to shake and quiver on the screen and horizontal lines moved up and down the screen. Paul addressed the problem quickly. "Space One, your on-board television camera needs to be stabilized." Hendry's calm, detached voice came back, "Control, we seem to be getting a little turbulence up here." Then, a bit more excited, he said, "Houston, something is not right."

Paul hurriedly scanned the indicator panel but all lights reflected green, signifying all systems were operating properly. "Space One, everything looks all right."

Hendry's voice became more excited. "I tell you something is not right. We're . . ."

His voice stopped and everyone watched the Mission Control Monitor as a strange phenomenon began to unfold. Knobs and switches were ripped out of the cabin mounts. Storage doors flew open and the contents were sucked out into the cabin. Debris was swirling around the capsule cabin, as if a tornado was ripping through the manned spaceship.

Colonel Hendry's voice screeched into his microphone. "Houston, what in the world is going on? The firing system is going to maximum power."

Major North, the co-pilot, yelled, "It's turning. What are you guys doing down there?"

Frantically, Paul looked from console to console but all he saw were shaking heads as technician after technician signaled a negative. "We're not doing anything, Space One. What is going on up there?" Again, Paul frantically scanned all gauges, looking for some clue as to what was happening.

From the capsule, Hendry's voice screamed again, "We can't control it." North screamed, "Control, we have a malfunction. I repeat. We have a malfunction."

Simultaneously, the alarm buzzer within Mission Control began to screech, indicating that, indeed, a malfunction had occurred.

Hendry's voice cracked over the speakers, "We're aborting the mission."

North screamed, "We can't. Something is wrong. Systems are not responding."

"Control, our systems are not wórking," Hendry yelled.

Behind Paul, General Snyder yelled, "Abort. Abort. Abort the mission."

Paul immediately reached over and pushed the emergency button. "Abort initiated," he screamed aloud.

"Negative," reported the computer programmer next to Paul's console. "Abort command failed. All systems still operational. Firing will commence in ten seconds."

Paul threw another switch and pushed the Emergency button again. "Number Two abort back-up initiated."

"Negative," yelled the computer programmer. "Abort back up failed. System still operational."

A third time, Paul reached forward, threw yet another switch and announced, hopefully, prayerfully, "Number Three back-up initiated." He turned quickly to the technician's console, checking for a status report.

The man shook his head. "Negative." Paul froze in his tracks for a precious few seconds. What could be done now?

Before he could reach an answer, a voice screamed from the audio monitors. "Control, the trajectory has changed. Our position has changed."

In the VIP room, Generals Petrie and Whiteside exchanged sly smiles but on the floor, there was pandemonium on the Mission Control floor. And there was panic in space.

North's excited voice screamed out, "Something has control of the ship."

Hendry yelled, "It's going to fire."

In Mission Control, all weapon systems indicator lights suddenly lit. The laser fired, followed instantly by the firing of the nuclear cannon. In space, Commander Cook, in the shuttle, watched the brilliant beam of light shoot from the capsule on a dead line to the moon, followed by an even more brilliant flash. His mouth sagged open as he watched the soundless explosion on the moon surface. Soundless, but unmistakably powerful, as the impacted energy twisted moon dust and rocks and debris into a miniature mushroom cloud, which was quickly swept away into space, leaving a giant hole in the surface of the moon.

Even as the enormity of what happened was registering on those watching in the control center, voices screamed out from both the capsule and a weapons analyst in the center. "Radioactivity on the increase. Fissionable material has become extremely unstable."

"Houston, shut the reactor down. It's getting hot up here. It's not stable. Shut it down now!"

Hendry, panic in his voice, screamed hysterically, "Houston, do something. Do something quick. It's going to . . . "

The monitor screen went blank.

From somewhere in the center, a voice yelled, "We've lost all contact with Space One."

Paul yelled into the microphone, "Space One, do you read? Hello, Space One, do you read?

A quiet, subdued voice announced, "There is no more Space One. She just exploded. She's gone."

There was a choked silence in the Control Center. No one moved. No one spoke.

Paul Marchand was the first to regain his composure. "Space Two, what is your status?"

Commander Cook replied, "Control, we appear to be all right. I don't know about Gilbert and Cannon."

A faint transmission crackled over the speaker. "We're all right," said the voice of Colonel Wayne Gilbert, pilot of the Lunar Landing Craft. "But, what happened?"

In the VIP room, General Whiteside, white-faced, was gesturing wildly to General Petrie. Obviously, an argument was underway, but no one could hear what the two generals were arguing about.

Downstairs, Paul Marchand, in a relieved voice, said, "LLC 1, we've had an accident with the capsule. Is your craft all right?"

"Roger, Control. We're fine. What happened?"

"One moment, LLC-1, we're trying to find out now."

Paul turned to General Snyder. "What do we do now?"

Snyder cursed under his breath. "First thing we'd better do is check for radioactivity on the moon. Lord, this is gonna make a stink all over the world."

He thought for a moment and then told Paul what to advise the lunar landing party.

Paul nodded understanding and relayed the message. "LLC 1, can you reach the impact area from your present position?"

"Affirmative, Control. It will take a little maneuvering, but we can get over there."

"Good. We'd like for you to discontinue the operation plan and proceed slowly to the impact area. Begin checking immediately for radioactivity."

"Roger, Control. We'll begin now."

Paul acknowledged their transmission and then addressed the shuttle. "Space Two, you will need to hold your position. Is that clear? Hold your position."

"Will do, Control. I can see the impact area now. There is a good-size hole in the surface from what I can see. Tell LLC-1 to be careful." "Will do, and thank you Space Two."

Again, Paul turned to General Snyder and, again, asked, "What do we do now, Sam?"

Snyder was asking himself that very question. Collecting his thoughts, the general began to make notes on his pad and after a few moments, looked at Paul.

"While Gilbert and Cannon are getting over to the impact area, I'm going to make a few calls. We have to let the president know what happened." Looking toward the VIP room, he said, in a resigned voice, "And I guess I should go talk to the generals. In the meantime, Paul, get a team to check every system on the shuttle. Check it and double-check it. We don't want anything else to go wrong."

- - - - - - - - - - - -

"What do we do now?"

"We don't change anything," General Whiteside answered. "We proceed as planned."

"Matthew, we just lost a spaceship, several astronauts, and shot a hole in the moon."

"So?"

"And we've lost our weapon. It was supposed to turn and shoot at the earth, not the moon. Without that laser cannon, we don't have much bargaining power." Whiteside laughed. "Norm, think about it for a second. We've got a major political problem here—major for the president. His image is going to go right down the toilet. Right where we want him. And as to losing the laser cannon, we still have Solomon." He added, "And we still have Davis' new force field, which he claims is more powerful and more functional than a laser cannon. Now, he'll get the opportunity to prove his theory."

General Petrie thought about that for a moment and then asked, "Do you think Davis may have sabotaged our plan? He had access to the computer program and could have changed it."

Whiteside shrugged. "What if he did? It doesn't matter. We have an international incident and a vulnerable president. Our plan proceeds exactly as we have it scheduled."

Petrie laughed. "I have to agree with you. Actually, maybe this is for the better. We win no matter what."

Whiteside nodded, looking pleased with himself. "And that's the important thing, Norm. That we win!"

------------

In Las Vegas, Ryan Abernathy stood impatiently in a long line at the rental car counter. He kept looking at his watch, then at the clock on the wall behind the two service clerks, comparing times. Ryan wanted to get on the road. But before he could do that, he had to rent a car. And it appeared that everyone arriving in Las Vegas had the same idea. Finally, however, Ryan reached a representative. He handed the clerk his driver's license and credit card, saying, "I'll need a car for several days. I'll be going to Hawthorne and back."

As the smiling service representative entered the necessary information into the computer, she asked, "Is there a number where you can be reached in Hawthorne, Mr. Abernathy?"

"No, I don't think so. I'll be staying at a motel and I've never been there before."

"All right, that's no problem. Would you like one of our state road maps to help you?"

"That would help," Ryan replied.

When the paperwork was completed, Ryan pocketed his license and credit card, picked up the keys to the late model sedan, and walked outside to wait for the car to be brought up from the agency lot. While he waited, Ryan studied the map and quickly established the best route to get from the airport to the highway leading to Hawthorne. He estimated he had a two-hour drive at most, assuming that the traffic was light and the roads fast. Finally, Ryan was on his way.

As he drove, his thoughts were naturally on Pamela. Ryan felt a sense of urgency, a need to get to Hawthorne as soon as possible, and extricate Pam from whatever she was involved in. He had no doubt she was an unwitting participant in whatever was going on. And what was going on? Ryan had no idea. With a little luck he might run into Jack Clayburn and, he hoped, Jack would fill him in. Assuming, of

course, Jack made it to Hawthorne.  A lot of ifs.  A lot of questions.
And the answers were waiting for him at Piaute Mountain.

# 12.

course, Jack made it to Hawthorne. A lot of it... A lot of...
And the answers were waiting for him at Plastic Mountain...

# Chapter Twelve

"**P**aul, do you think Clay Davis may have tampered with our program?" General Snyder asked.

"I have no idea, Sam," Paul replied.

"He was dead-set against us doing this experiment. And you know how far some of these self-righteous eggheads will go when they think they're right."

Paul Marchand shook his head. "I don't know. That makes as much sense as anything else right now."

Paul turned back to his console. A dark sense of gloom and sadness hung heavily over the Mission Control Center as the more than seventy technicians, engineers, and specialists struggled to maintain self-control while they continued to perform their assigned duties. The crew members of the capsule, David Hendry and Fred North, had been popular astronauts, quick with a smile, quick with a joke. More importantly, their sincere appreciation of each individual's efforts in their behalf won the hearts of virtually everyone in the room. Their loss now evoked feelings of guilt and helplessness. A few cried. Many just cursed. Most, however, sat dejectedly in their seats, silent, trying to figure out what went wrong.

Paul Marchand was especially upset. As he sat at his control console, he searched frantically for some clue, some insight, that might have caused him to react in any manner that might have stopped or prevented the death of his two friends. He knew that he had responded as quickly as humanly possible and everything he had done was right out of the textbook. Whatever had happened, for whatever reason, he felt responsible, although he was, in fact, blameless.

In an effort to further understand what happened, despite the obvious reluctance to review the tragedy, Paul spoke into his intercom: "Records, let's have a replay of the capsule tape prior to the malfunction, please."

There was a long pause and the technician at the Records Retention Desk finally answered, "A replay, Sir?"

"That's correct. I know it isn't going to be pleasant, but we have to find out what happened. Let's look at it again." Then he added, "Leave the sound off. Just give me the video."

"Roger. Replay coming up on the monitor."

The huge screen lit up and after a moment or two of garbled images, video of the capsule interior appeared on the screen. Paul watched in maddening and helpless frustration as the scene unfolded. He saw the panic on Hendry's face and the frantic efforts of North to stabilize the situation. Even more disturbing was the physical turmoil displayed within the capsule cabin. He watched pieces of equipment, container boxes, and tools, which were strapped, ripped from their moorings and flung around the cabin. Doors to storage cabinets and drawers, normally secured by twist locks, were ripped open and their contents sucked into the swirling mass of material. What he failed to understand was the source or reason for the turbulent force creating havoc inside the capsule. There did not appear to be any logical reason for what he was watching. It was, he thought, very strange.

A voice behind him said softly, "Doesn't make any sense, does it?"

Without turning, Paul replied, "you're right, Sam. Everything was normal. All systems checked out in the green. It's crazy."

A third voice chimed in. Mark Huffman, standing behind General Snyder, said, "For your information, we've run checks and re-checks on every computer program and there are absolutely no bugs in the programs. There's no earthly explanation for what happened."

Snyder retorted, "There's an explanation, Mark. We simply have to keep looking. Run checks on those programs again."

"Chief, we've already checked and rechecked."

"Then do it again. And if you don't find anything, do it again. We need some answers because when there's an inquiry on this thing, what do you want me to tell them? It was an act of God? The capsule was possessed?"

"All right, Sir." Mark turned and headed back to his terminal, signaling for his assistants to join him.

"You have any theories at all?" Paul asked.

"None. I'm convinced that it has to be in the computer somewhere. Mark and his boys will have to try a little harder to find the bug." He paused and continued. "I talked to the president. He really didn't have much to say. Said he would get back with me and told me to leave my line open. We need to put someone on that phone and the minute we have anything, we need to notify him."

"Did you call Davis?"

"Yes, but he wasn't in. He and his girlfriend were out for dinner, but his security director left to get him. He should be calling us in thirty or forty minutes and maybe we can get his computer on the problem." He flexed his tired shoulder muscles and added, "We may never find out what went wrong up there, Paul. Our primary concern now is to get the shuttle back intact and without any problems. What's their status?"

"Let's find out." Paul swung his chair around, pushed the transmitter button and said, "Space Two, how do you read?"

"Loud and clear, Control." "What's your status?"

Commander Cook's voice came right back. "We're fine. We ran a check on everything inside and out and all systems are normal."

"LLC-1, this is Control. Can you read?"

"Roger, Control. We read you and Space Two loud and clear."

"LLC-1, can you give us an estimate on your arrival to the impact area?"

"Roger. I think we should be there in five minutes."

Paul raised his head and focused his attention on the large monitor screens, trying to ignore the blank white screen on the left, which had been filled with life but was now void. The center screen still displayed flashing cursors but they represented two—not three—space objects, the shuttle that was holding its stationary position near the moon and the LLC, which was resting on the moon surface.

The right-hand screen was receiving video from the camera attached to the Lunar Terrain Vehicle, the LTV, which resembled a golf cart with oversized tires. The small vehicle plodded along at a rate of several miles an hour, heading in the direction of the impact area. There was no need for commentary from the two because, despite a slight fuzzy distortion in the pictures, everyone in the Center saw exactly what the astronauts were seeing.

And, as on previous lunar surface expeditions, the sight was transcendent to any view ever seen by man. There was a certain ominous, even ghostly quality of the terrain. Watching the scene on the monitor, Paul felt a cold chill run over his body as the deadness of the earth's satellite passed before his eyes. He realized he was looking at sights never before seen by man; it was a glimpse of the past, perhaps even a glimpse of man's beginning, and, most certainly, he felt, if man did not soon change his ways, it was perhaps a symbolic look at his future.

Colonel Gilbert's voice, crackling over the loudspeakers, jolted him back to reality.

"Control, we believe we're approaching the impact area and it would appear that the radioactivity level is negligible. We have a reading, but it's nothing serious."

"Roger, LLC-1," said Paul. "Can you see the impact area yet? Can you focus the camera on it?"

"Negative, Control. There's a hill just ahead of us and we believe the impact area is over that rise, slightly to our left."

"We understand." Paul read the hastily written note handed to him by Snyder. "LLC-1, you're advised to use extreme caution when approaching the impact area. When the impact area comes into view, do not, I repeat, do not proceed until we have an opportunity to examine and analyze the video."

"Roger, Control. As soon as we make visual contact, we will hold our position until you give us the green." Those in the Control Center saw the small rise referred to by Gilbert. It appeared to be a mound of smooth lunar dust, swept into a hill and packed down by the explosion, to form a gently sloping incline. The LTV would have no problem climbing its face and holding a position on the peak while the television camera swept the horizon.

Within a matter of minutes, the LTV made its way laboriously and slowly up the incline. Stopping on the summit, Major Gilbert allowed the television camera to scan the valley below the hill until a large black spot was seen in the distance. As the camera zoomed in for a closer shot, it was obvious the impact area had been reached.

At first glance, the black hole was impressive. As the camera's eye automatically adjusted to the dim light, those watching in Control could see that the hole was much wider than expected and it appeared to be quite deep. Even more impressive, though, was the shiny material lining the rim of the impact area. A geologist, sitting in the Control Center, quickly identified the substance as glass, fused from sand and dust by the tremendous heat generated by the laser blast.

As the camera focused on the impact area, the controllers began analyzing the computer data and within a very short time, once it was established there appeared to be no dangerous side effects, General Snyder gave his approval for the astronauts to proceed. "LLC-1, this is Control and you're authorized to proceed cautiously. Use your discretion in leaving the LTV for examination of the area by foot."

"Roger, we understand. We will proceed to the large rock in front of us and approach the impact zone on foot."

Nervous tension again reigned with the Control Center as the astronauts approached the ominous looking black hole. Everyone sat tensely, waiting apprehensively for the two moon walkers to begin their examination of the impact area. They watched the monitors in tense silence while the picture grew larger as the astronauts moved closer and closer to the for bidding site.

Finally, the picture stabilized, suggesting the two men had stopped and were surveying the situation. As if to verify that assumption, Colonel Gilbert's voice shot through the silence.

"Control, are you receiving video?"

"Roger, LLC-1. We have video," Paul answered.

"I estimate the hole is approximately eighty to a hundred yards wide and very, very deep. That shiny stuff around the rim looks like glass."

"That's affirmative, LLC-1." Paul waved a salute to the geologist who had already voiced that opinion.

"Our Geiger counter registers minimum radioactivity but the temperature around here is extremely hot. We feel it, even in our space suits."

"How hot is it? Can you get a reading?" "Negative, Control. Dennis will have to go back to the top of the hill and get a temperature gauge from the LTV."

"Roger, LLC-1. If that's not too much trouble, we would like to have a temperature reading."

"Major Cannon is going back for the gauge." There was a short pause and then Gilbert spoke again. "Control, I'm mounting the camera on the tripod. How's your video?"

"Video is good," answered Paul.

The voice of Commander Cook, from the shuttle, interrupted the conversation. "LLC-1, on our video we seem to be picking up something on the backside of that rim. Can you see anything?"

"Negative, Space Two." A slight pause. "Where do you see it?"

"Just to the right and in front of you, behind the mound."

"Negative. There doesn't . . . Wait a minute. I think I see . . . What is that?"

"LLC-1, what do you see?"

"Hold on, Control."

Everyone in the Center now saw an eerie white mist creeping over the top of the mound.

"Control," the astronaut said in a hesitant voice, "I'm not quite sure I know what to make of this. Can you help?"

"LLC-1," asked Paul, "can you focus the camera on whatever it is?"

"Roger."

The astronaut moved the tripod a few feet and pointed the camera in the direction of the mysterious mist moving slowly down the sloping side of the small hill. Like a fog rolling in from the ocean, it began to inch its way across the floor of the shallow depression, or valley. As Gilbert stood watching from the opposite side, the mist moved to within several yards of the astronaut and then its forward motion slowly stopped. It became stationary. Swaying hypnotically in the airless atmosphere, it appeared to examine or measure Gilbert, as if the astronaut were some sort of prey.

"Control," Colonel Gilbert said nervously, "I'm not sure I like the looks of this."

"LLC-1, can you get a closer picture?"

There was a long pause before Gilbert answered. "You want a closer look?"

"That's affirmative."

"It's getting pretty hot up here, Control."

"Do you need to fall back?"

"I think maybe I should for a moment. Wait a minute. Hold it. Something is going on."

Before Paul could ask what the problem was, his eyes were drawn to the monitor. The mist began drawing itself together, as if caught between two opposing wind forces, and began swirling around in a rapidly increasing circular motion. Before their eyes, the gentle-looking mist became a swirling mass and its soft white color became brilliantly harsh with a whiteness that stunned and blinded the eyes. Ever whiter lights appeared within the vortex of the mysteriously twisting matter and blue white sparks began shooting forth like so many fingers, as if probing or searching.

Suddenly, without warning, an arrow of light shot forth and struck Gilbert's helmet. There was no sound, just the arching of the light from the cloud to the astronaut's headpiece. Instantaneously, Colonel Gilbert ceased to exist. Col. Wayne Gilbert became a lifeless, formless heap on the lunar surface.

Paul Marchand jumped to his feet. "My God, what's going on?"

Snyder screamed at Paul. "Tell Cannon to get out of there."

"Cannon, move it! Get out of there! Now!"

"Oh, no, it's coming after me," Cannon yelled, abject fear in his voice.

Cannon was not within the camera field and could not be seen but his voice could be heard. "Oh, please Lord, let . . ." Cannon's prayer was cut short. Silence.

Paralyzed with shock, Paul could not move. He sat there, unable to think, like a statue until he was jolted back into reality by someone shaking his shoulders and screaming into his ear. "Get the shuttle. Tell them to give us their camera shot." Paul looked into Snyder's face and as comprehension sank in, he nodded his head. "Space Two, this is Houston. Can you give us a video sweep of the impact area?"

"Roger, Control." Almost immediately the video on the screen changed as Wes Summerall, co-pilot of the shuttle, manipulated the controls to furnish NASA with video. As the camera scanned the area, the brilliantly white cloud funnel could be seen hovering over the lifeless and shapeless mass of what was formerly Dennis Cannon's body. The empty space suit was void of life or shape. It just rested there, in a pile, on the moon surface.

In shock, his composure shaken, Paul spoke to the shuttle commander, omitting all radio formalities. "Greg, see if Wes can zoom the camera on that. . . whatever it is."

Greg Cook replied, "Roger, Paul."

Wes quickly said, "Zoom lens activated."

On the monitor, the picture of the still whirling pillar of mist grew larger and flashes of light were seen within its white interior but it appeared that the brilliantly harsh white glare was adopting a reddish tint. Then, the screen went blank.

"I think the darn thing just killed our camera," Wes observed.

Snyder spoke to Paul. "I'm getting on the mike at my desk, Paul." He took several quick steps, sat at his console, and activated his microphone so he could be in direct contact with the shuttle.

Paul advised the shuttle, "Greg, General Snyder is now on line."

"Commander Cook, can you see anything on the surface?"

"Affirmative, General. That smoke cloud is expanding."

Snyder thought a moment and said, "Cook, direct your on board video camera at the cloud."

"Roger, will do."

The powerful lens of the camera aboard the shuttle zoomed in on the moon surface and the monitor filled with a clear shot of the cloud, which was moving in both a lateral and perpendicular direction, expanding as it travelled rapidly across the moon surface, its brilliant whiteness shaded with a reddish tint.

Snyder, more to himself than to anyone, asked, "What's going on here?"

A voice spoke over the intercom. "General Snyder, we are receiving data from the instruments on the LTV."

"Let me have them," Snyder barked.

"The temperature gauge was obviously activated before Dennis was. . . I mean, he managed to activate the temperature transmitter."

"What does it read?"

"We can't get a reading, Sir. It has jumped off the scale. Whatever that thing is, it's hot."

"Anything else?"

"There's no radioactivity but we are getting some very strong electrical signals."

"From the cloud?"

"Has to be, General. Wasn't here before and now we are receiving signals—there is a lot of electrical energy on the surface."

"Anything else?"

"Not at the moment, Sir."

"Keep me advised." Snyder leaned forward and said to Paul, "I think we better set the computers in motion to get those boys outta there as soon as possible."

"I agree with you." Paul threw the intercom switch and his voice boomed across the Center. "Attention, everyone. We are speeding up the departure. We're going to bring the shuttle home."

"Control, this is Space Two."

"Yes, go ahead," Paul answered.

"Our instruments are a little erratic. Please advise."

"Roger, will do. We have indications there is now a strong electrical field on the moon and that it is probably affecting your instruments." Paul added, reassuringly, "The computers can handle the compensation."

"Let's hope so, Control."

Paul continued. "Greg, we've speeded up the schedule. We want you to begin preparations to leave orbit. We hope to have the computer programs ready in five minutes. Do you read?"

"I'll second that, Control. Wes and I are ready to get out of here."

Snyder spoke. "Commander Cook, from our monitors it looks like that cloud is moving in all directions at once."

"Affirmative, General. At the rate it's going, the entire moon is going to be covered up shortly." He paused. "Anyone figure out what's going on yet?"

"Not yet," answered Paul. "We're working on it."

Snyder switched his microphone off and said to Paul, "I had better get the president informed."

"He isn't going to believe all this," Paul suggested.

"I'm not sure I believe it myself," Snyder retorted. "We've lost a space capsule, four astronauts and we don't have the slightest idea what is going on."

While General Snyder began calling the president, to explain what happened, Paul coordinated the schedule advance with the engineers and technicians and within five minutes the computers were reprogrammed to allow reentry and retrieval of the space shuttle. The increased activity somewhat diluted the numbing effects of the twin disasters and each individual, although still shaken and shocked by the events of the past hour, was determined that a third tragedy did not occur. To this end, meticulous care was exercised in the reprogramming procedure.

Snyder, visibly unnerved from his conversation with the president, handed the phone to his aide and walked over to Paul. "He's jumping up and down now. He wants us to start feeding data to Piaute Mountain as soon as we can to see if Davis and his crew can come up with any sort of explanation about what happened."

"Can that wait till after they leave orbit?"

"It will have to. I want everybody on the alert while we're bringing the shuttle home. Are we ready?"

Paul looked at his console and said, "All we need is to have Cook maneuver the shuttle into firing position and then we bring him in."

"Let's do it then."

Paul reached over, turned on a switch, activating the alert signal, and said into the microphone, "Space Two, this is Control. We want you to move into orbital trajectory and prepare for ignition."

"Roger, Control. We're ready. Firing engines in ten seconds."

Paul began the countdown. "Ten, nine, eight, seven, six, five, four, three, two, one. Ignition!"

There was a moment or two of silence. "Control, we have a problem. We do not have engine ignition."

Paul looked at the technician overlooking the reentry process but received only a shrug.

"Try again, Greg."

"We are trying, Paul," replied a nervous-sounding Greg Cook. "We're not getting anything." "Go to program override and fire the engines manually."

"Will do. Switching to manual ignition." Then, he announced, "Nothing, Control."

Paul took a deep breath. "All right, we'll just start over again. All personnel, reactivate your computer programs from the beginning. This is a reprogram."

From the shuttle came Wes Summerall's voice. "Am I seeing things or is that cloud getting closer to the shuttle?"

Paul snapped into the intercom, "Give me computer enhancement of the cloud and shuttle."

Slowly, the center monitor screen produced a computer enhanced picture of the area in space occupied by the shuttle and displayed a large red mass, representing the mysterious cloud on the moon. There was silence in the Center, as every one watched the screen. The cloud was, indeed, moving. And it was moving toward the space shuttle.

"Control," Cook said in a shaky voice. "Can you fellows hurry up a little?"

"Roger, Greg. We're hurrying," Paul encouraged.

On the other screen, providing video of the shuttle's interior, Paul saw Greg and Wes frantically working to get their engines ignited. As they worked, the red-shaded area on the center screen advanced rapidly, narrowing the distance between the shuttle and the outer edge of the cloud.

Mark Huffman spoke into the intercom to Paul. "We're ready to try again. All systems are go. Engines should fire." Paul tried to keep his voice calm as he spoke to Cook. "Greg, we are beginning the countdown. Engines will fire in ten, nine, eight, seven, six, five, four, three, two, one; you should have ignition."

The indicator light on Paul's panel showed green—ignition. But, just as he heaved a sigh of relief, he heard, "Control, we do not have ignition. Engines do not respond."

"That's impossible, Greg. Our sensors indicate the engines fired."

"I don't care what your sensors say. We do not have ignition."

"Try the override. Fire the engines manually."

"Affirmative." There was a pause. "Still no power."

Wes, with a trace of panic in his voice, broke in. "Greg, look out there."

"Oh, oh," Greg said in a resigned voice.

All eyes in the Center switched to the monitor where they saw Greg and Wes staring through the small cabin porthole. The fear in their eyes was clearly visible through their face masks.

"Houston, we have a serious problem," Greg announced calmly.

Paul could not think of anything to say that might ease the tension of the moment, so he continued to watch the monitors. From the left corner of his eye he saw, on the screen, the redshaded mass overtaking the shuttle. The obvious question: "Would the shuttle prevent the cloud from entering the cabin interior?" The question was answered by Wes.

"It's coming right through the hull of the ship," he screamed in terror.

Greg cried out, "Help us. Oh, God, please help us."

Horror-stricken, the center watched the mist, no longer red, transform into, again, a whirling, blazing, dazzling pillar of white with glaring blue-white sparks of electrical energy shooting forth from within its interior. Greg's face was contorted in fear as the alien cloud swirled before him and suddenly a brilliant shaft of light exploded across the cabin, striking Greg's helmet. The supercharged spark hung there for a split second and, then, just as suddenly, returned with an even brighter glow back into the mist. Commander Greg Cook ceased to exist.

Sitting in the adjacent seat, in uncontrollable fear, Wes Summerall screamed hysterically as the white tornado cloud engulfed his body, whirled around for a few seconds, and, then, just as suddenly as it had appeared, vanished. For a long minute, Wes sat rigid in his seat, unable to understand, or believe, the strange alien invader had passed him by, leaving him unharmed—and alive. But as the realization slowly crept into his brain, he regained some semblance of control over his thoughts and actions. Moving ever so slowly, he unbuckled his restraining belt, and, in a quiet, shaky voice, said, "Houston, I think...I think I'm all right. Are you still there?" With a sigh of relief, Paul answered him. "We're still here, Wes. Are you sure you're all right?"

Wes responded nervously. "I think so. I'm checking on Greg now."

He leaned forward, began unlatching the bolts holding Greg's helmet in place, and as they twisted free, he raised the helmet and looked inside the space suit.

Wes screamed in terror. Mission control watched the astronaut reach into the suit. Suddenly, Wes jerked his arm, trying to free it from something which appeared to be grabbing for him. Fear overcame him; feeling trapped, he strained and pulled his arm free, but the effort was too much. He grabbed his chest, shuddered once, then again, and slowly drifted away out of camera range.

The Center's medical technician, monitoring the vital signs, screamed into the intercom, "His heart has stopped."

With that, the room went deathly still. All eyes locked on the screen as everyone tried to comprehend what they witnessed. One astronaut vanished. One died from an apparent heart attack. As they watched in stunned, unbelieving silence, a finger of red-tinted mist drifted lazily across the cabin from Cook's lifeless space suit and slowly waved to and fro in front of the camera, as if looking through the lens to the screen. Suddenly, there was a brilliant flash of light and everyone watching the screen involuntarily jumped. Just as suddenly, the light vanished and the red mist was gone. The cabin was empty. Except for the body of Wes Summerall, floating lifeless above the spaceship's deck.

The center was deathly quiet. Not so, in the VIP room. There, Generals Whiteside and Petrie were engaged in highly animated conversation.

"Look at this as a golden opportunity, Norm. We've been planning this for months and now the perfect setting has been handed to us on a silver platter."

"You don't think we better wait and find out what we're dealing with?" General Petrie asked.

"What can we be dealing with we can't handle? The time is now. The public will be yelling for his head." He paused and added dramatically, "We can give it to them."

Petrie shook his head in agreement. "OK, then we need to alert our people."

"You're right. If we are ever going to do it, we need to do it now!"

# 13.

# Chapter Thirteen

"**C**ome in, Adam, come in!" the president greeted him. "I'm sorry we had to interrupt your plans."

"That's all right, Mr. President. I'm just thankful you caught me before we boarded the plane back to Washington." Adam Armstrong nodded to each of the president's staff members as he walked to a seat near the president's desk. Sitting down, he looked at the president and said, "I understand we have a slight problem."

"Not a slight problem, Adam. We have a Page One disaster." The president leaned forward and said quietly, "to begin with, I don't think anyone has had a chance to tell you that we had three calamities tonight."

"Three, Mr. President?"

"Yes, three," the president replied. "First something went wrong with the space experiment and instead of blasting an old satellite out of the sky, we shot a massive hole in the moon. Then, the laser cannon exploded, destroying the spaceship and killing the two astronauts on board. NASA had the two crew members scheduled for the moon walk investigate the impact site and they were killed. And just a few minutes ago we received word from Houston that the two men in the shuttle are dead also."

Armstrong leaned forward, disbelief in his eyes, and said, "You mean to tell me we've lost six astronauts tonight?"

"That's right. Six good men are dead, one spaceship destroyed, and we have a billion dollar shuttle floating around in space with no one on board."

"What the blazes happened?" Adam wanted to know.

The president shook his head. "We don't know. That's why we're here. That's why I called you back in. You might call this a preliminary inquiry. We need some answers and we need them fast."

Armstrong looked around the room and asked, "Exactly what do we know at this minute?"

The president looked over at his press secretary. "Tom, give him the story."

Tom Barksdale looked at the notes on the tablet in his lap for a moment and then looked up at Armstrong. "We don't have all the details yet, Sir, but this is what NASA has given us so far."

He then proceeded to bring Armstrong up-to-date on what happened in space. Armstrong listened intently and as Barksdale described the mist and its deadly behavior, he became even more interested. Interrupting the press secretary, he asked, "Was NASA able to obtain any data on the mist at all?"

Barksdale answered, "Only that the mist, or cloud, or whatever you want to call it, emits a tremendous amount of electrical and heat energy. Temperatures and electrical energy readings were absolutely off the scale."

Armstrong, listening intently, leaned back in his chair. "And you said death was instantaneous?"

"As near as we can tell, it was POOF! They just ceased to exist. Nothing remained as far as we can tell. One second the astronauts were scared out of their wits, and the next second they were dead! Gone! Vanished. Nothing left but their space suits."

General Curry added, "I mean they were dead and gone in a hurry. Snyder and General Petrie both told me it was so quick they weren't even aware it happened."

The president slammed his fist down on the desk. "I should never have authorized this experiment." His shoulders sagged and he continued. "I just knew that a successful Star Wars demonstration in space coupled with my appointment of you, Adam, as the new vice president would put all our problems behind us. I was counting on this to unite the country. Restore a sense of pride. Make people forget the scandal and the mistakes I've made in this administration." He added weakly, "I never should have gone through with this." He sighed. "Maybe my enemies are right. Perhaps I should resign from office."

Adam Armstrong said, "Nonsense, Mr. President.' These are only momentary setbacks. I think if we all work together on these problems, we can restore the nation's confidence. I urge you not to mention the word 'resign' again!"

The president smiled his thanks to Armstrong, looked around the room at his staff members and with a shaking voice, his confidence fading rapidly, asked, "Does anyone have any suggestions on what we should do first?"

Tom Barksdale spoke up. "I should begin drafting some sort of press release. I don't know how much longer we can keep this under wraps." He shrugged and continued, "By tomorrow morning every reporter in town will be camped out on the front lawn looking for details."

Aaron Wheeler, the National Security Director, asked, "How have you managed to keep this hushed up so far?"

The president answered "Snyder has literally sealed off NASA. No one in. No one out. He will not allow any leaks." He paused, and said thoughtfully, "You're right about something for the press, Tom. Go ahead and get started on that right away."

Tom shook his head in acknowledgement and started out, but Adam Armstrong's strong, firm voice stopped him. "Mr. President, I would like to suggest you hold off on issuing the press anything for a little while."

The president looked at him curiously. "Why, Adam? They're going to find out anyway."

"True. But at the moment we don't really know anything concrete and all we can tell them is that we lost six astronauts and that we don't have any idea what happened. We will look pretty stupid."

The president motioned for Barksdale to return and said, "What do you suggest?"

"I suggest we wait a few hours. Give NASA an opportunity to go over their data. Maybe they missed something in the preliminary reports." Armstrong looked around the room and asked, "What does the military think happened?"

Aaron Wheeler spoke up. "Mr. President, the War Room in Washington has not totally discounted the theory that maybe a foreign power might be involved."

Armstrong snorted. "I doubt any foreign power has the capability to pull off what happened tonight."

General Curry offered, "We're still running everything through the computer now, and shortly we'll have Clay Davis and his computer on it. It's my understanding that they are feeding data from NASA to Piaute Mountain right this minute."

Colonel Nix said, "We think Davis and his staff will come up with something. They always do. Besides, he invented the thing."

The president asked, "What exactly are we talking about? Did that hole we made with the laser cannon release some sort of energy or force we don't know anything about?"

Wheeler took advantage of the silence following the president's question to ask, "Is it possible that the atomic explosion of the capsule had something to do with it?"

General Curry responded to Wheeler's question. "We, of course, don't know for sure at this point, Aaron, but it is highly unlikely. There have been other explosions out there in space and we have never had any negative results or reactions."

Wheeler quickly said, "Yes, but we've never had a nuclear explosion."

Curry said, weakly, "We'll just keep checking on it."

The president had another question. "What about these reports I've been getting the past week concerning meteor showers, earth tremors, radio and radar interference? Is there a connection?"

General Curry looked at Colonel Nix, who took his cue and replied, "Mr. President, we have no idea what has caused the disturbances, but we doubt if there is any connection to our accident."

"Well, did the laser cannon cause the release of some sort of energy force that was trapped beneath the surface of the moon?"

Colonel Nix said, "That's another theory we need Clay Davis to explore, Sir. We know the hole in the moon is about a hundred yards deep but quite frankly, in all our previous moon experiments, we never encountered anything that would suggest energy of this magnitude was locked beneath the moon."

"Well, if the cloud didn't come from the hole," the president continued, "where did it come from?"

No one answered for a moment and, then, in a tentative voice, General Curry said, clearing his throat first, "There is also a theory being tossed around down in Houston and in the War Room that maybe this thing came from deep space."

"Deep space? Are you trying to suggest this was caused by a space monster?"

Nervously, the general answered, "Mr. President, we haven't completely discounted the fact that this might well be an alien from outer space."

The president looked at Adam Armstrong. "Do you have any thoughts or theories on all this, Adam?"

"I might, Mr. President, but I need more data."

"Can you share your thoughts with us?" the president asked.

Armstrong shook his head. "Let me request your patience for a while, Sir. I may be wrong. Would you object if I go to another room and make a few calls?"

"No, Adam, go ahead."

Brandon Miles spoke up, obvious distrust in his voice. "I should think that if Mr. Armstrong has a valid theory about all this, he would want to share it with us so we can toss it around for discussion."

Armstrong looked at him and, in a condescending tone, said, "It's not a valid theory yet and it's all pretty complicated. But as soon as I work it out in my head, I will be happy to put it in layman's terms so you can understand what I'm talking about."

The president quickly interceded. "Well, Adam, see what you can come up with and let me know. Warren, show Mr. Armstrong the den and let him use the telephone in there."

As the two men left the room, Tom Barksdale entered from another door, leading to an outer office. He walked briskly to the president, leaned down, and whispered something in his ear. The president looked up at Barksdale, then nodded. He rose from his desk and addressed his staff. "Gentlemen, you'll have to excuse me for a moment. I have a phone call." As he turned to leave, he suddenly remembered something and asked, "What are we doing about the wives and families of the astronauts? Do they know what happened?"

General Curry answered. "General Snyder is awaiting word from you before calling them, Sir. And Tom thinks that as soon as they are contacted, you might want to consider calling each and expressing your sympathy and condolences."

"Yeah," said the president thoughtfully. "Lord help them through all this." He added, "Make sure we contact them before we release anything to the press. I want them to hear it from us, not the radio or television. Now, Gentlemen, let's get in touch with people and get some facts coming in. Aaron, you put some pressure on the folks in the War Room. Brandon, you get hold of your boy over in Nevada and tell him we need some help from that computer of his as soon as possible." Turning to General Curry and Colonel Nix, he said, "I would appreciate it if you would speak to your bosses at NASA and see if they can speed things up down there."

Each nodded and rose to leave the room. When the room was empty, the president turned to Tom and asked, "Exactly what did he say, Tom?"

"That it was an emergency and he could talk to no one but you."

The president frowned. It was highly unusual for the FBI Director to call him direct. He looked at Barksdale and said, "Tom, I want you to get on the extension while I talk to him and take notes."

Barksdale nodded approvingly, walked to a small desk, and at the president's signal, lifted the receiver simultaneously with the president. "Hello, Ralph, how are you tonight?"

Five minutes later, an ashen-faced president hung up the phone and for several minutes sat perfectly still, staring into space. Finally, he turned to Tom Barksdale and asked, "I think we're really in the soup now, Tom."

Barksdale didn't say anything for a moment. He was too shocked at what he heard in the conversation between the president and the Director of the FBI. Finally, he broke the tense silence of the room. "Mr. President, how do you want to handle this?"

The president shook his head and answered, "I'm not sure. Now I don't even know who I can trust." He nodded toward the main office of his home and added, "There are at least four men out in my office who might be involved in this. I just don't know."

"What about Adam Armstrong?"

The president considered his new vice president for a moment and then answered, "He might be the only one I can trust right now. Tell Adam I need to see him. In private."

- - - - - - - - - - - -

Two hundred miles east of Los Angeles, four men seated around the conference table were ribbing and teasing Diane about her dinner date. Karl Liederman, the oldest of the three and Clay's chief assistant, suggested, "Diane, you might be able to submit this date to the World Records Book as the shortest dinner date in history."

Sean MacTavish, the center's top programmer and the one who wrote most of Solomon's programs, added, "You might even submit it as the cheapest dinner date a girl ever had."

Laughing, Chuck Valens, Karl's assistant, observed, "If I had known how little money a guy needed to spend on a date with you, I would have taken you to dinner myself." Diane looked at the four, wrinkled her nose at them a few times and smiled. She still wasn't in the mood for any bantering or joking, but she felt herself becoming more calm. Admittedly, she had been furious with Clay. Not only because of his arrogance while explaining Solomon's capability but his naiveness concerning the power he had within his control. She shuddered to think what was possible if Solomon's capability became known to the wrong people. She realized, however, that her anger really stemmed from the frustration she felt when Clay talked about "getting away for a while." The thought crushed her. She knew that Clay was preparing himself to propose and she decided that when and if he ever did, she would accept. Even angry, she would accept. She loved the man.

MacTavish turned around to look across the room at Clay's office. "He's been on that phone for a while, hasn't he? I wonder what's up?"

"Diane, you have any idea what's going on?"

"Nothing more than I told you. Houston has a problem. Clay and I were sitting in the restaurant when Butterly came in and told us we had to return." She shrugged. "We came back and he told me to call you guys. And that's all I know."

Karl spoke up. "Well, we know it has something to do with the space experiment. That's the only thing they have on at this time. I wonder if something went wrong?"

"What a pessimist," MacTavish said. "What makes you think something went wrong?"

"Why else would they call us? Our only involvement with this mission was to double-check their computer programs and insure they were bug-free. So, the only reason they would contact us now would be to bail their backsides out of deep water."

"You have a point there, Karl," Chuck said. "Just last week when. . ."

Diane interrupted him. "Here he comes."

They all turned to look. Clay was headed their way, notes flapping in his hand as he walked across the room. "Well, folks, I'm sorry to ruin your evening, but it looks like we have a little work to do."

He continued. "I've just been on the phone to Houston and there has been an accident in space. Six astronauts are dead, the space capsule blew up, and the shuttle is orbiting the moon without any crew members left alive."

He paused as the enormity of his announcement registered with those seated at the table.

Karl was the first to speak. "You mean to tell me that six astronauts are dead?"

"That's right." And he added, "They were killed in three separate incidents."

Everyone began to speak and ask questions at once.

"What happened?"

"Are they sure every one of them is dead?" "Do they know for certain they're dead or do they just have a communications problem?"

Clay waved his hand to silence them. "There's no doubt all six are dead. NASA Control watched them die right on the monitor. Now, let me explain what happened.

"I know you've heard the rumors about testing the laser cannon. Well, they're not rumors. The Defense Department built one and this latest mission was to test the cannon on a target in space. The cannon was to be fired at a dead satellite, but something went wrong. The cannon fired a nuclear charge at the moon instead."

Karl interrupted Clay, "You mean someone authorized an atomic explosion in space?"

"Yes, and we now have a deep hole in the moon." He continued. "What happened next is our concern. First, the capsule exploded and killed the two men on board. Then, the two astronauts on the moon were sent to examine the impact area and they were killed by what appears to be some kind of energy field. Finally, the energy cloud attacked the shuttle, killed one of the crewmen, and the other apparently died of a heart attack."

"You call it an energy field. Exactly what kind of energy field?" MacTavish wanted to know.

Clay shook his head. "I don't know. I only know what Houston told me. They're going to feed us video and we can watch what happened. Maybe then we can figure what they're talking about."

He paused for a moment before continuing. "I've talked to General Snyder, Generals Whiteside and Petrie. Here's what we have to do."

Everyone began taking notes as Clay explained. "We have a lot of things to work on. First, what went wrong? Secondly, we have to make sure some error wasn't made when we ran NASA's computer programs through Solomon."

Karl shook his head vehemently. "No way. All we did was double-check their programs."

"I know, but they want reassurance."

MacTavish chimed in. "Maybe those clowns at NASA think we sabotaged their mission or something." He added, "Maybe someone down there changed the program or made a mistake after we checked it."

Clay waved the idea off. "That's not important. The area we need to concentrate on right now is what caused the energy field and where did it come from? Also, since it attacked the shuttle, we have to determine if it poses a threat to earth. And if it does, how can we neutralize it?"

"This could keep us here all night," suggested Diane.

"And all day tomorrow," added Chuck.

"Well, that's what we get paid for," Clay said.

Looking at his notes, Clay issued instructions. "Diane, I want you to make a video phone connection to the president's California office and then set up a line for us to receive the video feed from NASA."

Turning to MacTavish, he said, "Sean, set up our computer to give us an enhanced picture of that thing on the monitor. And begin trying to establish radio contact with it just in case it is or represents an intelligent life form."

"Karl, I'd like for you and Chuck to access NASA'S mainframe and let Solomon analyze all the available data and see what we come up with."

Pausing for a moment, Clay concluded with, "Let's see if we can get something to work with, and then we'll figure out our next move. OK?" He studied each of them and when no one made any suggestions, he said, "All right, let's get it moving and see what happens."

- - - - - - - - - - -

Back in Los Angeles, the president's aide ushered Adam Armstrong into the president's private office. He felt the stares of distrust and jealousy on his back when Tom Barksdale announced that the president wanted to see him—alone. Smiling, he accompanied the aide, curious, of course, why the president wanted to see him without anyone else present. He did not have to wait long to find out.

The president started explaining the moment Adam seated himself.

"Adam, I have to talk to you. I feel at the moment you're the only one I can totally trust. And, since you're now the number two man, you need to know what might be going on."

Visibly shaken, the president continued. "The Director of the FBI called and informed me there is a strong possibility that high-ranking members of the government and military are involved in a conspiracy and plot to overthrow the government. Furthermore, the Director is convinced the attempted overthrow might involve our assassination."

Adam leaned forward, listening intently.

"The FBI became involved in this investigation when a network newsman accidentally stumbled onto the conspiracy. Do you recall the murder of Dr. Floyd Thacker and the discovery of his body by Jack Clayburn?"

"I not only recall it, I was contacted by Mr. Clayburn several days ago. He asked me some rather strange questions."

The president nodded understanding. "He was undoubtedly trying to track down Solomon. The FBI knows that before Thacker died, he mentioned the name Solomon to Clayburn. When Clayburn asked an agent to run the name through the FBI computer, the military was alerted. That's when things started popping.

"There have been several attempts on Clayburn's life, two other people were murdered, including Dr. Thacker's wife, and three FBI agents were killed while conducting an investigation into all this."

He paused. "What tied everything together was a secret meeting held at Aaron Wheeler's Maryland farm. The FBI has photographs of everyone who attended and it's all pretty suspicious. A number of high-ranking government officials and military officers were there, including General Wheeler, General Whiteside, and General Petrie. Also at that meeting were the heads of six major communications networks and high-ranking government officials from at least a dozen foreign nations."

"Quite an assortment of dignitaries," Adam observed.

The president continued. "The FBI thinks that those behind the conspiracy plan to create chaos in the economic market by disrupting all banking, monetary, stock market, and financial transactions to such an extent that the nation would virtually collapse financially."

"Secondly, all the networks and news media would begin to call for our resignations." He paused, took a deep breath and said, "When the networks and news media have focused on the loss of my effectiveness as a leader, the FBI believes I will be assassinated, certain key government officials loyal to me will also be assassinated, the military will stage a coup and seize the government under the pretense of restoring financial stability; and there is even the possibility that some sort of nuclear blackmail will be used against the rest of the world in order for the new government to obtain world power." Adam interrupted him. "Mr. President, with all due respect to the FBI's efficiency, such a program would require not only a lot of assassins but thousands of people would have to be involved to make the coup work."

"Not necessarily, Adam. You're right about one thing. It would require a number of assassins. But let's talk about General Wheeler's farm. It's used as a school for security and body guards who are employed by corporate executives to defend against kidnapping,

terrorist activities, and whatever else corporate executives have to
guard against.

"When Wheeler retired, and became my Security Adviser, his
Special Forces Command was broken up by the army and all personnel
were either reassigned or discharged. The FBI learned that of the one
hundred eighty-five men in that command, seventy-two left the army,
fifty-six went to work for the government in various agencies
throughout Washington, and the remaining one hundred thirteen were
transferred to bases all over the world. However, in the past year every
one of the one hundred thirteen was quietly reassigned to a post in or
near Washington.

The president paused dramatically. "The one hundred thirteen
soldiers and fifty-six ex-soldiers, all trained killers and specialists in
urban terrorist warfare—all associated with General Wheeler's
school. What we have is one hundred sixty nine potential assassins
living and working in the nation's capitol. And every weekend these
ex-commandos meet at Wheeler's farm to participate in training
exercises that, according to the FBI, strongly resemble offensive, not
defensive, exercises."

"Mr. President, whoever is behind any conspiracy would have a
great deal of difficulty recruiting enough people, and keeping them
quiet, to be involved in such a move."

The president shook his head sadly. "No, Adam, we created our
own monster. When I authorized you to fund the development of Clay
Davis' super computer, I sealed the fate of this nation. Clay Davis'
Solomon is capable of not only implementing a conspiracy and ruining
the government, it is capable of running the country once the overthrow of the government is obtained.

"The FBI has learned that for the past two years Solomon has been
accessing, culling, and storing information from data banks all over
the country and the world. There is reason to believe that what we
have over on Piaute Mountain is a central computer operation with
information on every person, office, business, financial institution,
and every government agency in the United States."

"And one man running the computer," Adam injected.

"Right. Clay Davis. The FBI believes that Davis has been using
Solomon, with the permission of the army, to steal money from the
Russians to finance this project. They also believe very strongly that
Solomon can be utilized to neutralize or activate both the U.S. and
Russian nuclear arsenals."

"What do you want me to do, Mr. President?" Adam asked. "I
want you to go to Piaute Mountain and find out what's going on. At
the moment, all I have is a batch of veiled suggestions and theories
from the FBI. I want to know just how far Davis has carried this
Solomon project. I want to know how involved he is. Find out if
Solomon caused the space disaster. And, if possible, find out who is
the head of this conspiracy. Is it Davis? Is it Whiteside? Is it
Wheeler? Who is it? I need to know."

"When do you want me to leave?"

The president looked at Adam and answered, "Right away. I'm counting on you to find out what's going on and use whatever force is necessary to take control of Solomon."

"Take control of Solomon?"

"Yes."

Adam Armstrong returned the president's gaze and solemnly pledged, "You can count on me to do just that, Sir."

# 14.

# Chapter Fourteen

Locating the post office was no problem. Hawthorne's lone main street consisted of only several blocks of retail stores and offices, and the post office, a small brick structure, fronted by a flagpole, was distinctly Federal looking. It was the newest building on the block and the only one with the familiar red, white, and blue mailbox situated on the curb.

Jack drove by the building at ten o'clock and, when he did not see Ryan, returned to his motel room. Two hours later, at midnight, checking on the even hours as promised, he returned. Ryan was waiting for him. He barely acknowledged the Texan's presence but with a slight nod of the head, motioned Ryan to follow him. In his rearview mirror, he saw Ryan make a U-turn in the street and fall in behind him. On the outskirts of town, Jack, followed by Ryan, pulled into the motel parking lot, stopped in front of his room, and got out of his rental car. As Ryan stepped from his car, Jack welcomed him. "You don't know how glad I am to see a friendly face."

Ryan gave him a wide grin. "Well, I ain't gonna be friendly long if you don't tell me what's going on."

"Come on in," Jack said, "and I'll bring you up-to-date."

The two men entered the motel room and as Ryan grabbed one of the chairs, Jack asked, "Want me to grab a couple of cold drinks or something?"

"Nothing for me. You get one if you like. I've had at least a gallon of coffee and I don't really want any more liquids right now."

"I'll pass. Seems like I've been living on coffee myself lately."

Jack settled himself in the remaining chair, took a deep breath, and asked, "You go into Vegas or Reno?"

"I caught a flight right to Las Vegas, rented a car, and here I am," replied Ryan. "I made good time but it seems like it's taken me forever to get here." He added, "I'm just antsy. I want to get Pam out of there and get back to Houston."

"I did the same thing. I've been killing time, waiting on you and trying to figure out what to do."

Ryan leaned forward, resting his elbows on his knees, and asked, "What's going on, Jack?"

"I'm not even sure I know where to begin, Ryan." Jack thought a few moments and decided to give Ryan the entire story. Ryan was just about the last friend he had at the moment and he knew the two would have to depend on each other completely. He deserved to know everything.

Jack began the story, beginning with the Floyd Thacker incident. Slowly, methodically, unemotionally, he provided Ryan with every detail, right up to the shooting in the restaurant and the killing of Roger Grant. When he finished, he sat, waiting for the shocked Ryan to absorb everything.

Finally, Ryan spoke. "I want to say you're crazy, but I can't. Too much of it makes sense. You haven't heard what happened tonight, have you?"

Jack looked puzzled. "No, what happened?"

"I don't have all the details but I understand we had a mammoth tragedy in space. Just before I boarded my plane in Houston, I called my assistant and he said some experiment in space went crazy, six astronauts were killed, and a space capsule blew up."

"There hasn't been a thing on the news about it," Jack observed.

"No, and there won't be until they lift the lid. Right now, everything at Houston is nailed shut. No one in; no one out; and they aren't allowing phone calls. Probably won't release anything to the media until morning time."

"I wonder if the space thing has anything to do with the conspiracy."

Ryan shrugged. "Just a coincidence, I suspect. What would this have to do with any conspiracy?"

Jack thought a moment before answering. "It could create a very embarrassing and damaging situation for the president. Be sort of like another nail in his coffin. The media is sure to jump all over him. They'll point out that a disaster in space is just another example of his poor leadership."

Ryan asked curiously "Are you suggesting that someone might have planned a space disaster? Killed off six astronauts just to make the president look bad?"

"I don't know, Ryan. I really don't know."

"Do you think General Whiteside is at the head of all this?"

"I don't know that either, Ryan. It just looks like all of a sudden everyone is involved in this thing. From what I know and have learned, we have the military involved; we have the media involved; we probably have the CIA involved; and for all I know, the FBI may be involved."

"I thought the FBI was helping you."

"I thought so too but how did someone know I was meeting Roger Grant at that restaurant? He and I were the only ones who knew, yet two gunslingers showed up and tried to kill me. Somebody in the FBI must have passed the information along."

"Maybe somebody just followed Grant to the restaurant. Did you think of that?"

"True," Jack admitted. "I don't know. I don't know who we can trust. I can't even go to my network because they're up to their eyeballs in what's going on."

"How do you think Pam figures in all this?"

Jack shook his head. "I guess we won't know that until we ask her."

Ryan shook his head. "I still don't understand why Butterly didn't tell me Pam was at Piaute. He's supposed to be a friend and good buddy." He added, "I still don't buy the idea that she is any way connected to all this. I just don't think she knows what's going on. I don't doubt she's in there but I would bet a month's pay she doesn't know what's going on. I know her too well. This isn't her thing. She's not any political revolutionary or something. She's just a secretary working in a government office. There has got to be some kind of explanation."

Jack nodded sympathetically. "Well, somehow we have to figure out what's going on inside that mountain. And that's not going to be easy." He asked, "Any ideas?"

"I could call Butterly and tell him I'm passing through and want to visit with him, but that wouldn't get us too far."

"No, I doubt if that would help."

Ryan thought for a moment. "The only thing I can think of at the moment is just go up there and scope the place out. Maybe we'll get an idea if we see what's going on or what the place looks like. I don't know. Maybe we'll get lucky and Pam will leave the place to go to the store or something."

"Do you want to go up there now? I know how to get there."

"Too dark to see anything right now," Ryan answered. "I think we ought to grab a few hours sleep and head up there right at daybreak. Find us a good spot to hide and just see who comes and goes, and maybe something will happen."

"Makes sense to me." Jack looked around. "Well, we've got two beds. Why don't we catch a nap and I'll get us a wake up call bright and early."

"Good idea." Ryan stood up and headed for the bathroom. Before closing the door, he turned back to Jack and asked, "Jack, do you think the military could really take over the government and get away with it?"

Jack considered the question thoughtfully before replying, "A couple of weeks ago, I would have laughed at the idea. Now, I'm not so sure. Some powerful people seem to be involved and I don't think they'd be involved if they didn't believe they could pull it off. Maybe they have some white knight waiting in the wings who will be more acceptable to the public. Evidently, they know something we don't know or can't imagine. That's what bothers me. What is it they know that we don't?"

- - - - - - - - - - - -

The president studied the men gathered in his office and his face hid the emotional distrust he felt. Other than his immediate aides, he could not trust any of his advisers. Except his new vice president, Adam Armstrong. He glanced at Adam, standing on the far side of the room, pouring a cup of tea. He was an impressive man. His six feet, four-and-a-half inches still supported a running back's body—lean, muscular, and graceful. Soft black hair, neatly styled, framed an oval face dominated by piercing brown eyes and white, even teeth. His deep, resonant voice had a musical quality—some suggested a hypnotic quality—and when combined with his flashing eyes and disarming smile, he was a master at mesmerizing an audience. The president tapped his fingers on the desk, nervously, because he knew Armstrong would not mesmerize this audience tonight. He knew when he announced to the group his decision there would be a heated debate, but he was determined to discard all their arguments. His mind was made up, and he was determined to have his own way. He smiled to himself. There was still an advantage or two to being the president.

"Gentlemen, I'm sending Vice President Adam Armstrong to Piaute Mountain."

There was a stunned silence before General Curry jumped to his feet. "Mr. President, Piaute Mountain is our most classified defense facility. We . . . "

The president smoothly interrupted him. "You'll note I said Vice President Armstrong." Laughing aloud, he said, "Surely, Kenneth, you don't think the vice president of the United States would be a threat to our security, do you?"

Armstrong smiled. Curry continued to object. "Sir, I think both Generals Whiteside and Petrie would object."

"They probably would," said the president. "But that's why we have a president who is designated Commander-in-Chief, to override generals." He looked at Armstrong. "I want you to make arrangements to leave immediately for Piaute Mountain. Call and get transportation." Grabbing a sheet of presidential letterhead, he quickly wrote a brief message and handed it to Armstrong, saying, "This will authorize you to have complete access to Solomon." A sudden thought occurred to him. "And, Adam, I think you should have a military escort with you. Make arrangements to take a squad of soldiers with you."

Reaching for the note of authorization, Armstrong said, "Thank you, Mr. President. As soon as I know something, I'll call you." He added, "I'll leave as soon as possible."

He shook the president's hand and left the room, followed closely by Michael O'Conner. As they walked down the hall, Armstrong said, "Get the car, Michael. I'll be right out. I want to make a quick phone call."

Michael nodded and walked quickly to the front entrance, while Armstrong turned and entered one of the rooms where he knew he would find a telephone. He placed his call and, speaking in a hushed and confidential voice, explained quickly what he wanted done and concluded, "If you need me, I'll be at the Piaute Mountain Facility, but do not call unless it's an absolute emergency." He paused and added, "Now, whatever you do, don't panic. You'll be all right. You have my protection. You just keep calling until you reach all the people on your list and deliver my instructions. They'll know what to do."

He listened for a moment as the party on the other end was talking and, smiling, said, "You're right. This is a wonderful opportunity for me." He hung up the phone and walked outside to his waiting limousine.

- - - - - - - - - - - -

Level Four of the Piaute Mountain complex was referred to by everyone as "Solomon's Temple." The name evolved as a result of Diane's tongue-in-cheek dubbing of Clay's brainchild as "Solomon" because of its "all knowing—all wise" capability. More than one person agreed the name was appropriate in that Solomon cost a king's fortune to design, build, and house. Unlike the biblical king's home, however, the area housing the world's most advanced computer was not pretentious or opulent. In fact, it was sterile in appearance; distinguished only by the wall-to-wall, ceiling high unit housing the super sophisticated computer and data banks.

In the center of the spacious enclosure was a large computer console, fronted by an executive swivel chair, obviously intended to serve as a master control center for the operation. Three computer desks, with computer terminals and auxiliary monitors, flanked either side of the control center providing the computer director with a total of six stations that could either function independently as a master control center or provide support to the mainframe and console. At both ends of the room, mounted on the wall, two large video monitor screens, each of which could be utilized or controlled by any of the seven terminals, served as monitors for video feeds from within the complex or from anywhere in the world. This was Solomon's Temple; this was Clay Davis' domain.

Davis, staring at the computer monitor, was not aware of anyone standing behind him until he felt strong fingers dig into his tired shoulder muscles. Instantly, he leaned back, relaxed his body, and said, without turning around, "Ms. Williams, you certainly know the way to a man's heart."

Laughing, she continued to massage his shoulders, as she replied, "I'm going to have someone bring some tea and sandwiches down from the lounge in a little while. It looks like we won't be getting any breaks."

"Good idea," Clay said. "Have them set up a little snack bar or something on the conference table. Are you doing any good in your research?"

"Not yet, but we're plugging away over there. The feed from Houston is still coming in and we're still checking everything."

"Well, we should know what happened pretty soon. I haven't found a problem yet that Solomon couldn't solve. This might take a little more time, but we'll get to the bottom of it."

She patted him on the top of his head and turned to walk away, saying over her shoulder, "Of course we will. I'm back to work, Dr. Davis."

As she walked away, Clay unconsciously reached into his pocket to feel the ring box, which he was still carrying. He preferred to have the perfect romantic setting when he asked Diane to marry him but he was impatient. Perhaps, as soon as the problem was solved, he would ask her in his office or upstairs in the lounge. He really didn't care where he asked; he just wanted to begin making plans with her immediately for their future together.

# 15.

# Chapter Fifteen

**A**t seven o'clock Saturday morning, Clay Davis poured what he guessed was his tenth or eleventh cup of coffee and, as he slowly sipped the bitter-tasting liquid, looked around the room at his staff, who were still trying to find a few answers to their problem. The staff enjoyed the luxury of only one short break through the night and signs of fatigue—and frustration—were beginning to show. Looking at the clock again, Clay decided it was time for a break, which would provide not only a brief respite from the tedious work but an opportunity to assess the progress.

"All right, everyone, let's sit down and see where we are," he said in a loud voice.

Slowly, each of the staff moved to the conference table and sat, happy to be away from their computers. Clay took a seat, looked around the table and said, "I'm like you. I'm running out of ideas so I guess we need to stop for a moment and go over what we have. Perhaps, then, we can get an idea of what to do next."

Everyone exchanged glances and finally Karl Leiderman spoke.

"Well, we accessed the NASA computer and Solomon has analyzed all the data available. We know two things at this point. One, there is a gigantic mass of electrical energy out there. We can't even begin to estimate its full power because the readings transmitted from the moon and shuttle were far beyond the scale of the sensors. We can only say that its power is immeasurable."

He paused, looked at his notes, and continued.

"Secondly, as might be expected, the cloud contains a great deal of heat. Again, we are unable to measure its intensity because the portable sensors aren't capable of measuring that high. It does not, however, emit any sort of radio activity, which would tend to suggest that it is not nuclear powered in any way.

Liederman looked up from his notes and said, "I mention this because we have not been able to determine the cloud's energy source. We can see that it has form, but it apparently does not have any mass because early this morning NASA conducted a radar probe, using the shuttle's radar equipment, and the signals went right through the cloud and bounced off the moon."

Shrugging, he concluded, "As you can see, we still don't know very much. We've tried to analyze the physical nature of the cloud, mist, or whatever it is and we can't get a handle on its chemical makeup. The spectrometer cannot provide us with any information indicating whether the cloud is an optical illusion or if it contains chemical properties we're not aware of."

Clay smiled. "Well, I think we can rule out the optical illusion theory. We know it's there."

Looking over at Sean MacTavish, Clay asked, "Mac, what do you have?"

MacTavish shook his head. "Not any more than Karl."

Looking down at the notes on his yellow legal pad, he said, "As you know, we've put a grid on the screen depicting the moon and earth. Now, you can't tell right now by looking at the moon but we have superimposed a computer-enhanced configuration of the cloud over the moon. It's covering the entire moon at the moment but we're locked onto its electrical and heat transmissions and if it moves as much as a centimeter, we'll know because the tracking system will follow and display any movement on the grid."

"As you suggested, Clay, we've tried to establish radio contact with it on the outside chance that it might be an intelligent life form." Pointing to a thick pile of computer print outs, he said, "That's a list of the known languages in the world and I've had Solomon transmitting a message in each language over every known frequency. I have, of course, utilized the basic space communication system of integers and musical notes. We've had no response."

He paused, and added, "If it possesses any intelligence, it is an intelligence either far superior to ours or it's not as advanced as ours. There is, of course, a third possibility. Whatever it is may not want to communicate with us. At any rate, it either can't be communicated with, won't be communicated with, or we haven't figured out the correct way to communicate with it."

Clay leaned forward and asked, "How about the rest of the world? Have you monitored any activity on the airwaves that might pertain to our mysterious visitor up there?"

Sean looked over at Diane. "Diane, you want to answer that?"

She nodded and replied, "Well, the cat's out of the bag. Every major power knows what happened last night and they are just as nervous as us. They are utilizing all their resources to figure out what is going on, and I suspect they're as puzzled as we are."

She referred to her notes and added, "The Defense Department advised us that the U.S., along with Great Britain, France, Russia, and West Germany, and a few others have gone to semi-full military alert. Like us, everyone is simply waiting for something to happen." Clay looked at Karl. "What did your analysis of the NASA computer tapes reveal?"

Chuck spoke up. "I can answer that. We ran all their tapes through Solomon and everything checked. The programs were not changed or tampered with, as far as we can tell."

"Then, there is no way the program was sabotaged?" Clay wanted to know.

"Let me put it this way. If the programs were altered and there was sabotage, it was by someone smarter than us. I can't find any evidence that any alterations were made." Clay studied his notes and said slowly, "I've had Solomon analyzing the video tapes and I think we can pretty much rule out the possibility of the laser cannon being connected with the cloud. According to the video, the cloud did not originate from that hole in the moon."

He continued, "We've ruled out computer error, since NASA was in complete control of the mission, we have to rule out human error—the astronauts could not have made this thing appear. And we can pretty well assume it's not the work of any foreign power. What does that leave us?"

No one answered for a moment but finally MacTavish volunteered a suggestion. "I think we have to proceed on the assumption that the cloud, or mist, or whatever it is, is an alien and that it came from out in space."

Karl threw him a disdainful look. "Come on, Mac. This is supposed to be science not science fiction." "Do you have any other ideas?" Mac asked him.

"I just think we're overlooking something. There has to be a logical explanation for whatever that thing is."

MacTavish quickly said, "If we assume that there is . . ."

He was interrupted by the ringing of the soft bell of the video phone. Clay said, "I'll get it."

He walked over to his console, hit a switch, and the small video screen immediately projected the image of the president.

"Good morning, Dr. Davis," the president said pleasantly.

"Good morning, Sir. You're up mighty early."

"We haven't been to bed yet. How about you?"

Clay smiled grimly. "Neither have we, Sir. We've been up all night."

The president's face became more serious. "Dr. Davis, do you have anything to report?"

"Not much, Mr. President." He then proceeded to brief the gentleman in the California White House.

When he finished, the president asked, "So, as far as you can determine, sabotage is ruled out?"

"That's correct, Mr. President."

"And you don't have any concrete theories on what is up there?"

"None whatsoever, but the staff and Solomon are still on it." He paused. "Mr. President," he said hesitantly, "there is the possibility that this is an alien force. We have not ruled that possibility out."

The president's eyebrow arched. "An alien, Dr. Davis?"

"That appears to be our only viable theory at the moment."

"That's a little far-fetched, isn't it?"

"I just wanted you to know that we're exploring every possibility, Sir."

The president drummed his pencil on the desk and then said, "Clay, you're not going to like this but like you we are exploring every avenue also. What I've done is dispatch Adam Armstrong to your lab. I want you to provide him with access to Solomon."

"I beg your pardon, Sir," Clay said, stunned.

"I said Adam Armstrong is on his way to Piaute Mountain and should be arriving shortly. I have given him full authority to access Solomon."

Clay looked around and, not wanting his staff to overhear the conversation with the president, reached over and switched off the video, and said softly into the telephone, "Mr. President, I don't believe you realize the sensitive nature of our . . ."

The president interrupted him. "Dr. Davis, I really don't have time to debate this matter. Armstrong is on his way and I expect you and your staff to give him full cooperation and assist him in any way he requests. He has my written authority to take control of Solomon."

"Mr. President," Clay tried again, "I'm not too sure this is a good idea. To begin with, Adam Armstrong is. . ." Briskly, the president interrupted and said, "Is the vice president of the United States and operating under my direct orders. You will cooperate, Dr. Davis."

In a resigned voice, Clay answered, "I understand, Mr. President."

"If anything comes up, I'll be at my desk. Call me immediately."

With that the president hung up and as Clay switched the video phone off, he turned to face his staff. "Well, you heard that. Dr. Armstrong is on his way, and we are to cooperate with him fully."

Karl spoke up. "It won't be that bad, Clay. Maybe he can give us a little help."

"What kind of help can he provide?" MacTavish injected. "He's not a scientist anymore, he's a politician."

Diane, realizing Clay was very upset by the president's message, offered, "Clay, it won't be that bad. We'll be right here. What can he possibly do that we can't handle?"

Chuck tried to reinforce Diane's thought. "Hey, Chief, it won't be a big deal."

Karl had another point to make. "Listen, I've worked with the man and he knows what he's doing. He's a little secretive at times but he does know what he's doing. Maybe he has some theory he wants to check."

MacTavish butted in, "Well, if he has a valid theory, why not just tell us and we'll check it out for him." Chuck added, "Listen, if he has a theory, he comes in, feeds it to Solomon. Presto. Solomon either confirms it or rejects it, and Armstrong is out of here. Simple as that."

"You're right, of course. I may be overreacting." Clay sighed and added, "Maybe you've hit on it, Chuck. If he's here to check out one of his theories, we let him have access, and then he'll leave. I just have a little trouble with the idea of an outsider accessing my baby."

Diane looked at him, walked over, and quietly said, "Clay, maybe you just don't like the idea of someone finding out what Whiteside and Petrie have had Solomon doing these past few years."

Clay flashed her a hard look. "That's not your concern, Diane. And I don't want to get into another discussion of right or wrong on the subject. They said do it, so that's exactly what I did."

Sitting back at the conference table, he said, "Well, he won't be here for a while so maybe we can solve the problem and eliminate any need for him to access Solomon."

Looking around the table, he asked, "What's next? Who has a suggestion?"

Karl started to speak but was interrupted by MacTavish, who had jumped to his feet. Pointing at the monitor screen depicting the computer-enhanced configuration of the cloud covering the moon, he yelled, "That thing is starting to move."

- - - - - - - - - - - -

On a bluff facing the Piaute Mountain Facility, Jack Clayburn and Ryan Abernathy were concealed among the rocks and bushes trying to determine their next move. They arrived at daybreak and, thanks to Ryan's skill in locating motion sensors and remote television cameras, penetrated the facility parameter to lie concealed less than a hundred yards from the entrance of the facility.

Jack looked at his watch and observed, "It's almost half past seven and nothing is going on."

Ryan, looking through a pair of binoculars, studying the outside security devices, suggested, "Well, with all the cars in the parking lot, I would guess everyone who works in the facility has been there all night."

Jack kept fiddling with the small transistor radio he remembered to bring, trying to find a detailed news report on the space disaster.

"I don't think we're going to get any details. I can't get a station in clear enough or long enough to get anything."

"Probably the mountains," Ryan suggested. "Signal can't get in from the big cities."

"Well, what we heard this morning coming in was pretty bland."

Ryan shrugged. "You can bet NASA isn't giving out any details, so whatever we heard came from the military or the White House."

"And that wasn't too much," Jack added.

"Darn."

"What's the matter?" Jack asked.

"I'm sitting out here, about a hundred yards from Pam and can't do anything about it. I'm tempted to just walk in, say hello to Butterly, find Pam, and drag her out of there."

"That wouldn't be too smart, would it?"

"No," Ryan admitted. "But we're going to have to think of something. This sitting around out here in the bushes ain't going to get anything done for us. We need to get inside."

"Let's just be patient. Something is bound to happen. I can feel it getting ready to happen."

"I hope your feelings are right," Ryan said. "I'm getting tired of just sitting here, watching."

Jack smiled. The impatience of youth. He knew, from experience, that if one waited long enough, something always happened.

- - - - - - - - - - - -

Inside the facility, everyone on Level Four turned to look at the big screen and it was immediately obvious that the mysterious cloud covering the moon was indeed moving. As they watched, the moon appeared to look like a giant glass container and liquid was draining from it as the configuration melted away, sliding quickly from the top of the moon and emptying from the bottom, as if falling through a hole, into space, directly beneath the moon.

Fascinated, and spellbound, Clay and his staff watched in silence as the moon rapidly emptied and the cloud gathered itself into one condensed mass, stationary in its new position, as if waiting, menacingly in space. Within a matter of minutes, the surface of the moon cleared of the uninvited covering and, then, as those in the Piaute Mountain Facility watched, it began to move through space, away from the moon.

Sean MacTavish broke the silence as he yelled, "Look! That thing is heading towards Earth."

Everyone rushed to their consoles, and Clay yelled at Sean, "Mac, give us a grid map of the world and have Solomon track that thing. As soon as possible, give me an estimated time of arrival."

Turning to Karl, he barked, "Karl, step up the communications process. Do everything you can to establish contact with it. Try everything."

"Will do, Clay," Karl yelled back.

"Diane," Clay said, "Get the president on the line. Use the video phone; and then call General Whiteside or General Petrie at NASA. Also, alert the Defense Department. I'm sure they know what's happening, but call them anyway."

Seating himself at the command console in the middle of the room, Clay activated Solomon's synthesized voice system. He ran a few quick checks and then spoke into the microphone, "Solomon, this is Dr. Davis. Please acknowledge."

"Dr. Davis, this is Solomon."

Diane caught Clay's eye, motioned to the phone, and gave him a salute to indicate the president was on the line. Clay nodded, flipped the switch on his video monitor, selected the right channel, and the president's image appeared. "Hello, Mr. President."

"Hello, Clay. You have something for us?"

Clay answered quickly, "Mr. President, the cloud is moving."

The president leaned forward and asked, "Toward earth?"

"It would appear so, Sir. We're tracking it right now but unless it changes direction, it will intercept earth on its present course."

The president started to say something but Clay interrupted. "Pardon me, Sir, Dr. MacTavish has something."

"Clay," MacTavish announced, "the alien is moving in the direction of earth and should reach our atmosphere within fifty two minutes. As near as we can make out, the alien force is moving at a speed of two hundred forty-nine thousand miles per hour and will enter the earth's atmosphere over California. And if it continues on its present trajectory, it will travel in a westerly direction."

"Did you get that, Mr. President?" Clay asked.

The president had a curious look on his face as he asked, "Did I understand correctly? That thing is moving at two hundred forty-nine thousand miles per hour?"

Clay looked over at Sean, who nodded confirmation.

"That's the figure we estimate, Sir."

"Clay, it can't be moving that fast."

Clay turned around and studied his monitor with the grid map. The computer-enhanced configuration was moving down the screen, covering giant hunks of space at an incredible rate of speed.

"Mr. President, that is correct."

The president asked hopefully, "Is there any chance it will pass us by and continue on in space?"

"Mr. President," Clay answered sadly, "I don't think it will miss us." He added, "And if you'll forgive me, Mr. President, at the rate of speed it's travelling and on its present course, you might want to consider leaving the state as soon as possible. We have no idea what to expect as it moves into our atmosphere."

"We'll be considering that possibility, Clay. Has Adam Armstrong arrived yet?"

"No, Sir, he hasn't."

"As soon as he gets there, have him call me."

"Yes, Mr. President, I will." "Anything else, Clay?"

"No, Sir. That's it. We're still trying to establish contact with whatever it is and we're still trying to figure out what it is. If we come up with anything, we'll let you know immediately."

"Thank you, Clay. I have to leave the line now. Keep me advised." The monitor went blank.

Clay turned toward Sean and said, "Mac, give me a time reference on the alien's arrival."

MacTavish looked at his note pad, made a quick calculation, and answered, "At its present rate of speed, Clay, it should be reaching our atmosphere in forty-nine minutes. That will be roughly about 8:19 a.m."

Diane spoke from across the room. "Clay, I can't reach Whiteside or Petrie at NASA. They've left and no one knows how to contact them."

Clay muttered under his breath, "Why is it when you need a general you never can find one? I wonder where they are?"

- - - - - - - - - - - -

The two generals were at that moment only thirty miles away, in a small military jet, taxiing to the apron of the small airport that serviced the Hawthorne Munitions Depot. Throughout the flight from Houston, the two men reviewed the detailed plans of the final phase of their covert operation. Occupying their interest primarily were two lists of names, which they studied and discussed at length. One list, of more than eighty names, represented the nucleus of their plan. They were the names of individuals who would be immediately eased into key government positions the moment the final phase began.

The second list, consisting of more than one hundred thirty names, represented question marks or potential problems for their plan. It had been decided long ago, that if the men and women on this list did not cooperate fully and immediately, they would be terminated. A special termination squad was already on alert, awaiting word from either general, ready to eliminate any or all of the names on the list.

By the time the plane landed, the two generals were finished reviewing their plans and as the small jet pulled to a stop in front of the Operations Center, both men were ready to implement the final steps that would eventually, they thought, restore their country to greatness.

General Whiteside got off of the plane first and walked immediately to the small office adjacent to the hangar. There, waiting to greet him, was a nervous colonel, not quite sure what to expect from the unannounced arrival of a four-star general at the crack of dawn. As the general walked up, the officer snapped to attention, saluted smartly, and said, "Good morning, Sir. I'm Colonel Morrison. This is an unexpected pleasure."

"Colonel, I'm in a hurry. I'm going to need transportation, ten of your best military policemen, and I want to leave here as soon as possible. We'll chat later but right now, get moving."

The surprised colonel managed to stammer a few "Yes, Sirs," and hastily moved inside to phone the barracks and motor pool of the general's requests. As Whiteside paced the small office and the nervous colonel stood near the phone, General Petrie entered the door, followed closely by the two aides who had accompanied the generals from Houston.

Petrie walked immediately to the telephone, picked it up, and announced to Whiteside, "I guess I'll call and let them know we're coming up. This will no doubt make their day."

"Yeah, call Davis and let him know he has company for breakfast."

Within thirty minutes, Gen. Matthew Whiteside and Gen. Norman Petrie, accompanied by ten armed soldiers passed through the Hawthorne Munitions Depot gate. Neither general paid any attention to the three large combat helicopters passing over their heads as they left, but the Colonel watching their departure observed the craft immediately. He wondered what surprise was in store for him next as he watched the helicopters slowly descend to the apron in front of his office. Then, he nearly swallowed the cigarette in his mouth. On the side of the lead helicopter, clearly identifiable, was the presidential seal. "What the heck is going on?" he muttered aloud.

He watched in amazement as a tall young man jumped from the helicopter and ran in his direction. Close on his heels, jumping from the remaining two helicopters and following the running man closely were more than a dozen armed soldiers. Confused, the officer snapped to attention and said crisply, "Good morning, Sir. I'm Colonel Morrison."

"Colonel, I'm Michael O'Conner, aide to Vice President Adam Armstrong. Sorry for dropping in on you unannounced like this, but we need a staff car and two vans to carry us up to the Piaute Mountain Facility."

The Colonel, a little flustered, answered immediately, "Yes, Sir. Of course. I'll get what you need right away."

As he disappeared through the doors of the Operations Building, Adam Armstrong made his way across the rampart and as he approached Michael, asked, "What time is it, Michael?"

"Twenty past eight, Sir."

"Call the facility and tell them we'll be there in twenty five minutes."

"Will do, Sir." He opened the door, allowing Armstrong to enter and followed, looking around for the nearest phone. The Colonel, sensing his needs, pointed to one on a desk. Before he could pick up the phone, however, a bell began to ring furiously on the office Teletype machine. The Colonel froze, stared at the machine, then rushed over to read the incoming message. He studied the typed words for a moment, then spun around, almost yelling, "It's from Washington. We've gone on full military alert."

Armstrong walked over to the printer and read the message. "It doesn't offer any reason or explanation," he observed.

"Whatever the reason, Sir, it's pretty serious. The code name being used means this is not just a drill. We're on full military alert because something serious has happened." The Colonel turned quickly to his desk, grabbed his phone and began issuing orders to someone in another office.

At that moment, a car and two vans arrived. Armstrong looked at Michael, nodded his head, and the two made their exit, leaving the Colonel barking into his phone at a junior officer.

Armstrong spoke to the driver of the staff car. "Do you know where the Piaute Mountain Facility is located?"

The army private nodded.

"That's where we want to go."

As he entered the car, the soldiers quickly climbed into the vans and, at a signal from the vice president, proceeded toward the main gate and Piaute Mountain.

# 16.

# Chapter Sixteen

At 8:17 a.m., Saturday morning, the alien cloud entered the earth's atmosphere at a point high in the sky above the western edge of the Rocky Mountains. Sean MacTavish yelled, "Clay, check the monitor."

Clay turned to face the wall monitor and watched in fascination as the cloud became stationary, holding a position just above the western United States. Then, the computer-enhanced configuration began to expand in a longitudinal direction until it formed a thin band stretching from the north polar region to the opposite pole.

"Clay, if that thing drops to earth it will land right in the area that includes all the coastal regions of Washington, Oregon, and California." He paused and added, "That includes the city of Los Angeles."

"Diane, get the president," Clay barked. Looking over at Chuck, he asked, "Any luck on the communications?"

"Not a thing, Clay," Chuck answered. "We've tried everything in the data bank and we've received nothing. I don't know what else to do."

"Keep transmitting something," Clay ordered. "Karl, how about you? Anything on your analysis of the cloud yet?"

"No," Karl fired back. "But we're beginning to get some very strange readings from NASA. Their weather satellite is reporting extremely hot temperatures in the atmosphere and a tremendous amount of electrical energy."

Diane waved her hand at Clay. "President's coming on the line." She added, "Butterly just called from upstairs. He just received word that General Whiteside and General Petrie are on their way here from Hawthorne."

Clay looked at her, confused. "Armstrong's coming. Now those two. What are we having here? A convention?"

"What's going on, Clay?"

The president's voice drew Clay's attention back to his console. Looking at the monitor and the president, he said, "Sir, the alien cloud is now hanging over the western part of the country and if it settles to earth, Los Angeles will be in its path. I suggest you take cover immediately."

"We've already received word to that effect Clay, and we plan to leave in about ten minutes. Has Armstrong arrived yet?"

"Not yet, Sir. But I've just been informed that General Whiteside and General Petrie are on their way."

"Whiteside and Petrie? Were you expecting them?" "No, Mr. President."

The president turned away from the video camera and said something to another person in the office. When he returned on camera, he said, "Clay, I want you to turn off your video and pick up your telephone. I need to talk to you in private."

Clay did as he was told and said, "All right, Sir, we're on a secured line."

"Clay, I want to ask you something and I want you to be completely candid with me."

Puzzled, Clay replied, "Of course, Mr. President."

The president hesitated, then said, "Clay, there is the possibility, remote I admit, but still a possibility that the appearance of this mysterious cloud might somehow be connected to a conspiracy to overthrow the government of the United States."

"A conspiracy, Mr. President? To overthrow the government?"

"Yes, Clay. I can't go into details but I need to know where you stand?"

"Where I stand, Mr. President?"

The president hesitated, then continued. "If a problem develops within the government and we have a situation to contend with that demands we have complete trust and loyalty from you, am I going to be able to count on your support?".

"Of course, you can count on me, Mr. President," Clay assured him. But, puzzled, he asked, "However, I'm not sure what you're trying to say." "Clay, I have to know where your priorities are in terms of loyalty. Where does your first loyalty rest? With the military? With your computer? With your government?"

Clay didn't hesitate. "My first loyalty, Mr. President, is to God and then my government or president."

The president was not expecting such an answer from Clay, but as he thought about it for a moment, he seemed satisfied. "That's good enough for me, Clay. Now, here's what I want you to do." He quickly explained his wishes and when he finished, he asked, "Do you understand what I want, Clay?"

Grim-faced, Clay replied, "Yes, Sir. I understand completely. You can count on me and my staff."

"Good. Now, I want you to leave this line open so we can be advised immediately of any changes by the alien cloud. Thank you, Clay."

Clay replaced his telephone, switched the channel back to video, turned to Diane, and said, "We need to keep the line to the president open, so don't change channels."

He started to say something else but was interrupted by Mac-Tavish, who yelled out, "Here she comes. The alien is dropping to earth and beginning to move."

Simultaneously, the facility's Red Alert system sounded an alarm. The proximity of the alien force field, even though more than two hundred miles away, was close enough to trigger the warning and Solomon immediately activated the facility's defense system. As the siren sounded the alarm, Solomon shut down and sealed the underground facility. Within a matter of seconds, all doors and gates were secured, the great steel wall slammed shut, all emergency power generators were activated, and the facility was completely sealed off from the rest of the world. No one could leave—or enter.

James Butterly's voice crackled over the intercom. "Dr. Davis, what's going on? We're sealed off up here."

"I know, James. Solomon activated the defense system."

Butterly asked, "Are we under attack? My alert systems indicate everything is normal."

Clay answered, "We have a potential threat in the atmosphere, but I don't think it's going to affect us. This is just a precaution."

Art Gibson's voice, coming from the basement, interrupted the two men, "Dr. Davis, our generators are running, but we still have power coming in from the outside. Want me to shut them down?"

"No, Art," replied Clay. "Keep them operating and on stand-by. If we lose power from the outside, we won't have an interruption if the generators are functioning, right?"

"That's right, Doc. A circuit breaker will automatically switch from the outside source to our own power sources."

"That's what I thought. Keep them. . ."

Clay was interrupted by MacTavish. "The alien has landed," he screamed out excitedly. "It's at ground level and it's moving."

Clay glanced at the monitor to confirm MacTavish's observation and immediately yelled out to Karl. "Karl, interface the communications system in Denver and see what the Defense Department is getting on this."

He looked over at Chuck and barked, "See if you can hook up to the West Coast Defense Network."

"Mac," Clay called out. "Where is that thing and how fast is it moving?"

"It's somewhere near Los Angeles. I don't have an exact fix yet and I can't get a ground speed until I get another reference point."

"Stay on it," Clay said. Turning to Karl, he asked, "Do you have that. . ."

Clay was interrupted by a shriek of terror. Everyone looked in Diane's direction. She sat in front of her computer monitor, hands clasped prayer-like to her face, struggling to control the spasms shaking her body. Finally, in a shaking, quiet voice, almost a whisper, she announced, "The president is dead."

"What?" Clay screamed out.

"What happened?" Karl wanted to know.

She shook her head. "It all happened so fast, I'm not sure I know what happened. I just know he's dead."

"Chuck, stop the recorder a moment and rewind the video tape on the video phone monitor," Clay ordered. "And you need to play it back at a slower speed."

They waited as Chuck made the adjustment and then watched, horror mounting in their unbelieving eyes, at what they saw taking place in the president's office.

The president was talking to three men in his office, and as he talked, his housemaid or cook was arranging a tray of food on his desk. For a split second everyone in the room froze and those watching the monitor saw the tray of dishes begin to shake, as did the lamp, telephone, and other items on the president's desk. It was obvious the room was being shaken, as if by an earthquake. Suddenly, shattered glass exploded across the room as the windows in the president's office disintegrated. The explosion was accompanied by a loud whir-ring noise, filling the room with an ear-piercing sound. The screen revealed the picture of a cylindrical finger of cloud-like vapor shooting through the entire room. Clay and the staff watched as the smokey finger, emitting blue-white sparks of energy, paused for just a second and then expanded into a large mass.

Fear filled the eyes of those present but things happened so quickly, no sound left their lips. A blue-white dart of electricity shot forth, striking the Mexican-American cook standing by the president. Her body was jerked into the air and sucked upward where it slammed into the ceiling; then, it fell back to the floor in a lifeless heap. At the same instant, a fiery dart struck the president. He, too, was jerked into the air, lifted toward the ceiling, and, when his ascent was prohibited by the ceiling, fell to the floor. His body had disappeared and only a pile of smokey, smoldering ashes remained. A third person, quickly identified by Clay as Aaron Wheeler, was leaning down in front of the president's desk to pick up something and the blast from the exploding windows threw him under the desk, where he laid face down, unable to move but obviously untouched.

The two remaining men in the office, Warren Boyd, the presiden-tial aide, and Tom Barksdale, the press secretary were also attacked by the alien. Clay and the staff watched as they too were killed by the creature in the same manner as the president and his cook. First, a bolt of energy struck the men, and then their bodies were jerked into the air, off the floor, and lifted to the ceiling where, unable to continue, they fell back to the floor. There were no screams, no signs of pain. They simply ceased to exist. They disappeared.

Clay asked Chuck to play the tape one more time and as they watched the tragedy in slow motion a second time, Clay yelled out, "Freeze that frame, right there. Freeze it."

Chuck hit the pause button and the image frozen on the monitor was that of the president.

"Chuck, see if you can zoom in on his eyes." As this was done, he yelled out, "OK, that's good. Look at that. What do you make of that?"

Everyone studied the magnified section of the president's face. The eyes had ceased to appear human; instead, the pupils appeared only as two brilliantly bright shining lights.

Clay spoke to Chuck. "Now, advance it just a hair. Just a frame or two."

Chuck did as he was instructed and, suddenly, the eyes were without light. They were closed, lifeless.

"What do you make of that?" Clay asked again.

No one had an explanation for the sudden blinding light which obviously lasted only a millisecond. "All right, Chuck, speed up to the point where the bodies just disappear."

They watched, in silence, as Chuck fast-forwarded the video tape to the point where the bodies fell to the floor. Zooming in on the lifeless forms, it was apparent the body mass had disappeared.

"There's nothing there," MacTavish said.

"Nothing but ashes," Karl added.

Diane spoke up. "Aaron Wheeler is on the video phone."

Clay turned around and said, "General Wheeler, are you all right?"

The image on the monitor shook his head and said in a trembling voice, "I think so. What happened?"

"We don't know yet, Sir."

Wheeler looked around. "Everyone's gone." He looked into the camera. "Where have they gone? Why am I still here?"

Clay answered. "We don't know that either, Sir, but we're working on it." Clay thought a moment and then suggested, "General Wheeler, you'd better get word to Congress right away. Are you all right? Can you handle that? Someone needs to be advised that the president has disappeared."

Wheeler nodded affirmative. His voice still trembled when he replied. "I'll do it. I'll do it now. I need to get word to the vice president. Has he arrived there yet?"

Karl observed, "He's in shock."

Clay answered Wheeler. "No, Sir. He's on his way but he hasn't arrived yet. I'll advise him what has happened as soon as he gets here."

Mac caught Clay's attention and said, "The alien has moved off the coast of California now."

"Diane, start scanning all communications systems and see if you can get some damage reports or eyewitness reports or anything." Clay added, more to himself than to anyone in particular, "We need data. And we need it in a hurry."

Butterly's voice came over the intercom. "Doc, we have company."

Clay flipped the two-way switch on the intercom and asked, "Who's there?"

"General Whiteside and General Petrie are outside the main gate and they can't get in. And I can't let them in. Solomon has everything secured."

"Right, James, I understand. I'll have to deactivate the system and that's going to take a minute or two. Explain to the generals that it will take about five or ten minutes."

"Roger, will do."

Clay reached down to type a message to Solomon. Overriding the security system was a simple process but Clay had no intention of letting the visitors in. He was merely stalling for time. As he thought about what he should do, Mac spoke up.

"Clay, the alien is about a hundred miles off the coast of California and moving in a westerly direction at a speed of roughly twenty four thousand nine hundred miles per hour."

Clay digested that for a moment and observed, "Wow, that means the alien will be able to cover the entire earth in exactly one hour."

Karl yelled out, "Look at the screen. That thing seems to have a rear guard."

Clay looked up and watched as the computer-enhanced configuration inched its way across the Pacific. It was obvious that the alien's size and shape were expanding from its original position. It was not just moving, it was expanding, traveling forward, but as it moved, it was leaving the area in its wake a wall stretching from pole to pole.

"You're right. I didn't even notice that. I just thought maybe it was moving too fast for the computer to fix its position."

Clay studied the monitor for a moment. "It could be doing what it did on the moon," he suggested. "Maybe it's going to completely encircle the earth."

Mac made a quick calculation and said, "If it is, at the speed it's traveling it will do that in less than an hour."

Clay glanced at the clock. It was 8:40. "If that's what it's doing, it'll be arriving back here in less than forty minutes."

Butterly's voice interrupted again. "Doc, we have more company Dr. Armstrong just arrived and he wants in now."

"James, tell them we have to override Solomon's defense system. It will take a minute or two longer for me to do that."

Solomon's voice broke in: "Alien energy field is proceeding across the Pacific Ocean. If it maintains its present heading, it will reach Hawaii in four minutes and on its present course, Tokyo in thirteen minutes."

Chuck's voice yelled out, "I'm picking up a message from the West Coast Defense Center. A nuclear submarine in the Pacific has been ordered to fire a missile at the alien."

Diane reported, "The Soviet Union has scrambled a squadron of jet fighters to intercept the alien."

Butterly's voice came back on the intercom. "Doc, those people outside are getting a little impatient. What do you want me to tell them?"

Clay knew it was time to inform the Security Chief of what was happening so he said, "James, I have orders from the president of the United States not to let the generals into this facility. For your own information, they may be involved in a conspiracy plot and if that is true, you may have a fight on your hands. They are not to be allowed entrance. Can you handle that?"

There was a long pause at the other end and then James's excited voice replied, "You better believe I can."

Clay quickly added, "Just expect the worst and keep me advised on what's going on up there."

Karl looked over at Clay and asked, "What about Armstrong? The president told you to admit him and now, with the president gone, Armstrong is the president. You can't deny access to the president, Clay."

Clay shrugged. "I can't let one in without letting in the others. Armstrong will just have to wait outside with the generals."

"Clay, you can't do that. Armstrong is the president. That might be certain death for him out there in the open."

Clay knew Karl was right. But he also knew that if a conspiracy was in the making, and the two generals were indeed involved, he could not allow them access to Solomon. Too much power rested within those data banks.

Fortunately, a decision was postponed by Chuck, who announced, "Switch on your audio monitor, Clay. Something is coming in on the submarine."

Clay reached down, pushed a button, and immediately the room was filled with crackling static and a voice. They had to strain their ears to hear the faint voice as it reported, "All I know is that the commander of the submarine said he fired a nuclear warhead at the alien and then he yelled that nothing happened. I could hear him screaming into the microphone that his ship was being lifted out of the water. That was the last thing I heard."

"What kind of power are we dealing with here, Clay?" asked MacTavish. "I can't believe all this is happening."

Solomon's voice reported, "Alien is now passing through the islands of Hawaii. Alien will reach Tokyo in ten minutes."

Butterly's voice came back on. "Dr. Davis, you're going to have to do something. They're demanding that I let them in and I keep explaining that you're the only one who can open the facility. And they're demanding to talk to you. What do you want me to do, Doc?"

"Hold on a second, James." Clay ran the problem through his mind. Armstrong had the authority to enter, no doubt about that. His orders from the president, however, were explicit. The generals were not to be allowed access. Something else bothered Clay but he couldn't put his finger on it. And things were happening so fast he couldn't stop to retrieve the nagging thought from the recesses of his mind. He hesitated, and then instructed James, "Tell them we're having trouble overriding Solomon. Tell them we're working on the problem."

Karl looked at Clay. "That's a lie, Clay."

Clay shrugged.

Karl continued. "I don't understand you. That's the president of the United States out there."

"Karl, leave me alone. I need to think this out."

Meanwhile, outside the complex, standing at the entrance, were Armstrong, Whiteside, Petrie, Armstrong's armed escort, and Whiteside's Special Forces team. Armstrong and the two generals were trying to decide what to do.

"I don't understand the problem," Whiteside said.

"Neither do I," added Petrie. "All he has to do is program the override and the facility will open."

"I don't understand what's going on either," Armstrong said. "He has his orders direct from the president."

At that moment, Whiteside's aide came running from the staff car, yelling, "General, General Whiteside. We've just received a radio message from the Operations Officer at the Hawthorne Munitions Depot."

Impatiently, Whiteside asked, "What does he want? I don't have time..."

The aide interrupted him. "Sir, they just received a report from Washington. The president is dead."

"What?"

"The president is dead, Sir. It's been confirmed by Gen. Aaron Wheeler."

Whiteside exchanged quick glances with Petrie and Armstrong, then smiled. "I guess that means you are now automatically the president of the United States, Mr. President," he said, addressing Armstrong.

Petrie's face broke into a wide grin. "Suddenly everything is looking good."

Armstrong gave them a serious look and replied, "That does sort of make me the commander in chief, doesn't it? And I think my first official act will be directed toward this facility. Gentlemen, I think Clay Davis has succumbed to the pressure of the moment. I don't think he has any intentions of letting us in.  Therefore, I suggest we force our way inside."

"How are we going to do that, Mr. President?  This place is like a fortress," observed Petrie.

Armstrong smiled.  "My men have explosives with them.  I think we need to blast our way in."

Petrie shook his head approvingly.  "But, how do you plan to get past the wall.  Nothing is going to blast through that."

Whiteside patted him on the back.  "I have a little surprise for you, Norman.  First, let's just get past the first obstacle and the security guards."

- - - - - - - - - - - -

Jack and Ryan had no idea what was going on.  First, two generals arrived with an armed guard.  A short time later, another convoy arrived, carrying more armed soldiers and two men, one of whom Jack recognized as Adam Armstrong.  He and Ryan watched as they approached the entrance and, curiously, both wondered why they were acting so strangely.  Even more odd was the fact that it appeared the entrance was locked and the generals, with their contingent of soldiers, were being denied entrance.

"What do you think?" Ryan asked.

"Beats me, Ryan.  What I don't understand is why two generals and a member of the president's staff can't gain access to that place. I think they're locked out."

They watched the party below, obviously arguing with someone on the inside, and then one of the generals stomped away, gesturing wildly, angrily.

Ryan chuckled.  "Never thought I'd see the day when old Whiteside would lose his cool. Boy, he's mad."

Jack failed to see the humor because he sensed something was seriously wrong.  "Ryan, something is definitely going on down there and I don't like the looks of it.  First of all, why are they all here?"

Ryan reminded him, "They're all part of the conspiracy, aren't they?  Maybe your fears and assumptions are coming true."

"Lord, I hope not but I have to agree with you."  Cursing under his breath, he said, "What I can't figure out is this alien thing.  How does it connect with the conspiracy?  If this radio would only pull in another radio station or two,  maybe we could find out what's going on.  Heck, the president could be dead for all we know, and we wouldn't even know it."

# 17.

# ChapterSeventeen

Inside Solomon's Temple, Clay Davis and Karl Liederman studied the printout from Solomon in an attempt to understand the data that seemed to defy all normal laws of physics and chemistry.

"It just doesn't make sense, Karl," Clay said, puzzled.

"No, it doesn't. There is absolutely no clue here on what the thing is composed of, where its energy source is, or why it's behaving the way it is."

Diane's voice interrupted their discussion. "First ground level video reports are coming in." She quickly identified the source of the video. "This is coming from Los Angeles from one of the television stations. There is no sound, just video."

All eyes in the room focused on the screen as the dense cloud, like a giant fog bank, rolled in at treetop level from the hills east of Los Angeles. Jagged fingers of blue-white lightning shot forth from the low-flying cloud, probing and searching the city; and in its wake, as it passed over the city, at random intervals, soundless explosions erupted on the screen with a burst of fire and smoke. The earth could be seen trembling, shaking, splitting open, and the tremors added to the devastation being wrought. In a matter of seconds, even in slow motion, the leading edge of the cloud passed over the giant city, but a churning, swirling mass of lightning-filled whiteness remained, hanging stationary over the city like a threatening storm cloud.

It quickly became obvious to those watching the video film that the enormous damage and carnage depicted on the screen was being caused not only by the cloud but because of the cloud. Panic-stricken people were leaping from buildings, landing in a sickening, soundless jolt on the pavement below. Fear-filled motorists slammed their cars into each other with metalwrenching, often death-dealing, consequences. Pedestrians, in a futile attempt to escape the onrushing cloud, darted into the paths of moving trucks and cars and busses and their mangled and lifeless bodies were flung and thrown about like so many sacks of wasted rags. Others, streaming from buildings into the streets, knocked down those who got in their way, trampling over their bodies in crazed fear. But even as the terrified populace was killing not only themselves but each other, it was apparent that the alien cloud was wreaking its own type of annihilation. In what appeared to be a haphazard manner, lightning bolts searched out and destroyed. In automobiles, car tops were ripped open with a burst of electricity, killing the passengers instantly, sucking their bodies out of the vehicles and into the swirling cloud mass. Supercharged tentacles of energy sought out and attacked pedestrians standing in the streets, running for cover, in hiding, and, in some cases, even attacking the mangled and lifeless bodies of those struck down by vehicles rolling amuck.

Slowly the scene changed as the cameraman panned a large area of the city. Random and isolated pockets of destruction appeared on the screen. Small portions of the city remained untouched but there were areas where the devastation was complete. It was as if the alien had specifically designated certain targets for destruction, while leaving huge parts of the city untouched and free from its wrath. Even more strange was the fact that graveyards had been decimated by the alien. In its gruesome attempt to—what appeared to be—feed upon dead bodies, havoc had been wreaked as vaults were opened and headstones overturned in its unexplainable and ghastly search.

Clay and his staff watched in stunned silence as the scene of death and destruction left in the alien's wake paraded past their eyes. The seemingly wanton carnage of the huge city held them spellbound and speechless. Finally, Clay broke the heavy silence of the room and quietly said, "It's incredible."

For the first time, fear began to surface within the room as those watching the monitor realized they were dealing with something that went beyond man's understanding and knowledge.

Sean MacTavish nervously offered, "I don't know about you people, but if I wasn't watching it, I wouldn't believe it and I'm watching it and I still don't believe it."

Clay struggled to calm himself, not trusting his voice to comment but, finally, said, "Well, we now have a little more to work with. Let's get busy and analyze what we have."

Turning to Diane, he said, "I don't know how you're going to do it, but we need the identities of as many dead and living as possible. Maybe the Los Angeles police can give us a hand in this. Tell them we have to have that as soon as possible. We don't have much time."

"What do you plan to do, Clay?" asked Chuck.

Clay answered, "We'll run all the names through Solomon and see if we can arrive at some logical explanation for the alien to attack some but ignore others. It may be just an indiscriminate selection by the alien, but it also may mean that some people are immune."

He continued. "If we can compare personal histories or physical characteristics of the victims and survivors, maybe Solomon can detect a pattern or reason for its behavior." He thought a moment and added, "If we can come up with a defense against it, we can then figure out how to destroy it." Looking at Diane, he said, "We need the names of the victims and survivors so Solomon can compare and contrast any similarities or parallelism." He stopped for a moment and, catching Diane's eye, added in a firm tone of voice, "All that information stored in Solomon's data banks will come in handy now. Maybe we can get a handle on the alien's behavior."

As Diane jumped to follow Clay's instructions, Solomon's synthesized voice interrupted Clay. "The alien is now approaching the coast of Japan and will be reaching Tokyo momentarily. On its present course and at its present rate of speed, the alien will reach Calcutta in eight minutes."

MacTavish shook his head. "That sucker is covering some ground in a hurry."

Karl chimed in, "Clay, I think you need to reconsider your position and get Dr. Armstrong down here. At the rate that thing is moving, it's going to be here in just over a half hour."

"Karl, you need to concentrate on analyzing the data we have. I'll worry about Armstrong."

Chuck Valens yelled out, "Clay, we're getting a news report from one of the television networks."

Everyone turned to face the screen as a network commentator began reporting on the alien visit.

"We don't have much at this time, but what we do have is staggering. The alien cloud touched down at 8:19 a.m. Pacific Standard Time and the results, although sketchy, defy belief. For an on-the-spot, up-to-the-minute report, we now switch you to our reporter in San Francisco."

The picture on the screen changed to that of a newsman, on a hill, with the Golden Gate Bridge in the background. He somberly began: "This is Edward Albritten in San Francisco and we're on a hill overlooking an unbelievable scene. In the background you can see the tremendous traffic jam on the Golden Gate Bridge. Over a hundred automobile collisions have brought traffic on the bridge to a standstill. No one can move. The story is pretty much the same on the major thoroughfares of the city. We estimate that literally thousands have died, their bodies littering the streets, and we understand that thousands more have simply vanished into thin air. Fires are scattered across the city, blazing uncontrollable as fire workers are either unable to reach the scene because of the traffic jams or because the fire stations themselves were decimated by the alien. We'll have more to report in a minute but right now let's switch you to Charles Murray in Seattle."

Again, the picture changed but the scene remained the same. Charles Murray, a news reporter, stood in downtown Seattle, in an area similar in destruction to San Francisco. He spoke in a shaking, hysterical voice: "Here in Seattle, we have been unable to verify the extent of damage and loss of life but it appears destruction has been massive. In downtown Seattle, buildings are burning, people are still

dying and rescue teams are virtually nonexistent. Bodies line the
streets as far as the eye can see and all that remains of those directly
attacked by the alien are piles of smouldering ashes. It seems that those
attacked by the alien creature were destroyed in just a matter of
seconds. We've just been told that . . . "

The report ended, the screen went blank, and a few more seconds
passed before the network anchorman came back on the monitor: "We
apologize for the interruption in that report. We take you now to San
Diego and Roger Murphy for this report."

A new face appeared on the screen and the reporter, almost
hysterically, announced, "We don't know what is going on at this
time. All communications within the city have been disrupted. We
can only report on what we see at the moment. There are dead bodies
everywhere. People jumped to their death from high-rise buildings.
All vehicular traffic went berserk, smashing into each other, running
over pedestrians, crashing into buildings. In the background you can
hear the screams from those still trapped in burning or wrecked cars.
All across the city, houses, buildings, schools, even a few churches
and synagogues are burning. As far as we can determine, the alien
cloud is using electrical projectiles to kill and destroy. Overhead, the
cloud is still here but it has calmed down."

The anchorman suddenly appeared on the screen as the network
cut away from the San Diego report. "We interrupt this report to bring
you an up-to-the-minute account from our studios in downtown Burbank."

The image of another reporter filled the screen. He began to speak
in a calm, unhurried voice. "Authorities are now beginning to assess
the damage done by the invading force. Eyewitness reports from those
who managed to escape the alien attack indicate that death from the
alien is instantaneous. Whatever it is approaches with a loud whirring
noise and seems to select victims at random and those selected are
literally lifted off the ground and sucked into the cloud."

Solomon's voice cut across the laboratory: "Alien is now leaving
Japan and moving into the Soviet Union and China. Estimate alien to
reach Calcutta in seven minutes."

"Clay," Chuck yelled out. "Switch the monitor over to channel
seven. This is weird."

Clay reached over, hit a switch and as the picture filled the screen,
Chuck said, "This is an airborne video from an army helicopter. I think
we're getting a view of the rear guard of the alien."

In appearance, it looked like a cloud line formed by a cold front.
In a straight line, the cloud stretched north and south as far as the
camera eye could see, holding a position just above the ground at
treetop level. Unlike the cloud of a weather front, though, it was
perfectly perpendicular as if someone had taken a giant cleaver and
sliced away a part of it, leaving a towering vertical wall reaching
skyward. Clay watched, puzzled at first, and then the realization of

what he was viewing registered. "Good grief," he exclaimed. "It's a force field keeping people out."

The alien was, indeed, prohibiting entrance to the area covered by the cloud. The monitor clearly revealed that vehicles were leaving the area, and there was a steady stream of those, propelled by panic-stricken people who escaped the initial onslaught of the alien and were trying to leave the area in case the creature attacked again. However, what captured Clay's attention were the cars and trucks trying to enter the area, no doubt to reach loved ones or homes, or, perhaps, simply unaware of what had happened. These were being repelled by an invisible barrier or wall. Vehicles attempting to enter the area simply crashed headlong into an unseen, invisible barrier.

The highway was strewn with crushed and mangled automobiles that were obviously the first to reach the scene and had driven unsuspectingly into an invisible steel wall. Other cars slowed, stopped, and, as Clay and the staff watched the monitor, a gigantic line of stalled bumper-to-bumper traffic stretched east along the highway.

"Look at that," yelled out Chuck.

One soul, braver than the rest, walked cautiously to the point where the barrier was located and was trying to put his hand through the transparent wall but it was perfectly obvious to those watching that whatever was there, was impenetrable. Another man, encouraged no doubt by the bravery of the first, walked up to the barrier and tried the same experiment. Instantly, a blue-white missile of energy shot from the cloud and his lifeless, seemingly weightless body was sucked into the cloud.

The picture on the monitor became an instant scene of panic as hundreds jumped into their cars, sped across the median and attempted to force their way into the eastbound lane of traffic. Cars sideswiped each other, crashed into each other, forced one another off the road; and, as if to demonstrate that escape was impossible, the alien began attacking vehicles at random. Fingers of lightning shot forth from the wall, striking cars with an unbelievable force, ripping metal open like paper, and seizing the passengers inside.

Within a matter of seconds, the entire area became a blazing inferno, a living nightmare, as gasoline tanks began to explode and burn out of control.

Clay managed to detach himself from the scene and with a mighty effort returned to the immediate reality of his task. "Chuck, can we make contact with that helicopter?"

"I don't know, Clay," Chuck answered. "I can try."

"See if you can and see if he is reporting anything unusual on his instrument panel."

"Clay, we got lucky," Diane yelled out. "The Los Angeles Police Department can provide us with the names of all the policemen killed or spared. The names are coming in now and I'll feed them directly to Solomon."

"Good!" exclaimed Clay. "But keep trying to get more because all these names are linked together—they're policemen. Try to get a more diversified listing of victims and survivors."

"I'm working on that." Diane looked at her notes. "One of the hospitals is feeding me a list of the patients who survived the attack and that will include their medical histories."

"Great," Clay said. "As soon as the info is fed to us, get everything compared. Blood types, age, nationality, race, sex, whatever. Compare everything and see if there are any common threads among either the victims or the survivors."

He then turned to Chuck. "Any luck with that helicopter pilot?"

"Clay, I can't get the pilot but I can hear him talking to his commanding officer and you were right. His instrument panel has gone haywire. None of his instruments are reacting properly and, get this, his magnetic compass is pointing west, not north."

"I thought that might be the case," Clay said. "The alien is creating a force field just like ours, with electrical energy." He allowed himself a hopeful smile. "Now, it's using something I understand."

MacTavish asked, "Why are people allowed to leave the area but no one is allowed to enter?"

"Your guess is as good as mine, Sean." Clay added, "What intrigues me is that the alien will attack one, skip one, attack another. Is there some design or plan we're missing? Why are some people immune? That's what we have to find out."

Turning to Karl, Clay asked, "Have we exhausted every possible means of communicating with the creature?"

"Yes. It hasn't responded to anything we've transmitted."

Chuck volunteered, "Maybe it doesn't have intelligence. Maybe it's just a freak of nature, a physical force born in outer space."

"Then where does it get its energy?" asked Karl. "It seems to be feeding on humans."

Clay glanced at his watch, checked the time against the large clock on the wall. Then, with a sudden thought, he reached over to flip the intercom on and paged Art Gibson. "Art, you down there?"

"I'm right here, Chief."

"I want you to come upstairs and connect the force field generators."

"Right now?"

Clay looked at the clock again. "Yes. Let's get it done as quickly as possible."

"I'm on my way," Art responded.

Clay flipped the intercom switch to its neutral position, signaled to Diane, and, with a wave of his hand, indicated he wanted her to go to his office. She nodded.

Clay looked over at MacTavish and said, "Sean, watch the board a moment, please. I need to tell Diane something." "Gotcha, Chief," replied Sean, stepping over to the main console.

Clay followed Diane into his office and once they were inside the darkened room, he shut the door.

Obviously frustrated and needing support, he turned and pulled her into his arms. As their bodies pressed together, he reached, raised her face and kissed her gently on the lips.

"We don't have much time in here."

"I know," she answered. "We'll have to get right back."

In a concerned voice, Clay said, "I have no idea what's going to happen in the next half hour so I wanted just a minute alone with you."

"I'm glad," she said softly.

"Are you afraid?" he asked.

"Yes, a little."

"Don't be," he assured her. "Nothing can get inside this facility. Not even the alien. And I'll figure out a way to stop it."

"What if you can't? And what if it does get in here?"

"We still have the force field. That can stop anything."

He kissed her again. "I probably don't say it often enough, but I love you very much."

"I know," she said, laying her head on his shoulder.

Clay took a deep breath and said, "About last night. I want you to understand that it wasn't my idea to steal that money from the Russians. The whole plan was authorized by General Whiteside and practically all of the money went to the Defense Department. I really didn't see any harm in taking from the bad guys. I just didn't think of it as stealing. I'm sorry that it ever happened."

She cuddled deeper into his arms. "Let's not talk about it any more."

Then, nervously, not wanting to approach the subject in a dark office four stories beneath the ground, he said, "Last night I wanted to walk you to the top of the mountain after dinner but we started arguing and then Butterly showed up. Well, listen, I know I have a lot of faults and sometimes I'm not too easy to get along with but I love you so very much. I can't envision going through life without you by my side."

Clay slipped to one knee in front of her and reaching into his pocket to retrieve the ring box he had been carrying since the previous evening, said, "Diane . . ."

He was interrupted by Sean opening the door. He stuck his head in and said, "Clay, I hate to bother you but Butterly has an emergency upstairs."

Clay stepped quickly through the door and followed Mac to the main console. He switched on the two-way intercom and asked, "What's the problem, James?"

I think Whiteside and his people are getting ready to blow the main entrance."

"You gotta be kidding."

"I'm not. The gate intercom is still on and I can hear them talking. They're putting plastic explosives on the entrance."

Clay reached over and hit another switch, which connected him to the people standing outside. "Armstrong, what are you doing?"

Armstrong's voice came back. "You've been told to let me in and since you won't, I'm letting myself in."

Clay's voice replied urgently, "Adam, you don't understand. I have my orders from the president."

"The president is dead, Davis. I am the president and I am ordering you to let me in. I need access to Solomon."

Clay continued. "Adam, you don't understand. The president told me not to allow Petrie and Whiteside into this complex. Adam, I would let you in but you're with them. I can't let them in."

There was a loud expletive over the speaker and General Whiteside's voice boomed through. "What are you talking about? I don't believe the president issued those orders."

Armstrong barked, "We're coming in, Davis. With or without your assistance. This is your last chance. Are you going to open the gate?"

"No," Clay answered.

"So be it," Armstrong said.

James Butterly broke in. "Chief, what do I do if they manage to break through the gate?"

"James, if they get through and penetrate as far as the main security gate, what are the chances of keeping them from gaining access to the elevators?"

"Chief, I think we could take them if we had to. They have to come through that narrow walkway and they'd be sitting ducks."

He added, "Even if they did get this far, the wall will hold them. Nothing they have can penetrate solid steel."

"James, let me know the second they come through the outside gate. Is that clear?"

"I understand, Doc."

Solomon spoke. "Alien force has now reached Calcutta. It is still moving on a westerly course and will reach Rome in eleven minutes."

As Clay looked at his watch, Art Gibson stepped from the elevator. It was 8:46 a.m. and if the alien was encircling the globe, only thirty minutes remained before it returned to its original starting point, which would include Piaute Mountain. Clay wondered if the facility would be immune from the alien's attack and as he began to instruct Art on where he wanted the force field generators placed, he wondered also if they would be able to stop the invader.

# 18.

# Chapter Eighteen

**J**ames Butterly was on an adrenalin high. Ever since joining the super-secret Piaute Mountain facility, he had envisioned how he would react in the event of an emergency—particularly one involving an intruding force. It appeared that he would get the opportunity to find out. Quickly gathering his men around him, he explained the situation, assigned them to strategic points in and around the main security entrance, and then sat back to wait. The monitor was still operational, and he could see a group of men huddled around the main outside gate. From bits and pieces of their conversation, he was able to deduce that they were planting an explosive charge.

He wasn't worried, or scared; he was excited. Even if they managed to open the main gate, which was doubtful, the group outside still had to maneuver over an area nearly sixty feet long and only twelve feet wide. The open walkway provided no obstacles or obstructions which could be used as a shield and he knew it would be like shooting ducks in a gallery. If by some miracle the military contingent did penetrate as far as the Security Office, they would be halted by the fourteen-feet-thick steel wall, with an equally thick vault door, guarding access to the facility's interior.

Meanwhile, several stories below, in SOLOMON's Temple, Diane was speaking to Clay: "We are getting something from Tokyo now." She listened for a moment, then said, "No video, just audio."

Clay reached over and switched on the loudspeakers so all could listen to the report, but the static was too bad. "Diane, can you make out anything?"

Straining to listen through the headset on her ears, she began to share what she was hearing: "The U.S. Embassy reports that nearly twenty percent of the staff has been killed by the alien, and the air base outside of Tokyo is reporting almost thirty-five percent casualties. The U.S. Trade Mart is also reporting heavy casualties." She continued to strain her ears, then remarked, "The Japanese Defense Department is reporting only scattered casualties and damage."

"MacTavish said, "It's overlooking the Orientals.""

Karl observed, "Well, shortly it will be moving into Europe and maybe we can get a more clear picture of what is going on."    Clay started to say something, but sirens began to sound throughout the room and he knew immediately that security had been breached. Armstrong and the generals had obviously managed to blow the gate open.

Clay flipped the intercom switch and asked, "James, what is going on?"

Butterly quickly replied. "They've blown the main gate, but they still can't get in. We're watching them on the television monitor, and it looks as if they're putting another explosive charge in place. I don't think the door is going to hold, Doc."

Clay reached over and flipped the surveillance monitor on. He could see Armstrong and General Whiteside leaning over two soldiers and it was obvious they were planting another charge. "Adam, can you hear me?"

There was no response and Butterly said, "I think that explosion knocked the speaker system out, Doc."

"James, is the remote control on the television camera still operative?"

"As far as I know."

"See if you can tell how many of them there are," Clay instructed.

"I already know, Sir. Counting the two generals and Armstrong, there are more than twenty-five people." He added, "They're all armed."    Clay asked, "How many security people do you have in the complex, James?"

Butterly, who had already figured that out, answered, "Twelve, counting myself."

"How many people in the complex altogether?" Clay wanted to know.

"Let's see, Chief," Butterly began, "there's twelve of us, Art Gibson, the five of you downstairs, and I think Mary Beth and Kathryn are somewhere down there. I guess we have twenty people inside."

The president had been very specific. He could not let Whiteside and Petrie take control of SOLOMON. Clay sighed. "James, they must not penetrate the complex."

"Chief, don't worry about a thing. My boys know their business. We'll keep them out."

Clay flipped the switch off and turned to Karl. "Karl, have you finished the analysis?"

Karl shook his head. "Clay, we're still analyzing everything, but we're getting nowhere. There doesn't seem to be any common threads that can pull this together."

"Nothing matches?" Clay asked.

"Nothing corresponds. We've tried every imaginable factor and nothing matches."

Clay suddenly remembered something they might have over-looked and he said hopefully, "Karl, remember that news report we had? Someplace in California. Maybe it was Burbank. Anyway, the reporter said the cloud seemed to have a whirring noise, like a low frequency hum or something."

"Yes, I remember that," Karl said excitedly as he realized what Clay was going to suggest.

"Let's analyze that noise. Run it through a sound wave spectrum, and let's identify the frequency of that noise. Then, try transmitting on that frequency and see if we can establish communication."

Karl nodded in agreement and began to work on the problem while Clay leaned back in his swivel chair, trying to analyze and separate logical possibilities from the illogical ones.

SOLOMON's voice softly announced, "The alien force has reached Rome. It will reach London in three minutes. Estimated time of arrival on the eastern seaboard of the United States now fourteen minutes. If alien continues to travel at its present rate of speed, it will arrive this location in nineteen minutes."

Butterly's voice cracked excitedly over the intercom: "They've blown the gate open. They're coming in. We're standing by."

As Butterly finished, Art Gibson said to Clay: "The force field generators are all hooked up, Dr. Davis. You can turn them on anytime you want, by hitting this switch." He pointed to a switch on the console. "They'll come on automatically."

"Thanks, Art." Then Clay had an idea. "Art, can you make the elevator inoperative?"     "Sure, that's no problem. I can have the computer downstairs turn it off."

"Do it. Get downstairs and turn that elevator off." He added, in a softer tone, "And please hurry."

Art smiled grimly and left for the elevator. As he waited for the elevator to come back down, he wondered why Davis wanted the force field generators connected. Art knew that the Piaute Mountain facility was theoretically impregnable and that no one could break into the complex once everything was sealed and secured, so he assumed that Davis was simply adding a little extra insurance by installing the force field generators in the Temple.

The elevator arrived and as Art stepped in, he was surprised to see Mary Beth. "Hi, little girl. Where are you going?"

Flustered and scared-looking, Mary Beth said breathlessly, "I was looking for you, Mr. G."

The elevator doors closed and began to descend. "For me? What in the . . .?" Before Art could finish his sentence, he gasped then broke out coughing. He looked at the cigar he was smoking earlier and observed, "I used to enjoy these things, but they're beginning to taste terrible. I don't even want to smoke them anymore."

Mary Beth looked at him curiously. "You know, Kathryn and I noticed the same thing with our cigarettes. In fact, I haven't smoked one today. They taste too repulsive."          "Well, maybe we're getting rid of a nasty habit. Now, why were you looking for me?"

"I'm scared."

Art tried to reassure her. "There's not a thing to be scared of. Nothing can get in this place."

"That's what scares me," Mary Beth said. "If nothing can get in, nothing can get out."

Art looked at her, puzzled. "Why would you want to get out?"

"What if that alien thing breaks in or something else goes wrong and I'm up in my office by myself? How can I get out of here?"

Art studied her for a moment and said, "I shouldn't tell you this, Mary Beth, but if it will make you feel better, there is a way to get out. On the wall by the vault door is a fire alarm switch. It's right by the door and says, IN CASE OF FIRE, BREAK GLASS AND PULL SWITCH. It's not a fire alarm. If you have to get out, all you need to do is break the glass and pull the switch three times. That will open the vault door."

"Oh, Mr. G.," she said in a relieved voice, "that makes me feel better."

The elevator stopped on the basement floor, the doors opened, and Art stepped out. He turned, put his hand on her shoulder reassuringly and said, "Don't worry. Nothing is going to happen." The doors closed, leaving him, and the elevator carrying Mary Beth returned to the upper levels.          Back in SOLOMON's Temple, Karl turned to Davis. "Clay, we have that whirring noise frequency isolated."

"Great, Karl. Start trying to establish contact with the alien on that frequency."

"Clay, we've already tried," Karl said. "We're getting no response. The frequency is a dead end."

A hushed voice came from the intercom. "Chief, they're coming down the walkway now. I'm going to leave the intercom on so you can hear what's going on." Butterly added, "If you want to watch, plug into the security video system."

Clay immediately threw the appropriate switch and the monitor screen displayed a split-screen image of what was happening on the main level. One side of the image depicted Butterly and his security guards placed strategically around the main entrance way and the other side of the screen displayed the walkway leading to the main level entrance from the outside.

Ten soldiers moved stealthily and cautiously along either side of the narrow walkway, their small automatic weapons held in ready position. James Butterly, crouched behind a metal retaining wall guarding the path to the vault door, raised up and yelled out, "That's far enough, soldiers."

The soldiers stopped, looked at each other, and then continued, hugging the wall of the walkway.

Butterly repeated his warning. "I said that's far enough. This is your last warning." The soldiers again stopped, looked to their rear, as if for instructions, then continued forward.

Butterly lifted his pistol, took careful aim, and fired over their heads. The explosion of the small weapon was magnified tenfold within the closed confines of the narrow passageway and everyone, soldiers and guards, jumped in shock. The soldiers threw themselves on the floor, weapons ready to fire, but they could not see the concealed security guards.

From behind them, an urgent voice was commanding the soldiers to continue forward and, after exchanging looks, they began to slowly crawl forward. Butterly watched them carefully, debating on whether to afford the men another warning and, then, deciding that a warning would be useless, took careful aim and fired twice in rapid succession. The first soldier collapsed, dead instantly. A brief gun battle followed, but the soldiers didn't stand a chance. Butterly's security forces eliminated the first wave with no casualties.

A loud cheer went up from the security guards, but a withering look from Butterly silenced them quickly. There was a hurried conference between the two generals and the army sergeant in charge of the attack force. They appeared to be in agreement over some matter, because the sergeant yelled to one of the other soldiers who came running up with a small satchel grasped in his hand. Butterly watched the soldier pull something from the bag and then as realization registered, he screamed out, "Grenade. Take cover!" His warning was too late. The specially designed scatter grenades were thrown and within seconds, several immense explosions thundered through the security control section, scattering smaller explosions and fragments of killing steel in every direction. As the noise and smoke subsided, a dazed Butterly raised himself up, looked around, and saw not only the center in ruins but the lifeless bodies of six of his best men as well.

Furious, he reached under his desk and grabbed the automatic machine gun he had cached and raised himself up over the desk just as all fifteen remaining soldiers charged up the walkway. Screaming at his remaining guards to shoot, he began firing burst after killing burst, dispassionately mowing down the charging force. Two of Butterly's men were killed immediately in the vicious exchange of gunfire and then a stray bullet tore into Butterly's chest, spinning him around and slamming his body against the wall. There, even as he was sliding to the floor, dying, his weakened legs no longer able to support his bleeding frame, he reached into the holster for his .45 pistol and managed to squeeze off three more shots, killing another of the charging soldiers before he slumped to the floor dead.

The remaining defenders continued firing at the charging invaders, dropping many of them in their tracks, but a few finally reached the protection of the inside security gate which provided them with a certain amount of cover from the security guards. One of the soldiers again reached into the lethal canvas bag and pulled out a grenade. He pulled the pin and lobbed it in the direction of the concealed defenders. There was another loud explosion and then, silence. Cautiously, the remaining attackers raised their heads and peered through the smoke, trying to determine if anyone had survived. Only one had. Wounded, and realizing he was alone in the fight, the bleeding security guard elected to lay his pistol down and raise his hands in the air, surrendering. The three surviving soldiers, all that remained of the attacking forces, quickly reached him, spun him around, and slammed the unresisting security guard up against the wall. There he stood, with his hands raised, as Armstrong, Generals Whiteside and Petrie, Whiteside's personal bodyguard, and Michael O'Conner walked up.

Armstrong, with a pistol in his hand, asked the guard, "Are there any more of you up here?"

The guard shook his head.

"How about downstairs? On the other levels. Any other guards?"

"No," the guard replied weakly.

Whiteside asked, "How many people in the facility?"

"Five in the computer room and Art Gibson who is probably in the basement."

"What about Mary Beth Raleigh?"

"Oh, yeah," the guard remembered. "She's in the office with Kathryn."

"How do we call the office?" Whiteside asked.

"Just dial extension 1104."

Whiteside looked at him a moment, then raised his pistol without any warning and shot the guard in the head.

Turning to Armstrong and waving the gun menacingly, he said, "Now, Adam, we need to get into the computer room. I'll get Mary Beth up here to open the vault."

Meanwhile, as the battle had raged, Davis and his crew caught only bits and pieces of what was going on. They saw the trespassers charge, saw the exchange of gunfire, then the camera was destroyed in the fire-fight and they had no idea what was happening on Level One. The sense of urgency throughout the room increased, because just as Whiteside was shooting the guard in cold blood, SOLOMON announced that the alien had reached London and was continuing across the Atlantic Ocean.

Seconds later, Diane yelled over to Clay, "We're getting a report from Rome." She added, "We have video and audio."

Clay changed the selector switch and the monitor screen leaped alive with burning buildings, and the ever-present low-flying alien cloud. A voice, in English, was describing what had happened:

"Ladies and gentlemen, it's horrible. The entire Vatican is a shambles. We do not know at this time if the Pontiff is alive, but it would appear to me that no one could possibly live through such a holocaust. It's the same story all over the city of Rome. Fires

everywhere.  Dead everywhere.  Devastation everywhere.  It's unbelievable.  We can only estimate that thousands have lost their lives."

The hysterical announcer paused to catch his breath and then he
continued.

"The alien arrived here in Rome with a whirring sound and
thunderbolts flashing from within its cloud.  Within a matter . . ."

Clay yelled out to Karl, "There's that whirring sound again."

The transmission suddenly went off and the monitor screen went
blank.  Automatically, Clay whirled around to look at the other
monitor, but he could see that it was functioning.  His eyes lingered
on the screen for a moment, looking at the computer-enhanced configuration of the alien which now covered nearly three-fourths of the
globe.  It was spreading relentlessly across the Atlantic, moving in the
direction of the United States.

"Clay," MacTavish yelled out, "I think we finally have something
from Cairo."

Clay turned back around and the English-speaking Egyptian
newsman was pointing to a large map on the wall: "In Beirut, damage
is said to be minimal and the same story is being reported from Iran,
Iraq, and Saudi Arabia.  Tel Aviv is also reporting only token pockets
of destruction and very slight casualties."   Clay turned the audio off
and watched the video film.  Although the alien cloud could be seen
hanging at treetop level over the city, there were no scenes of massive
death and destruction.  Only widely scattered smoke pillars suggested
that anything was amiss.  It was a peaceful and undisturbed setting.  It
just didn't make sense.

Turning to MacTavish, he asked, "How long before the alien
arrives in the United States?"

Mac looked at his watch, made a quick calculation and answered,
"Close to . . ."

He was interrupted by Solomon.  "Facility has been penetrated."

Clay rushed to the video console and switched to the camera
focused on the entrance protected by the steel walls.  His heart sank.
The giant door was open and Whiteside, and his men, were entering.
"That's impossible.  How did they penetrate the steel wall?"

Clay's mind was racing when SOLOMON spoke: "Alien creature
has arrived in London.  Estimated time of arrival in the United States
is nine minutes."

"Davis," Whiteside was yelling into the intercom, in an irritated
voice.

Clay knew immediately what Whiteside wanted.  He had discovered that the elevator was inoperative.

"Davis," Whiteside's voice boomed over the loudspeaker, "Reactivate your elevator.  We don't have time to take the stairs."

Clay ignored him.

Then the general said in a threatening voice:  "Clay, are you
watching the monitor?  Look at what I have."

Clay looked down at his monitor, and his body went stiff. Mary Beth and Kathryn were being held by a soldier and General Petrie, and guns were being pointed at their temples.

"You have exactly ten seconds to turn the elevators on. In ten seconds, these soldiers will turn these pretty girls' heads into mush."

Clay knew he wasn't bluffing. He would kill the girls, but he stalled for time. "Just a minute. I'll get maintenance to turn them on."

Turning to his staff, he said quickly, "Listen, if any of you want to try to get out of here before they come down, you need to get up to the second floor and the emergency exit. Take the stairs, push code number 4257, and that will blast the emergency door open. But you'll have to leave now."

They exchanged glances. Karl and Chuck nodded at each other and Karl said, "I think Chuck and I will give it a try. There's nothing more we can do down here."

Diane looked at Clay and said, "I'm staying."

"So am I," Sean MacTavish announced. "We're in this with you all the way, Clay." Clay smiled and reached over, hit the intercom switch and said to Art Gibson, "Art, are you watching the monitor?"

"Yes," the answer came back.

Clay sighed and said. "Reactivate the elevator, Art. Let them have access to it."

"All right, Dr. Davis."

Whiteside's voice came out of the speaker. "Tell your man to come up with the elevator, Davis."

"Did you hear that, Art?"

"I heard, but I'm not coming up there. Do you think I'm crazy?"

Whiteside motioned for the soldiers to open the stairway doors and to go down and get the maintenance man. As they left, Clay looked around the room at his remaining staff and realized that there was very little left to do. They had failed to establish contact with the alien, had failed to discover some means of stopping the alien, and now it was apparent they had failed to prevent Whiteside, Petrie, and Armstrong from taking over the compound. There was only one thing left to do. The inevitable could be postponed. He glanced at the four force field generators which Art had located around the computer room. Although they were small, only prototypes, each was capable of creating an impenetrable and invisible barrier the complete width and length of the room, providing a more than adequate defense against any intruding force. Once activated, nothing could penetrate the magnetic field generated by the apparatus, making it the most effective defense system ever devised by man.

"All right, everyone," Clay said, "I'm going to activate the force field generators. Make sure you remain within the confines of the lines on the floor."

They each acknowledged his announcement and he reached down and pressed the button. Immediately, the engines fired up and the conical reflectors began to glow with a white-hot heat as the generators began to produce the invisible ray or energy field. To insure that it was working properly, Clay picked up a small note pad and threw it in the direction of the force field. Almost magically, it stopped in midair and fell to the floor in flames.

Clay sighed and then sat down in his chair, looking at the elevator door, waiting for the intruders to emerge. As he waited, despondently, SOLOMON's voice unemotionally announced: "Alien is still moving across the Atlantic Ocean. It will arrive on the eastern coast of the United States in seven minutes."

Clay glanced at the clock, mentally calculating the time remaining before the alien reached Piaute Mountain, and at that moment, he heard the faint sound of gunshots from above.

- - - - - - - - - - - - -

Art Gibson, in the basement below, was also waiting for the intruders. He deactivated the elevator's access to the sixth floor, but he knew it would only be a matter of time until somebody came down the stairs to get him. He was scared, but there didn't seem to be anything he could do. Looking around, he walked to the rear of the basement to the fire exit, locked the door, and as an added precaution, he moved a heavy file cabinet up against the door. Then, with a mighty effort, he pushed one of his heavy work benches up against the file cabinet. That, he figured, would slow anyone coming by way of the stairs. He had only one other alternative. He went to his locker, opened it, and pulled out his twelve-gauge shotgun. Several weeks previously, he had brought the gun to work, intending to replace the worn butt plate on the stock, but he had never managed to find the time to fix it. Now he was thankful it was in his locker. Grabbing a handful of shells from the box, he loaded the gun and sat down to wait.

Within a few seconds, he heard banging on the stairway doors as they opened, and then a voice yelled out, "Gibson, come on out and we won't hurt you."

Art didn't say anything. He had never aimed a weapon at anyone in his life, but he was well aware of what had happened upstairs and he wasn't about to be shot without first defending himself.

The soldier walked into view, carrying an automatic weapon. He yelled again. "Gibson, where are you?"

Crouched behind his desk, Art did not reply. His heart was beating faster, he was breathing with difficulty, and the sweat was beginning to pour from his forehead. Tense, he watched as the soldier walked cautiously through the engine room, taking advantage of every affordable cover, until he reached the area leading to Art's office.

Once again, he spoke. "Gibson, come on out. You don't have a chance, and no one will hurt you. We'll all just go upstairs."

Behind Art, there was a sudden burst of gunfire as someone in the other stairwell shot the lock off the door. The noise momentarily distracted the soldier, and as he froze, Art rose up and fired. The twelve-gauge blast reverberated through the basement, but accomplished its goal. The load of buckshot ripped into the soldier, throwing him backward and to the floor in a bloody heap. Another burst of gunfire came from the stairwell as whoever was in there shot out the small glass window in the door. Art spun around and ducked behind the front of his desk, and as he did, his computer caught his eye. He had distinctly remembered turning the computer off, but it was now on, flashing a message across the monitor screen. He stared at it, open-mouthed, eyes disbelieving, and then a wide smile spread across his face. The excitement overcame him. He had to relay the message. Art grabbed for the intercom switch, pushed it, and yelled into the mike, "Dr. Davis, I know what's happening. It's on my computer. I know what's happening. It's . . ."

Another burst of gunfire ripped through Art's body and interrupted his excited message to Clay. He slumped to the floor, stared for a moment at the face of the man standing over him and, oddly, smiled at his killer. Then his eyes closed and he died.

# 19.

# Chapter Nineteen

On the bluff facing the Piaute Mountain Facility, Jack and Ryan observed the scenario unfolding in the facility parking lot and in disbelief watched as two of the soldiers began to plant what appeared to be explosive charges around the doorway. Everyone took cover and there was a muffled explosion, which obviously did not open the door because the soldiers planted another series of charges and there was another explosion. This time, the gate was blown from its hinges and several soldiers entered the door. Ryan thought he heard several gunshots and then he watched as all the soldiers rushed through the doorway, followed a few moments later by Whiteside, Petrie, Armstrong and another civilian whom Jack recognized as Michael O'Conner, Armstrong's aide.

Then, from within the facility, they heard the faint popping sounds of gunfire, then several dull explosions from within, and finally there was silence. As they sat there, trying to figure out what was going on, Ryan said, "We have to go in there and find out what's going on."

Jack disagreed. "Listen, we can't tell the good guys from the bad guys. It might be a good idea for us to just sit tight and see who comes out on top."

"You can sit out here if you want, but I'm going inside." Jack hesitated and then said softly, "Then you need to know something about Pam."

Ryan jerked around. "What do I need to know?"

"She may be involved in this, more than we know. Roger Grant, my FBI friend, told me she was General Whiteside's step daughter. So, be careful."

"Whiteside's step-daughter? That might explain a lot of things." Ryan turned and began to walk cautiously toward the entrance. When he reached the doorway, he paused, peered down the passageway, shook his head at what he saw and, with a shrug of his shoulders, darted inside.

Jack watched him disappear and, unable to curb his curiosity by waiting outside, ran to join Ryan.

- - - - - - - - - - -

With a feeling of helplessness, Clay looked around the computer room. Fear permeated the room, and it was etched on the faces of those watching him expectantly, waiting for some word of reassurance that everything was going to be all right. Clay groped for words and finally said, "I'm sorry that it came down to this. If I had known it was going to go this far, I would have done things a little differently."

He paused for a moment, then added, "Now, when they get down here, don't worry. Remember, we're protected by the force field, so we won't be in any immediate danger. Stay at your consoles, and stay within the marks on the floor so you don't get too close to the force field. We should be all right. Maybe I can talk some sense into Whiteside and we can avoid any problems."

Clay directed his attention to the countdown clock mounted on his work station. Adjusting the digital face to read 14:00, he activated the instrument and immediately the seconds began ticking off, numerically descending, providing an instant reference to the time remaining before the alien's arrival.

Then Clay addressed SOLOMON. "SOLOMON, this is Dr. Davis. Please activate your voice responder."

"Voice responder is activated," SOLOMON acknowledged.

"There they are," announced Diane.

Clay rose from his chair, checked the instrument panel to insure that the force field was working properly and seeing that it was, turned around to face the intruders. Kathryn and Mary Beth were shoved through the door first, followed by Michael O'Conner who had frustration and fear written across his face. Directly behind them were the soldiers, each holding an automatic weapon. Adam Armstrong was the next to step into the computer room. He had a semi-automatic pistol slung casually over his shoulder and arm. Next, General Petrie was followed by General Whiteside, armed with a .45 pistol and a look that seemed to invite someone to try something.

Clay, still concerned about being disconnected with Art, asked, "Where's Art Gibson?"

Whiteside, with a sly smile, said, "If you're referring to your maintenance man, he's still downstairs."

Clay whirled around, flipped the intercom switch and yelled into the system, "Art?" He paused. "Art Gibson. Are you there?" Receiving no answer, he turned back to Whiteside and asked, "What did you do with him? If you've hurt Art . . ."

An unfamiliar voice on the intercom interrupted Clay. "General Whiteside, this is McElroy. I've eliminated two men in the stairwell and one in the basement. We also lost one man. I'm now bringing the elevator up to join you."

Whiteside shrugged his shoulders and observed, "Obviously, your people presented a problem to my men. That's regrettable."

Clay stiffened and pain flashed across his face as he realized what had happened. Art, Karl, and Chuck murdered, obviously, in cold blood. A look of disgust spread across his face as he turned to confront Armstrong and said angrily, "Adam, you obviously don't know what's going on. The president explained everything to me, and Whiteside is up to his crooked little neck in some kind of conspiracy to kill the president and take control of the government. You don't know what you've done in bringing this madman down here."

Armstrong quickly answered, "I didn't bring him down here, Davis. I'm here because the president of the United States sent me, but now that he's dead, I'm the president and I'm ordering you to turn Solomon over to my control."

"Adam," Clay screamed out. "You still don't understand. Whiteside and Petrie were part of a plot to assassinate the president of the United States. You could be next if they get control of Solomon."

Whiteside shook his head. "That's ridiculous."

"It's true. The president himself told me less than an hour ago," Clay declared.

Mary Beth, listening intently, suddenly developed the uncomfortable feeling that her role in the unfolding drama might be somewhat less glorious than she had envisioned. As they argued, a sense of comprehension flooded her consciousness and she blurted out, startling everyone, "You lied to me, Daddy."

Everyone turned to look at her and as her eyes flashed angrily at Whiteside, she continued, "You told me I was being sent here because the president wanted to keep an eye on Dr. Davis. You lied to me."

Whiteside threw her a condescending look and shook his head, dismissing her accusation with, "It was expedient at the time for me to have someone loyal inside this facility. You were available. Nothing personal, honey. I just needed you."

Mary Beth, realizing that she had been duped and used by the general, shot him a look of contempt. "And to think I was the one who let you inside the wall."

Whiteside smiled. "Yes, you did, and for that I'm very grateful. That steel vault door would have presented us with a slight problem."

"Dr. Davis," she said apologetically, "it's all my fault. Mr. Gibson is dead, my dad is down here, and if . . ."

She was interrupted by SOLOMON. "The alien is now five minutes away from the east coast of the United States. It is now ten minutes away from this location."

As the guard from the basement arrived on the elevator, Armstrong, standing off to one side, looked anxiously at Clay and repeated his question. "Are you ready to turn SOLOMON over to me?"

Sean MacTavish said nervously, "Clay, we don't have much time."

"Adam, the president was very adamant about not allowing Whiteside and Petrie access to SOLOMON."

Whiteside sneered, "Let's see how good your little toy is, Davis." He grabbed a desk chair and threw it into the force field. There was an immediate reaction as steel, plastic and metal melted and vaporized simultaneously. Within a split second, the chair had disappeared. As soon as the general saw the chair fail to penetrate the invisible shield, he raised his pistol and fired at Clay Davis, but the force field deflected the bullets, causing them to disappear into nothingness.

- - - - - - - - - - - -

Upstairs, on the main level, Ryan Abernathy was resisting the urge to dash headlong into the facility in search of Pam. Instead of throwing caution away, he was carefully making his way through the narrow passageway leading from the main entrance of the facility. At first, he couldn't believe his eyes. The scene stretched out before him had all the appearances of a war zone. Dead bodies were everywhere and the smell of gunpowder and explosives still permeated the confined area. Upon reaching the first body, Ryan stooped down, picked up the dead soldier's weapon and, as he checked the magazine to see how many rounds remained, he heard a noise to his rear. Spinning around with the weapon at the ready, he relaxed when he saw it was Jack Clayburn.

He raised a finger to his lips, signaling Jack to remain quiet, and as the newsman walked up he whispered, "Can you believe this? It looks like a war went on."

Jack nodded his head and, seeing the gun in Ryan's hand, reached for a weapon of his own from another dead soldier. "What the heck's going on?"

Ryan shook his head. Whispering, he suggested, "Your conspiracy must hedge on taking over the place." His lips tightened and he added, "I don't care what they do, but they'd better not hurt Pam." He paused, looked ahead, and added, "Let's make our way up to the office. Be careful and stick close to me. We're too exposed." Jack nodded agreement and the two men continued forward until they reached the small retaining wall separating the main lobby from the passageway. Ryan couldn't see anyone on guard, so he motioned Jack to follow and they crossed the lobby to the door to the main Security Room. There, slumped in a dead heap, was the body of James Butterly.

Distracted by his obsession with finding Pam, Ryan had totally forgotten the problem his buddy had been facing, but as he was jerked back into reality by the dead body of his friend, he fought to hold back the tears. He felt a wave of despair and guilt sweep over him as he remembered thinking that James had lied to him about Pam's presence. With a trembling voice, he quietly said, "Looks like you put up one heckuva fight, old friend." Ryan covered James with his jacket and, straightening up, his face hardened, his resolve strengthened and now the need to find Pam became even more urgent. Stepping over his friend, he entered the main Security Room and immediately his attention was drawn to the monitors. Ryan's face went white. He blinked they to insure his eyes weren't deceiving him, and then jumped for the nearby desk where he began to frantically pull drawers out, searching wildly through the mass of papers and file folders.

Jack stepped up beside him and asked, "What's wrong? What are you looking for?"

Pointing to one of the monitors, Ryan snapped, "That's Pamela. She's in here someplace, and I have no idea where. I'm trying to find some kind of map or floor plan to this place." Both men began to rapidly search through drawers and file cabinets until Jack yelled out triumphantly, "I think I have it."

Ryan grabbed the folder from Jack, searched through the papers, and then matched the monitor number to the corresponding floor. "She's on the fourth level."

Ryan walked over to the console, studied the control panel for a moment and, within a matter of seconds, had determined which switch controlled the audio for the computer room monitor. Turning the audio up, sound immediately filled the control room and the first voice he heard was Whiteside's. "You have fifteen seconds to make up your mind, Davis, or this girl is dead."

Ryan watched in horror as the general grabbed Kathryn, pulled her up close, and put the pistol to her head. Ryan slammed his fist on the console and wheeled around. "Whiteside's history." He reached down and picked up another automatic weapon lying on the floor next to his dead friend's body. Anger, out-and-out fury and fear for Pam's safety, completely dominated his being and, shedding all feeling of caution, he looked at his dead friend and said, "It ain't over yet, James, and I promise you someone's going to pay." Glancing again at the monitor, he sprung for the elevator door, yelling over his shoulder,

"Jack, if anyone comes up this elevator other than me and Pam, shoot first and ask questions later."

- - - - - - - - - - - -

Meanwhile, down on the fourth level, SOLOMON's voice was adding to the tension. "The alien is now three minutes away from the eastern coast of the United States, and it is now eight minutes from this location."

"Clay," Armstrong said in a calm, reserved voice. "We're running out of time. Let me have SOLOMON."

Wearily, Clay asked, "What can you do that we haven't done, Adam?"

"I can do plenty. Certainly more than you've been able to do," Armstrong replied.

Clay felt helpless. There didn't appear to be any alternative except to turn SOLOMON over to Armstrong, but he was still worried that doing so might result in a disaster. "Adam, it's too late. The alien is only eight minutes away, and nothing anyone has come up with can stop it."

Smiling reassuringly, Armstrong said confidently, "I can stop it."

Whiteside spoke up. "You have fifteen seconds to make up your mind, Davis, or this girl is dead."

A voice boomed from the monitor speaker. Diane had inadvertently left a channel open and a video report was automatically feeding into the monitor system. Everyone, startled, turned to look at the monitor and continued to watch dumbfounded as an announcer sitting at a news desk began to speak in a sober tone. "This is Roger Evans in New York. It cannot be stopped. Every weapon known to man has been used against the alien invader and neither nuclear nor conventional weapons have had any effect. All have failed. The European continent has been devastated. Millions of people have vanished from the face of the earth. They were just sucked into that cloud of death. Even as I speak from our studios in New York, we can see the alien energy field rapidly approaching. There is panic and confusion in the streets below as . . . "

The reporter's voice was cut short as the studio windows exploded. His eyes suddenly flashed with a blinding light and he was jerked from his seat, sucked out of the studio and heaved through the window of the building. He was gone—and so was the video report.

The room was deadly silent. No one spoke for what seemed an eternity as the full meaning of the video report began to sink in. Time did appear to be running out.

For the first time, General Whiteside saw the devastation the alien was causing on earth. He began to panic, fearing that the alien would soon be attacking the facility. "Can you really stop that thing, Adam?"

Grinning, Armstrong replied, "You and General Petrie give me your weapons. It's the only way Davis is going to let me in."

Bewildered by the request, Whiteside asked in a strained voice, "Are you sure you know what you're doing?"

Adam smiled at the general, and with a wink, answered, "I've always known what I was doing."

Reluctantly, Petrie dropped his weapon as General Whiteside tossed the pistol across the room into the waiting hands of Adam Armstrong, who handed the gun to Michael O'Conner. "Keep them covered," he said, and turning to face Clay Davis, he began to plead, a sense of urgency in his voice—with Clay. "The conspiracy is under control. Now drop the force field.

Clay, however, was still not convinced that he should relinquish control of SOLOMON. "How do I know you're not part of the conspiracy, Adam?"

"Clay," Armstrong said in a condescending voice. "I am now the president of the United States. What am I going to do? Overthrow myself? Turn the force field off."

Clay shrugged. He had no more arguments. He walked over, threw the switch, and the generators ground to a halt. The force field melted away.

Whiteside wasted no time. He barked an order to the soldiers. "Shoot them! Shoot him now!"

The soldiers responded and began firing their weapons indiscriminately in the direction of the scientists standing across the room.

Clay and Diane both dove for cover as one bullet smashed into Sean MacTavish's throat, nearly decapitating him. As the murderous gunfire swept across the room, a wild-eyed Ryan Abernathy jumped through the elevator doorway, a gun in each hand, leveled and aimed. One of the soldiers spun around to cover the unexpected intruder, but before he could bring his weapon around, Ryan squeezed off several rounds. The shots reverberated in a series of deafening explosions and the bullets tore into the soldier's body, killing him instantly. In that split second, another soldier swung his weapon around, but before he could get off a shot, Ryan fired again. Shells ripped into the thug's body, the impact jolting him off balance, and as he was falling, his finger instinctively squeezed the trigger of his automatic weapon. In one last effort, the dying man tried to aim his weapon at Ryan, but even as he was bringing his weapon up, Ryan shot him. As the soldier's life ebbed from his body, his finger, in a final reflexive move, squeezed off a final burst, hitting Michael O'Conner, killing him instantly.

In that split second of gunfire, Whiteside pulled another pistol from inside his jacket and tried to aim at Ryan, but Kathryn, struggling to free herself, hit his arm, spoiling his aim. The general wheeled around and, without a thought, shot her. During all this, Mary Beth took advantage of the confusion and darted behind the door, where she huddled in fear.

A soldier, standing beside Petrie and Whiteside tried to get a shot off, but Ryan squeezed off a final burst and emptied his weapon. The soldier fell against Whiteside who shoved the dying man away.

Petrie and Whiteside both smiled as they realized Ryan's weapons were empty. Ryan, now vulnerable and helpless to defend himself, stood there, waiting for the inevitable.

Suddenly, the door to the laboratory was flung open. Jack Clayburn stepped through the door, an automatic weapon blazing way. The first burst cut Petrie in half. Whiteside jumped for cover, and from behind a desk, recognized Jack Clayburn. "Clayburn," the general stated. "You should have stayed out of this."

"I should have, General, but I didn't. Please drop your gun."

Whiteside smiled, stood up from his crouched position behind the desk, and said, as he backed up a step, "I don't think you have the stomach for killing someone in cold blood, Clayburn." As the two men glared at each other, Clay Davis recognized his opportunity. With all eyes focused on Jack and Whiteside, Clay reached his hand over his console, felt blindly, searching for the generator switch, and when he found it, reactivated the force field. The generators fired up and the deadly electrical charge shot out of the conical-shaped reflector. Whiteside never knew he had lost the game. Multi-amplified mega-volts shot through his body like a hot knife, and then as the full power of the energy field surged through his body, he literally disintegrated. He was simply vaporized, as his ashes fell to the floor.

Armstrong watched in curious astonishment as Whiteside disappeared from time and space, but Clay paid him no heed. The moment he threw the switch, he searched the room for Diane and when he saw her body crumpled on the floor, he screamed out in pain, jumped to her side, and cradled her body in his arms. He saw immediately that she was not dead, but badly wounded. Tearing open her blouse, he ripped a handkerchief from his pocket and pressed it softly against the mangled skin of her body in an attempt to stop the bleeding from her chest.

On the other side of the room, Ryan and Jack stared in disbelief at the spot where Whiteside disappeared. Ryan blinked his eyes several times, unable to comprehend what had happened. One moment Whiteside was there; the next moment, he was gone. Jack, still not sure who were bad guys and who were good guys, pointed his weapon at both Armstrong and Davis.

"Don't be nervous, Jack. It's all over. I'm not with them." Armstrong blurted.

Mary Beth, realizing that the shooting was over, jumped to her feet and immediately ran to Ryan, who was rising to his feet. The two embraced and she buried her face into his shoulder and began sobbing. "Ryan, I've been such a fool."

He caressed the back of her neck with his hand and asked, "Pamela, are you all right?"

"I am now," she answered. "Oh, Ryan, I had no idea what I was getting into." She sobbed uncontrollably while trying to explain what had happened. "He told me I was being assigned here on special orders from the president and I couldn't tell anyone—not even you—what was going on. You don't know how bad I've wanted to be with you . . . look at what I've caused."

Ryan, relieved that she was all right and no longer in any danger, calmed her. "It's all right, Pam. It's all over."

"But he used me. And I nearly got us killed."

"Calm down, Pam. I'm going to get you out of here and everything will be all right."

Armstrong started to move, but Jack quickly warned him, "Stay where you are, Adam. I don't know what's going on down here, but nobody moves until I find out."

Armstrong looked at him for a moment and then said, "I think . . ."

He was interrupted as SOLOMON's voice unemotionally announced, "The alien will arrive at this location in five minutes."

# 20.

# Chapter Twenty

**A**s Jack pointed his weapon at the two men, the floor began to move. Pam tightened her grip on Ryan as the computer terminals and monitor screens quivered. Roof tiles suddenly came crashing down around them and the electrical conduit and water sprinkler lines burst, creating a shower of sparks and spraying water. The facility was built to withstand both atomic explosion and earthquake shocks but the power of the tremor shook the very foundation upon which the facility was built and everyone froze as the walls trembled, shook, and threatened to collapse.

For an agonizing minute, the quake continued and as Clay held Diane, he wondered if there was any connection between the quake and the alien. He didn't dwell on the question long—Diane began to stir in his arms and he immediately gave her his full attention.

As the tremor subsided, Ryan looked at Armstrong, then at Davis. He had no idea what was going on, but he knew the foundations of the underground facility were weakening, and if there was another tremor, it could suddenly become a very dangerous place to be. He decided that the best move would involve getting out of the facility and leaving the two scientists to resolve their problem. He gently guided Pamela toward the exit, but he suddenly remembered something. He stopped and looked at Clay Davis, who was still kneeling on the floor beside Diane, and asked defiantly, "Davis, James Butterly told me he caught you putting something on the sugar. What was it, and will it hurt Pamela?"

Clay, momentarily shocked by the question, stammered, "It was only a nicotine inhibitor—a chemical—I made to stop Art from smoking." He added, "It won't hurt her."

Ryan looked at Pamela, and her face brightened with understanding. "That's why I haven't wanted a cigarette."

Relieved, Ryan said, "Come on, Pam, let's get out of here." He grabbed her hand and pulled her into the elevator. "Jack, you coming with us?"

"No, I'll take the stairs. You turn the elevator off when you get to the top," he said over his shoulder. Jack's weapon was still pointed at Armstrong, but he kept an eye on Davis also. He had not yet resolved in his mind who was the bad guy and who was the good guy.

As the doors closed and the elevator began to rise to the safety of the upper levels, Adam Armstrong turned and once again pleaded with Clay. "Clay, you've got to lower the force field now, or it will be too late for me to stop the alien."

Clay looked at the countdown clock on his console and saw that he had less than four minutes left before the alien would arrive. Quickly, he began to check off his options. There was still a chance that the alien would not be able to penetrate the airtight compartments of the complex, in which case, he and Diane would be safe. On the other hand, if the alien was able to reach the computer room, he had no way of knowing if the alien would bypass the two of them, or if they would be killed.

Therein was the dilemma. Stay within the confines of the complex or try to leave. Either action was a gamble. He could not help but remember that the alien had been able to penetrate an airtight, sealed space capsule without any trouble, and he had to assume that the same possibility existed for the complex. Therefore, he had to believe that if the alien was going to kill them, it could do so as easily inside the complex as outside. However, if the alien bypassed them inside, he would have lost valuable time getting Diane to the hospital, and he knew that it was imperative he get aid for her as soon as possible or she wouldn't make it. She had lost far too much blood. There was another option, of course. He could allow Adam access to SOLOMON. Perhaps Adam could stop the alien.    Suddenly, however, Clay became aware of an additional problem. He realized that throughout the entire ordeal with Whiteside, not once had Adam interfered or offered any assistance in dealing with the general; nor had Whiteside ever threatened or addressed Armstrong. Something didn't ring true. It was almost as if Armstrong knew what Whiteside was doing—he had made no effort to prevent him. There was not time, however, to dwell on the subject. It was obvious that he had to get Diane to a doctor, alien or no alien.

A voice penetrated Clay's consciousness, and he was slowly drawn back into the reality of the moment by Armstrong yelling at him from the other side of the still active force field. "Clay, you have to let me in. Turn the force field off."

Jack joined Armstrong with a plea. "For crying out loud, Davis, let him do what he thinks he can do. I'll keep him covered. Just let him try to stop that thing out there." Clay turned slowly, staring at Armstrong but didn't speak.

Armstrong, realizing that he had only a matter of minutes to accomplish his goal—thereby fulfilling his destiny—continued. "Unless you let me in right this second, you and Diane will both be killed by that thing. I will survive, but you and Diane won't. You have to let me access SOLOMON now!"

Clay shook his head, bewildered. He was having a great deal of trouble comprehending what Armstrong was saying. "How do you know we'll be killed and you won't? What makes you so sure you know what's going to happen?" Adam retorted, "Believe me, Davis, I know exactly what's going to happen."

Jack tried again to convince Clay to let Armstrong in. "Davis, your girl needs medical attention. You can't stay behind that force field too much longer. She might die. And Armstrong might be able to do something. You'd better decide quick. There isn't much time."

"I don't want to see you die, Clay," Armstrong said. "Together, we can chase the alien away. Clay, we can share credit for saving the world." Pleading, he begged, "Clay, let me in. Lower the force field."

Clay glanced at the countdown clock and then looked over at Diane. The blood had soaked through the handkerchief and was spreading rapidly through her clothes. He had to get medical help, or she would bleed to death. He knew that if he lost her, nothing would matter anyway. She had come to mean the world to him, and he could not bring himself to even think of living without her. Slowly, realizing that he had only one logical choice, he walked over to the generators and turned the switch off. The force field fell away and Adam, obviously relieved, rushed to the console and began to feed data into SOLOMON.

Clay returned to Diane, and as he knelt to lift the fragile, unconscious body, her eyes opened and she smiled weakly. She tried to reach up and put her shattered arm around his neck, but the pain swept through her body and she involuntarily cried out. He felt a spasm of fear shudder through his body as he realized she had lost far too much blood. Her clothing, in the back where he was holding her up, was drenched with blood, and Clay suddenly realized that there was not enough time remaining to get her to a hospital or doctor. He was holding a dying woman in his arms. Fighting to hold back the tears threatening to flood from his eyes, Clay tried, in a choking voice, to soothe her. "There, Angel. Just lie still. You're going to be all right."

Shaking the cobwebs from her muddled, pain-filled brain, she asked in a shaking voice, "Is it all over? Is everything all right?"

A sense of urgency gripped him as he looked into her trusting eyes. He had to take her mind off the pain and not allow her to realize the hopelessness of her condition. Smiling, he lied to her. "Everything is just fine. We'll be leaving in just a moment."

She looked at him and said weakly, "Last night, you wanted to get away from everything. Does that include me?"

Puzzled, Clay didn't understand what she meant, but then he realized that she had misunderstood him. He also suddenly understood why she had become angry with him. If the situation had been less serious, he would have laughed, but under the circumstances it was all he could do to keep from breaking down completely and crying. Looking into her eyes, he said softly, "Diane, I love you, and I want to live the rest of our lives together."     She asked, "Are you saying you planned to take me with you all the time?"

Smiling, he answered, "Of course I did.  I assumed you knew I was talking about us—not just me."

"Oh, Clay. I didn't understand. I thought you were going to get away by yourself."

Reaching into his pocket with his free hand, he pulled out the small jewelry box. "I wanted this to be a lot more romantic." He added, "I had planned to walk you up to our favorite spot on top of the mountain where just you, me, God, and all the stars would be alone, but that walk will have to wait. Diane, will you marry me?"

Opening the small jewelry box with his hand, he said, as he displayed the ring, "I love you more than you'll ever know."

The pain was becoming unbearable, and she could feel herself growing faint and weak from loss of blood, but her heart pounded, her spirits soared, and with a weak, joyous cry, she answered, "You know I will, Clay. Oh, you know I will. Now you can't ever leave without me."

Clay laughed nervously, but he could no longer restrain his tears. "Diane, I would never leave you. I love you." As the tears streamed down his face, he realized he was losing her. He began to lift her and said, "Now hang in there. Heaven's going to have to wait a little longer for you." He smiled encouragingly at her, and then the smile faded from his face, a frown creased his forehead as a strange, unnatural feeling gripped him. He searched for something in his mind that was just triggered by his last words. There was something he had overlooked. He closed his eyes and tried to focus on whatever elusive clue he sensed he had. Quickly, he tried to isolate and analyze every bit of information he had absorbed since the arrival of the alien in the earth's atmosphere. He had been unable to piece the puzzle together, but sensed that somehow everything fit. He began to run questions through his mind.

If the alien had intelligence, why hadn't they been able to establish communication? Why was the alien discriminatory in its attacks throughout the world? Clay still did not understand why the Oriental and Middle Eastern nations enjoyed less devastation than other nations. Nor could he understand why graves had been split open. It was as if the alien could not distinguish the difference between live and dead humans, yet it was able to distinguish between animal and human life, because not one report received had mentioned an attack on an animal.

Even more puzzling to Clay was the power source of the alien. Where was all that electrical and heat energy originating, and how was it able to regenerate itself? More importantly, there was the question of how the alien was able to generate more power than anything known on earth—and obviously able to do so through some mysterious method unknown to earth science.  Clay remembered the printout figures on the magnitude of the alien's power, and they had been staggering—far beyond man's capability or understanding. He shook his head in frustration. It was almost as if the alien had the power of God. But why would God let such a terrible creature ravish earth? Nothing like this was ever in . . .

Something clicked in Clay's mind. What had he said to Diane, just moments ago? "Heaven will have to wait. . ." He turned, looked first at Armstrong, then Jack, and back at Armstrong. Thinking out loud, he said slowly, "Art Gibson tried to tell us something about his computer, but he didn't get a chance to finish whatever he wanted to tell me."

A smile began to fill his face. A breathtaking sense of understanding—or maybe it was hope, even wishful thinking—slowly crept over him, and as his mind raced, an immense surge of joy engulfed him, lifting the heavy burden from his shoulders.

His mouth popped open, and he exclaimed, "Of course. That has to be it. Art must have stumbled onto what was happening, and there is only one place where he could have found it." He leaned Diane against the cabinet and said reassuringly, "This won't take a second, Angel. I have to confirm something, and if I'm right, everything is wonderful." He laughed. "In fact, everything will be wonderful."

She looked at him and wanted to ask what he meant, but Clay had leapt to his feet and literally ran to his computer terminal. Lowering his body like a football player, he struck Armstrong with a fierce body block, catapulting him across the room, knocking him to the floor. Turning to Jack, he begged, "Jack, I don't know you and you don't know me, but you're going to have to trust me now." He turned back to his console and barked a command to SOLOMON: "Access Art Gibson's computer, retrieve and display all information concerning alien." Then he began typing on the keyboard, entering instructions to SOLOMON.

Armstrong raised himself from the floor, livid with anger, and rushed back to the computer terminal. He demanded, "What are you doing, Davis?"

SOLOMON's voice boomed out over Armstrong's. "File is retrieved and stored. Ready for search and evaluation. Alien is now two minutes from this location."

Armstrong's face contorted with fury. "Don't mess this up, Davis. I'm almost finished."

Clay grinned. "You're right about that, Adam. You are almost finished." He continued to type and Armstrong, sensing what Clay was up to, grabbed him by the shoulders and with supernatural strength, lifted Clay's body off the floor and flung him across the room where he slammed into the wall with a sickening thud. Clay felt something give inside his chest, followed by a blinding flash of pain, and as he collapsed to the floor, he knew several ribs had been broken. He laid there a moment, regaining his breath, clutching his chest, looking in astonishment at Armstrong, wondering how Armstrong had managed to pick him up and throw his body over thirty feet across the room. The man was inhuman.

Jack couldn't move. He simply stared in amazement at what was going on. He was a spectator, but he didn't understand the game he was watching. Slowly, Clay raised himself from the floor to a standing position and leaning against the wall in pain, he said in a voice shaky with the excitement of discovery: "I know what's happening."

Armstrong didn't acknowledge. He simply continued to type on the computer keyboard.

Clay managed a grin and offered, "I think you're wasting your time, Armstrong.

At that moment, a beeping noise began to sound, indicating that Art's computer files had been accessed and the evaluation was beginning. Clay, guessing at what was about to flash on the monitor, couldn't resist taunting Armstrong a little. He looked up at the monitor and as the data began to scroll across the screen, Clay asked, "Does that mean anything to you, Adam?" He looked at Clayburn. "How about you, Jack. Do you understand now what's happening?" Pointing to the screen, he read, "Only human life has been affected. Not animal life. What is so different about humans that the alien would ignore animals?"

"Probably just intelligence," Armstrong replied.

"And discriminatory selection of the alien indicates absolute zero percentage of followers of Hinduism, Buddhism, Confucianism, Shintoism, Islam, and Taoism suffered loss of life." Clay looked over at Armstrong. "What do you think, Adam? Why would that be? Why the discrimination?"

Armstrong didn't answer. He continued to type.

"Do you think it was a coincidence that the alien was moving from east to west with lightning bolts?" He laughed as he suddenly remembered something else. "And why was the ground exploding in the graveyards? Was the alien attacking graves—or freeing them?"

Armstrong continued to ignore Clay.

"And something else." Clay thought for a moment and quoted a scripture he remembered from the Bible: " 'In the last days the moon will turn as blood and stars will fall from the sky.' Adam, do you think that explains the red moon and strange meteor showers?"

Not even waiting for Armstrong to answer, Clay continued. "Now it all makes sense." He thought for a moment and then said, "Art Gibson figured it out first and tried to tell me. He remembered the verse from Zechariah. 'And his arrow shall go forth as the lightning and shall go with whirlwinds.

"Lightning in the cloud . . . a whirlwind. Everyone saw the lightning, but we thought of it as bolts of electrical energy, and we heard the whirring sound, but didn't know what it meant." With a contemplative look on his face, Clay said, "It just wasn't what I expected. I guess I was thinking it would be different—something else."

"Will someone tell me what's going on?" Jack asked. "Clay, what is going on? What are you talking about?"     Armstrong laughed. "All very mysterious, isn't it?"

"Not mysterious at all, when you don't try to make it complicated. Look at that," he said, pointing at the screen, "'The dead shall rise first. First Thessalonians 4:16.'

"And that's why the graves were exploding. The dead were being called home."

Armstrong nodded his head and said sarcastically. "Very good, Davis. You are beginning to understand." He added, contemptuously, "At least, you are beginning to understand part of it."

Clay smiled. "I understand because I remembered the scripture in First Thessalonians. The one that reads, 'Then we which are alive and remain shall be caught up together with them in the clouds.' The alien wasn't devouring or killing people. In fact, it was just the opposite. People were being given a new life. Not death. Life." He added. "And no one knows the time or hour. Hour. The alien has covered the earth in exactly one hour."

Continuing, Clay said, "But we missed the most obvious clue of all. The reason we could not establish any communications with the alien, even though Solomon tried everything, we failed to try the one thing that would work. Solomon was incapable of praying."

Diane, still lying on the floor, interrupted him in a weak voice. "Clay, is it really the Rapture?"

Turning to look at Diane, with a big smile, Clay said, "Yes, Diane. He is coming to carry us home!"

"Rapture? What are you talking about? What's the Rapture?" Jack wanted to know.

Clay turned back to Armstrong, frowned and said, "There's no way you could know what was about to happen. Unless . . ." He stared at Armstrong, a look of disbelief spreading across his face as he remembered something else. "There is no way you could know what was happening. You wouldn't be privy to something like this unless . . . unless . . ."

Clay finished his sentence, ". . . Unless you're not what you appear to be."

SOLOMON's voice interrupted: "Alien will arrive this location in one minute thirty seconds. There is now exactly 90 seconds left before the alien arrives."

Armstrong flashed a smile of triumph. "Well, you did figure it out, but what good will it do you?" He leaned against the computer, patted the metal frame, and said, "At this very minute, SOLOMON is arming two nuclear missiles that are programmed to strike the spot where the Rapture began. The Rapture will have ended with the explosions, I'll get credit for having chased it away, and there will be sufficient chaos throughout the world for my people to move quickly and easily into positions of power."

Jack finally understood what was happening. "It was your plan all along, wasn't it? All this stuff about being the great humanitarian was just a scam. Trying to help people and help nations was just a way of gaining control. You've got all these people all over the world who are loyal to you and will do whatever you say."

Armstrong sneered, "You've finally figured it out, haven't you, and now there's nothing you can do about it."

Clay offered, "The World Coalition is nothing but a front to enable you to gain control of the European nations. When the Rapture ruins them financially, you'll just step in and take over, won't you? You've been preparing for this for years, haven't you?"

Armstrong sneered. "Everything is ready for me. As soon as this is over, I'll be in control of not only the United States, but nearly a dozen other nations as well." With a sly smile, he added, "When this is over, Davis, I'll be the only one who can put this world back together again. SOLOMON gives me access to everything, everywhere in the world. I'll be able to step in and put the pieces back together again, thanks to your little toy." Smiling, he said triumphantly, "You fell into my trap and let me carry out my plan with SOLOMON."

Incredulously, Clay stated, "You were the head of the conspiracy, weren't you? You've been planning to take control of the government all along."

Smugly, Armstrong answered. "Quite right. When I heard about the alien, I knew immediately what it was, but I couldn't tell my people. I allowed them to think it provided an excellent opportunity to initiate our take-over plan. As it stands now, only you, myself, Clayburn, and her know what is really happening." He added, "Just like you Christians, I've been waiting for this for years. My birth forced this event to happen now. Your God had no choice but to come to earth at this time because He knows it's only a matter of time before we defeat Him."

Diane said weakly, "Clay, he's the Anti-Christ. We have to stop him."

Armstrong laughed. "You've been a blessing for me, Davis. You have sort of been my protégé, working under my wing, so to speak. Who do you think arranged for all the funding for your research projects? Who do you think arranged all this? Made Solomon possible?"

Sneering, he continued. "When Thacker told me about your idea for the super computer, Solomon, I knew it was perfect for my plans." With a sweeping gesture, he boasted, "I made all this possible."

Jack, listening intently, commented, "It's all making sense now. The military, the networks, the media, the financial world; all under your control and all controlled by that computer over there. First you destroy, then you take over, and then you rebuild under your control. You'll control almost every financial institute in the world."

"Jack, you still don't understand, do you? I don't care about controlling governments, banks, or networks. I want to control people. I want to own them, body and soul!"

"The space experiment was set up by you then?" Jack asked.

Armstrong chuckled. "Yes and no. I preprogrammed one of Thacker's looping chips to override the program, which was supposed to command the laser to shoot the earth. But when the Rapture began, it was a stroke of luck I had not counted on. Once I knew what was happening, all I had to do was take advantage of it."

Jack pointed his weapon at Armstrong. "I think your luck just ran out, Armstrong." He saw the evil in Armstrong's eyes and although he had never killed anyone deliberately, he knew he had to kill Adam Armstrong. He pulled the trigger. Nothing happened.

"That won't work now, Mr. Clayburn. It's too late. My power grows stronger with the loss of every Christian. There is no stopping me now."

Clay, listening to Adam's boasting, knew time was running out. He gripped Diane tighter, thankful she did not know that Solomon's self-destruct mode was activated the moment Armstrong programmed the nuclear strike. Within a short time, the secret explosive charges planted throughout the underground building would detonate and the Piaute Facility would cease to exist. He yelled to Clayburn, "Jack, you have to get out of here now. Leave. Don't wait another second. Get out. Tell the world what you've learned in here!" Jack, now filled with fear, needed no further urging. He turned and ran toward the open stairway door. Before he could reach it, however, Armstrong waved his hand and the door slammed shut.

Sarcastically, he asked, "You didn't really think I would let you live after telling you everything, did you?"

Jack stared at the door, turned and looked at the madman standing across the room and, realizing only a supernatural force could have accomplished such a feat, began trembling. He was scared. He was scared of dying, he was scared of Armstrong, and he was scared the hand of God would soon be upon him.

He sank slowly to his knees, and for the first time in his adult life, put his hands together, closed his eyes, and prayed.

"Dear God, forgive me for not accepting you, Lord. Forgive me for being so stubborn. Forgive me for all my sins, Lord. God, please spare me. Let me go. Let me tell the rest of the world what I've seen here today. Let me tell everyone what I know. What I've learned. God, let me tell them about you."

"It's too late for that mumbo-jumbo, Clayburn," Armstrong taunted. "I have triumphed over him."

As Jack continued to pray, Clay smiled at Armstrong. "You think it's mumbo-jumbo, huh? You think you've won?" God has never failed or allowed himself to be manipulated by your evil." Clay grinned at Adam as he walked over to Diane, lifted her in his arms, and stood looking excitedly around—awaiting the Rapture.

It suddenly occurred to the man of darkness that Davis did not seem overly concerned about the fact that at that very moment SOLOMON was sending signals to nuclear missiles. Then, in a panic, he suspected that there was a reason for Clay's calmness. "What have you done?"

Clay merely smiled, holding the weakened Diane in his arms. "I told you, accidents don't just happen. God obviously had this all planned out before you. It is you who fell into a trap, not him." He pulled Diane closer and as she pressed against him, her arm around his waist, he leaned down and kissed her gently on the lips and whispered, "I think he's in for a little surprise."

Diane knew Clay well enough to know something was up his sleeve. She gazed into Clay's eyes and with a tender squeeze, whispered back, "I love you, Clay Davis."

Armstrong scrambled to SOLOMON and began typing instructions, but SOLOMON's voice froze him in his tracks. "Ten seconds before the arrival. Doomsday Self-Destruct is now implemented. Destruction in ninety seconds."

Helplessly, Armstrong looked at Clay and Diane, realizing that Davis had beaten him. Jack felt more than helplessness. He felt panic. Solomon's announcement of the Doomsday Self-Destruct didn't need any explanation. Jack began edging his way toward the stairwell door.

A loud noise suddenly filled the room, and the four turned to look for the source of the strange whirring sound. Clay tightened his grip on Diane as they both watched a wisp of smoke, a delicately formed sliver of mist, coming out of the closed elevator door. Knowing that Jesus was about to take their human bodies, they became excited, closed their eyes and—as the mist spread across the room—they began to pray. Shiny, glimmering beads of electrical energy began to dance around them, fusing together to form an enveloping golden aura of brightness. Slowly, the white mist encircled the couple and two single bolts of energy shot around their bodies. A blazing bright light flashed in their eyes as they were slowly lifted upward while Adam Armstrong cowered on the floor, trembling in fear before the hand of God. Their bodies separated from their spirits as they reached the ceiling. Only their ashes fell back to earth.

Jack, still on his knees, felt the building begin to tremble and as he opened his eyes, he saw the stairway door suddenly fly open, as if pried from its hinges by an unseen power. He looked at Armstrong and then leaped to his feet and began running as fast as he could, taking the stairs two and three steps at a time. He was running for his life.

He heard footsteps behind him and knew Armstrong was either trying to escape also or was following him. He ran faster. Armstrong, however, was not following Jack. He was running for the second floor where he knew there was an emergency exit leading to the outside. His only thought was to escape the building and the hand of God.

After what seemed an eternity, Jack reached the first level. His lungs and legs cried out for rest but he knew time was running out so, without a pause, he headed down the long ramp leading to the outside. As he broke into the daylight, his heart was pounding and his breath was coming in gasps. He saw Ryan and Pamela standing on the rock ledge gazing at the amazing display in the sky. When he reached the ledge, Ryan held out his hand, pulled him up, and Jack painfully gasped, "Hide! Quick. The building's gonna go."

Ryan grasped the significance immediately, grabbed Pamela's arm, and began to run, almost dragging her behind him. The three frantically raced for the safety of the rocks and with only a split second to spare, flung themselves to the ground in fear just as a horrendous explosion shattered the stillness behind them. For several minutes, they crouched in fear, and when it appeared that the explosions had ceased, all three peered cautiously over the rock. Debris and chunks of the giant complex were falling in a steady stream across the immediate area and where there had been a facility, there was now only a large, gaping hole. Silently, they exchanged looks, agreeing with each other—nothing could have survived the blast.

Yet, as spectacular as the explosion seemed, their attention focused on a sight that made the detonation pale in comparison. Above them, lightning flashed, smoke billowed, and the heavens seemed filled with the sound of battle. Jack needed no one to tell him that he was witnessing God's forces battling evil and in his heart, he knew they were fighting for him, for his survival. He sensed an urgency to get away as quickly as possible, because in his heart he knew that Adam Armstrong, somehow, was nearby. He could feel his presence.

He motioned to Ryan and the three made their way down to the parking lot where Ryan commandeered one of the military vehicles. Within seconds they were speeding down the mountain road. They were escaping, but they had no idea where they were going or what they would do.

The alien—or as Jack now knew, God—was departing earth. He had lived through the Second Coming and as the realization of what he was viewing sank in, tears began to stream from his eyes and a feeling of hopelessness and helplessness swept over him. He, and his friends, had been left behind. Pam, Ryan, and Jack watched the departing mist fade into the sky and each, in trembling fear, felt an aloneness and abandonment never before experienced. It was at that precise moment that they began to give some thought to their future.

# Epilogue

Jack Clayburn was seated in the far corner of the dingy and dirty concrete cell, his chin resting on knees pulled up close to his chest. His eyes were closed, not because he was sleepy, but because there was nothing to see. His cell measured twelve feet by twelve feet and there was no light, but even if there had been, there was nothing to see. The dirty, grey, grimy, even blood-spattered, walls were completely bare and the hard floor upon which he sat was covered with the stench and filth of those who had preceded him. There was no cot or mattress upon which he could rest; there was not even a container or receptacle which could be used as a toilet. There was only concrete, darkness, and Jack Clayburn.

Over three years had passed since that day on Piaute Mountain when he, Pamela, and Ryan had managed to escape. At the time, they had not fully understood what they were escaping from, and only much later had they realized that they had not actually escaped. True, they had avoided death in the explosion that erupted from the mountain, but only later had they managed a full comprehension of the events of that fateful day. Sitting in the darkness, remembering, it was hard for him to accept the fact that only three years had passed. It seemed much longer than that. So much had happened—to him, to Pamela, to Ryan, to the world.

Following the first explosion at Piaute Mountain, the three had made their way into the mountains, and with some difficulty, had managed to get back to Hawthorne and Jack's motel room. There they had remained for several weeks, waiting for the chaos to subside, and while keeping a low profile, Jack obtained—and began reading—a small Bible. In his quest to verify his salvation and to discover the meaning of Clay and Adam's conversation, he read the scriptures carefully and began to understand the full impact of what had happened. Sharing his newfound knowledge with Ryan and Pamela, they soon realized that their lives were in danger because they knew the full truth about Adam Armstrong. They also acquired insight concerning what was to happen throughout the entire world following the Rapture.

Trusting no one, including Clay Davis, Adam Armstrong had secured the looping chip from Dr. Thacker prior to his assassination. He had also duplicated all plans and developmental procedures concerning the computer. He felt he should be prepared to re-create his own "facility" in the event that Piaute Mountain was wrested from his control.

Even with the most brilliant scientific minds at his disposal, it took over a year to re-create the system that would help coerce absolute submission from his subjects.

The subsequent events came as no shock to Jack, Pamela and Ryan. Adam Armstrong convinced the world that he had chased the alien away, and on the strength of that claim, combined with his carefully executed plans for world conquest, had moved himself into a position of unquestioned monarchial power with sovereign rule over not only the ten European nations, but the United States as well.

Surprisingly to Jack, Pamela and Ryan, Armstrong had proven to be an effective leader—at first. However, the three had learned from the scriptures what to expect. As the sins of corruption slowly crumbled beneath Armstrong's power base, Jack, Pamela and Ryan quietly made plans to retreat to the safety of the mountains, where they hoped to remain for the full seven years of the tribulation. Despite the fact that Armstrong mounted a massive campaign to have all humans implanted with his micro-chip monitoring system, they managed to evade the implantation and, gathering all the supplies they could obtain, disappeared into the mountains.

The three might have silently spent the remainder of their earthly lives living quietly and studying the Bible, preparing for His return, but their privacy was invaded by others seeking sanctuary and hope from the days of tribulation. Their small community grew, and within a year, their group numbered almost forty. Amidst this growing and questioning congregation, Jack slowly found himself assuming the role of spiritual leader and advisor. He joined Ryan and Pamela together in matrimony, and they assisted him in his pastoral functions. Although there was no official leader of the group, Jack was recognized as the standard bearer—or man of God—and as the group's Holy Man, he prepared all for the next Coming. The group lived in a constant state of caution, always on the alert for the special military search teams and the marauding bands of bounty hunters searching for just such groups as theirs, upon the orders of Adam Armstrong. Thanks to Ryan's prior security experience, elaborate security measures were installed and they were able to remain secluded from the outside world.

There came a time, however, when seclusion became their enemy. Throughout the world, crops failed, food supplies dwindled, and water supplies became contaminated or dried up. The small hidden community was forced to send foraging parties out to obtain food and water. On one such excursion, while Ryan was away with a small band of men, bounty hunters discovered the group's hiding place. In the darkness of night, they had captured the entire community, bound them in chains, and marched them to the nearest city.

Now, as he sat in his dark cell, he could only wait for the inevitable. He had made his peace with God, and he felt no fear. In fact, he felt somewhat relieved that it would soon be over, and he would not have to live through the rest of the tribulation, which he knew would last at least three more years. He had no way of knowing that even at that moment, Ryan and a small band of warriors were on their way to effect some form of rescue. Even if he had known, he would have felt no joy. He now knew the Truth and was ready, even eager, to meet that Truth. Heavy-booted footsteps sounded outside the door to his cell, and as he heard the key turn in the lock, he knew his time had come. Raising himself to a standing position, Jack Clayburn felt a peace settle over his being. He was ready for whatever Adam Armstrong's followers had planned for him.

# MORE GOOD BOOKS FROM HUNTINGTON HOUSE PUBLISHERS

***Inside the New Age Nightmare*** by Randall Baer

Now, for the first time, one of the most powerful and influential leaders of the New Age movement has come out to expose the deceptions of the organization he once led. New Age magazines and articles have for many years hailed Randall Baer as their most "radically original" and "advanced" thinker... "light years ahead of others" says leading New Age magazine *East-West Journal*. His bestselling books on quartz crystals, self-transformation, and planetary ascension have won worldwide acclaim and been extolled by New Agers from all walks of life.

Hear, from a New Age insider, the secret plans they have spawned to take over our public, private, and political institutions. Have these plans already been implemented in your church, business, or organization? Discover the seduction of the demonic forces at work—turned from darkness to light, Randall Baer reveals the methods of the New Age movement as no one else can. Find out what you can do to stop the New Age movement from destroying our way of life.

**ISBN 0-910311-58-7 $8.95**

***The Devil's Web*** by Pat Pulling with Kathy Cawthon

This explosive exposé presents the first comprehensive guide to childhood and adolescent occult involvement. Written by a nationally recognized occult crime expert, the author explains how the violent occult underworld operates and how they stalk and recruit our children, teenagers and young adults for their evil purposes. The author leaves no stone unturned in her investigation and absolves no one of the responsibility of protecting our children. She dispels myths and raises new questions examining the very real possibility of the existence of major occult networks which may include members of law enforcement, government officials and other powerful individuals.

**ISBN 0-910311-59-5 $8.95 Trade paper**
**ISBN 0-910311-63-3 $16.95 Hard cover**

***From Rock to Rock*** by Eric Barger

Over three years in the making, the pages of this book represent thousands of hours of detailed research as well as over twenty-six years of personal experience and study. The author presents a detailed exposé on many current rock entertainers, rock concerts, videos, lyrics and occult symbols used within the industry. He also presents a rating system of over fifteen hundred past and present rock groups and artists.

**ISBN 0-910311-61-7 $8.95**

***The Deadly Deception: Freemasonry Exposed By One of Its Top Leaders*** by Tom McKenney

Presents a frank look at Freemasonry and its origin. Learn of the "secrets" and "deceptions" that are practiced daily around the world. Find out why

Masonry teaches that it is the true religion, that all other religions are but corrupted and perverted forms of Masonry.

ISBN 0-910311-54-4 $7.95

*Lord! Why Is My Child a Rebel?* by Jacob Aranza
This book offers an analysis of the root causes of teenage rebellion and offers practical solutions for disoriented parents. Aranza focuses on the turbulent teenage years, and how to survive those years—both you and the child! Must reading for parents—especially for those with strong-willed children. This book will help you avoid the traps in which many parents are caught and put you on the road to recovery with your rebel.

ISBN 0-910311-62-5 $6.95

*Seduction of the Innocent Revisited* by John Fulce
You honestly can't judge a book by its cover—especially a comic book! Comic books of yesteryear bring to mind cute cartoon characters, super-heroes battling the forces of evil or a sleuth tracking down the bad guy clue-by-clue. But that was a long, long time ago.

Today's comic books aren't innocent at all! Author John Fulce asserts that "super-heroes" are constantly found in the nude engaging in promiscuity, and satanic symbols are abundant throughout the pages. Fulce says most parents aren't aware of the contents of today's comic books—of what their children are absorbing from these seemingly innocent forms of entertainment. As a comic book collector for many years, Fulce opened his own comic book store in 1980, only to sell the business a few short years later due to the steady influx of morally unacceptable material. What's happening in the comic book industry? Fulce outlines the moral, biblical, and legal aspects and proves his assertions with page after page of illustrations. We need to pay attention to what our children are reading, Fulce claims. Comic books are not as innocent as they used to be.

ISBN 0-910311-66-8 $8.95

*New World Order: The Ancient Plan of Secret Societies* by William Still
Secret societies such as Freemasons have been active since before the advent of Christ, yet most of us don't realize what they are or the impact they've had on many historical events. For example, did you know secret societies played a direct role in the French Revolutions of the 18th and 19th centuries and the Russian Revolution of the 20th century? Author William Still brings into focus the actual manipulative work of the societies, and the "Great Plan" they follow, much to the surprise of many of those who are blindly led into the organization. Their ultimate goal is simple: world dictatorship and unification of all mankind into a world confederation.

Most Masons are good, decent men who join for fellowship, but they are deceived—pulled away from their religious heritage. Only those who reach the highest level of the Masons know its true intentions. Masons and Marxists follow the same master. Ultimately it is a struggle between two foes—the forces of religion versus the forces of anti-religion. Still asserts that although the final battle is near-at-hand, the average person has the power to thwart the efforts of secret societies. Startling and daring, this is the first successful attempt by an author to unveil the designs of secret societies from the beginning, up to the present and into the future. The author attempts to educate the community on how to recognize the signals and how to take the necessary steps to impede their progress.

ISBN 0-910311-64-1 $8.95

*Hidden Dangers of the Rainbow* by Constance Cumbey
The first book to uncover and expose the New Age movement, this national #1 bestseller paved the way for all other books on the subject. It has become a giant in its category. This book provides a vivid exposé of the New Age movement, which the author contends is dedicated to wiping out Christianity and establishing a one world order. This movement, a vast network of occult and pagan organizations, meets the test of prophecy concerning the Antichrist.

ISBN 0-910311-03-X $8.95

*To Grow By Storybook Readers* by Janet Friend
Today quality of education is a major concern; consequently, more and more parents have turned to home schooling to teach their children how to read. The *To Grow By Storybook Readers* by Janet Friend can greatly enhance your home schooling reading program. The set of readers consists of 18 storybook readers plus 2 activity books. The *To Grow By Storybook Readers* has been designed to be used in conjunction with Marie LeDoux's PLAY 'N TALK phonics program but will work well with other orderly phonics programs.

These are the first phonics readers that subtly but positively instill scriptural and moral values. They're a joy to use because no prior instructional experience is necessary. The *To Grow By Storybook Readers* allows parents and children to work together learning each sound. Your child progresses through the readers and learns to appreciate his own ability to understand and think logically about word and sentence construction, thereby raising his self-esteem and confidence.

You can lead your child step-by-step into the exciting and fun world of reading and learning, without heavy reliance on memorization. Repetition and re-arrangement will leave your child begging to read page after page. Whether it's a home educational program or a phonics based program in school, these readers can substantially improve a child's reading capability and his desire to learn.

ISBN 0-910311-69-2 $44.95

*The Delicate Balance* by John Zajac
Did you know that the Apostle John and George Washington had revealed to them many of the same end-time events? It's true!Accomplished scientist, inventor, and speaker John Zajac asserts that science and religion are not opposed. He uses science to demonstrate the newly understood relevance of the book of Revelation. Read about the catastrophic forces at work today that the ancient prophets and others foretold. You'll wonder at George Washington's description of an angelic being which appeared to him and showed him end-time events that were to come—the accuracy of Nostradamus (who converted to Christianity)—and the warnings of St. John that are revealed in the book of Revelation—earthquakes, floods, terrorism—what does it all mean? No other author has examined these topics from Zajac's unique perspective or presented such a reasonable and concise picture of the whole.

ISBN 0-910311-57-9 $8.95

**Backward Masking Unmasked** by Jacob Aranza
Rock music affects millions of young people and adults with lyrics exalting drugs, Satan, violence and immorality. But there is even a more sinister threat: hidden messages that exalt the Prince of Darkness!

**ISBN 0-910311-04-8 $6.95**

Also on cassette tape! Hear authentic demonic backward masking from rock music.

**ISBN 0-910311-23-4 $6.95**

**Personalities in Power: The Making of Great Leaders**
by Florence Littauer
You'll laugh and cry as Florence Littauer shares with you heart-warming accounts of the personal lives of some of our greatest leaders. Learn of their triumphs and tragedies, and become aware of the different personality patterns that exist and how our leaders have been influenced by them.Discover your own strengths and weaknesses by completing the Personality Chart included in this book. *Personalities in Power* lets you understand yourself and others and helps you live up to your full potential.

**ISBN 0-910311-56-0 $8.95**

**The Last Days Collection** by Last Days Ministries
Heart-stirring, faith-challenging messages from Keith Green, David Wilkerson, Melody Green, Leonard Ravenhill, Winkie Pratney, Charles Finney and William Booth are designed to awaken complacent Christians to action.

**ISBN 0-910311-42-0 $8.95**

**The Lucifer Connection** by Joseph Carr
Shirley MacLaine and other celebrities are persuading millions that the New Age movement can fill the spiritual emptiness in their lonely lives. Joseph Carr explains why the New Age movement is the most significant and potentially destructive challenge to the church today. But is it new? How should Christians protect themselves and their children from this insidious threat? This book is a prophetic, information-packed examination by one of the most informed authors in America.

**ISBN 0-910311-42-0 $7.95**

**Exposing the Aids Scandal: What You Don't Know Can Kill You**
by Dr. Paul Cameron
Where do you turn when those who control the flow of information in this country withhold the truth? Why is the national media hiding facts from the public? Can AIDS be spread in ways we're not being told? Finally a book that gives you a total account of the AIDS epidemic, and what steps can be taken to protect yourself. What you don't know can kill you!

**ISBN 0-910311-52-8 $7.95**

**A Reasonable Reason to Wait** by Jacob Aranza
God speaks specifically about premarital sex. Aranza provides a definite, frank discussion on premarital sex. He also provides a biblical healing message for those who have already been sexually involved before marriage. This book

delivers an important message for young people, as well as their parents.

ISBN 0-910311-21-8 $5.95

*Jubilee on Wall Street* by David Knox Barker
On October 19, 1987, the New York Stock Exchange suffered its greatest loss in history—twice that of the 1929 crash. Will this precipitate a new Great Depression? This riveting book is a look at what the author believes is the inevitable collapse of the world's economy. Using the biblical principle of the Year of Jubilee, a refreshing dose of optimism and an easy-to-read style, the author shows readers how to avoid economic devastation.

ISBN 0-933-451-03-2 $7.95

*America Betrayed* by Marlin Maddoux
This hard-hitting book exposes the forces in our country which seek to destroy the family, the schools and our values. This book details exactly how the news media manipulates your mind. Marlin Maddoux is the host of the popular, national radio talk show "Point of View."

ISBN 0-910311-18-8 $6.95

*Dinosaurs and the Bible* by David W. Unfred
Every reader, young and old, will be fascinated by this ever-mysterious topic—exactly what happened to the dinosaurs? Author David Unfred draws a very descriptive picture of the history and fate of the dinosaurs, using the Bible as a reference guide.

In this educational and informative book, Unfred answers such questions as: Did dinosaurs really exist? Does the Bible mention dinosaurs? What happened to dinosaurs, or are there some still living awaiting discovery? Unfred uses the Bible to help unlock the ancient mysteries of the lumbering creatures, and teaches how those mysteries can educate us about God the Creator and our God of Love.

ISBN 0-910311-70-6 $12.95 Hard cover

*"Soft Porn" Plays Hardball* by Dr. Judith A. Reisman
With amazing clarity, the author demonstrates that pornography imposes on society a view of women and children that encourages violence and sexual abuse. As crimes against women and children increase to alarming proportions, it's of paramount importance that we recognize the cause of this violence. Pornography should be held accountable for the havoc it has wreaked in our homes and our country.

ISBN 0-901311-65-X  $ 8.95 Trade paper
ISBN 0-910311-92-7 $16.95 Hardcover

*Devil Take the Youngest* by Winkie Pratney
A history of Satan's hatred of innocence and his historical treachery against the young. Pratney begins his journey in ancient Babylon and continues through to modern-day America where infants are murdered daily and children are increasingly victimized through pornography, prostitution and humanism.

ISBN 0-910311-29-3 $8.95

### *God's Rebels* by Henry Lee Curry III

From his unique perspective Dr. Henry Lee Curry III offers a fascinating look at the lives of some of our greatest Southern religious leaders during the Civil War. The rampant Evangelical Christianity prominent at the outbreak of the Civil War, asserts Dr. Curry, is directly traceable to the 2nd Great Awakening of the early 1800s. The evangelical tradition, with its emphasis on strict morality, individual salvation, and emotional worship, had influenced most of Southern Protestantism by this time. Southerners unquestionably believed the voice of the ministers to be the "voice of God"; consequently, the church became one of the most powerful forces influencing Confederate life and morale. Inclined toward a Calvinistic emphasis on predestination, the South was confident that God would sustain its way of life.

Dr. Curry illuminates the many different activities in which Confederate clergymen engaged. He focuses on three prominent clergymen in the heart of the South. James A. Duncan, editor of the Richmond Christian Advocate, Moses I. Hoge, Honorary chaplain of the Confederate Congress who ran the Union blockade in order to get Bibles for Confederate soldiers, and Charles F. E. Minnigerods, a pastor of one of the most important parishes in the South.

Dr. Curry is a Virginian. He holds degrees from the University of Virginia, Duke University, and Emory University. While teaching at Mercer University's Atlanta Campus, his course on The Civil War and Reconstruction was always very popular.

**ISBN: 0-910311-67-6 $12.95 Trade paper**
**ISBN: 0-910311-68-4 $21.95 Hard cover**

### *Kinsey, Sex and Fraud: The Indoctrination of a People*
#### by Dr. Judith A. Reisman and Edward Eichel

Kinsey, Sex and Fraud describes the research of Alfred Kinsey which shaped Western society's beliefs and understanding of the nature of human sexuality. His unchallenged conclusions are taught at every level of education—elementary, highschool and college—and quoted in textbooks as undisputed truth.

The authors clearly demonstrate that Kinsey's research involved illegal experimentations on several hundred children. The survey was carried out on a non-representative group of Americans, including disproportionately large numbers of sex offenders, prostitutes, prison inmates and exhibitionists.

**ISBN 0-910311-20-X $19.95 Hard cover**

# Order These Books from Huntington House Publishers!

| | | |
|---|---|---|
| _____ America Betrayed—Marlin Maddoux — — — — — | $6.95 | _____ |
| _____ Backward Masking Unmasked—Jacob Aranza — — — | 6.95 | _____ |
| _____ Deadly Deception: Freemasonry—Tom McKenney ____ | 7.95 | _____ |
| _____ Delicate Balance—John Zajac — — — — — — — | 8.95 | _____ |
| _____ Devil Take The Youngest—Winkie Pratney — — ✎ — | 8.95 | _____ |
| The Devil's Web—Pat Pulling with Kathy Cawthon | | |
| _____ Trade paper ____ | 8.95 | _____ |
| _____ Hard cover ____ | 16.95 | _____ |
| _____ •Dinosaurs and the Bible—Dave Unfred — — — — — | 12.95 | _____ |
| _____ Exposing the AIDS Scandal—Dr. Paul Cameron — — | 7.95 | _____ |
| _____ From Rock to Rock—Eric Barger— — — — — — — | 8.95 | _____ |
| •God's Rebels—Henry Lee Curry III, Ph.D. | | |
| _____ Trade paper ____ | 12.95 | _____ |
| _____ Hard cover ____ | 21.95 | _____ |
| The Hidden Dangers of the Rainbow— | | |
| Constance Cumbey— — | 8.95 | _____ |
| _____ Inside the New Age Nightmare—Randall Baer— — — | 8.95 | _____ |
| _____ Jubilee on Wall Street—David Knox Barker— — — — | 7.95 | _____ |
| •Kinsey, Sex and Fraud—Dr. Judith A. Reisman & | | |
| _____ Edward Eichel — — — — — — — | 19.95 | _____ |
| _____ Last Days Collection—Last Days Ministries — — — | 8.95 | _____ |
| _____ •Lord! Why Is My Child A Rebel?—Jacob Aranza — — | 6.95 | _____ |
| _____ Lucifer Connection—Joseph Carr— — — — — — — | 7.95 | _____ |
| •New World Order: The Ancient Plan of Secret Societies— | | |
| _____ William T. Still — — — | 8.95 | _____ |
| _____ Personalities in Power—Florence Littauer— — — — | 8.95 | _____ |
| _____ A Reasonable Reason To Wait—Jacob Aranza — — — | 5.95 | _____ |
| _____ •Seduction of the Innocent Revisited—John Fulce | 8.95 | _____ |
| •Soft Porn Plays Hardball—Dr. Judith A. Reisman | | |
| _____ Trade paper— — — — | 8.95 | _____ |
| _____ Hard cover — — — — | 16.95 | _____ |
| _____ •To Grow By Storybook Readers—Janet Friend | 44.95 per set | _____ |
| Shipping and Handling | | _____ |
| TOTAL | | _____ |

•New Titles

AVAILABLE AT BOOKSTORES EVERYWHERE or order direct from:
Huntington House Publishers • P.O. Box 53788 • Lafayette, LA 70505

Send check/money order. For faster service use VISA/MASTERCARD, call
toll-free 1-800-749-4009
Add: Freight and handling, $2.00 for the first book ordered, and $.50 for each
additional book.

Enclosed is $ _____ including postage.
Card type:
VISA/MASTERCARD# _____ Exp. Date _____
Name _____
Address _____
City, State, Zipcode _____